"When I go home, I'll look for a house of my own in Red Wing." The corners of her mouth were turned down. **"Have to find a job first, though."**

"So, Minnesota is home now," Matt said. "It's been decided?"

Heather glanced away but nodded. "It's time I put down some roots and get myself a real life."

She may be petite but there was nothing dainty or fragile about her. "When you say you need to find a real life, what's your definition of that?"

"I want what most everyone wants. Satisfying work, a family, a place to call home and have it mean something."

His instincts were waging a battle with his urge to ask her to stay. Give them a chance to find out if this attraction between them was genuine or just a flirtation. But since Matt now lived where she had once been raised, he could argue that her roots were still in Adelaide Creek.

Dear Reader,

Welcome to Adelaide Creek, a Wyoming town named for one of its first sheep ranchers, Adelaide Stanhope, who happens to be Heather Stanhope's great-great-grandmother. When Heather and her brother lost their family's land, a big piece of Heather's heart went with it.

After being gone four years, Heather is back in Adelaide Creek for her best friend's wedding. She's in for a few surprises when she meets the best man, Mathis—Matt—Burton, who's raising sheep on what she still considers *her* ranch. It turns out Matt's blue-green eyes and friendly smile aren't so easy to ignore. Neither are the adorable six-year-old twins Matt's been raising since his sister died.

As the wedding approaches, Heather and Matt are running out of time to make new choices. Matt's bravado has taken a couple of hits that force a shift in his thinking, while Heather struggles to discover the true meaning of home.

The Rancher's Wyoming Twins is my first trip to Adelaide Creek, but it won't be my last, with its close families and colorful holiday festivals.

Please visit me on Facebook and Twitter, nd sign up for news and updates: giniamccullough.com.

ppy endings!

McCullough

HEARTWARMING

The Rancher's Wyoming Twins

—

Virginia McCullough

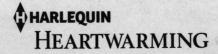

HARLEQUIN
HEARTWARMING

HARLEQUIN®
HEARTWARMING™

Recycling programs
for this product may
not exist in your area.

ISBN-13: 978-1-335-42668-0

The Rancher's Wyoming Twins

Copyright © 2022 by Virginia McCullough

For questions and comments about the quality of this book,
please contact us at CustomerService@Harlequin.com.

Harlequin Enterprises ULC
22 Adelaide St. West, 41st Floor
Toronto, Ontario M5H 4E3, Canada
www.Harlequin.com

Printed in U.S.A.

Virginia McCullough grew up in Chicago, but she's lived in many other exciting locales, from the coast of Maine to western North Carolina and, for the last several years, northeastern Wisconsin. She's enjoyed a long career writing nonfiction books as a coauthor and ghostwriter, but now she tells stories her fictional characters whisper in her ear. Six romance novels later, *The Rancher's Wyoming Twins* is the first of her latest miniseries, Back to Adelaide Creek, for Harlequin Heartwarming readers. When she's not writing, Virginia reads other authors' books, wanders on trails and in parks near her home, and dreams about future road trips.

Books by Virginia McCullough

Harlequin Heartwarming

Girl in the Spotlight
Something to Treasure
Love, Unexpected

Back to Bluestone River

A Family for Jason
The Christmas Kiss
A Bridge Home

Visit the Author Profile page
at Harlequin.com for more titles.

To Lynda McDaniel, a lifelong writer and a close friend and colleague for many years and across long distances. A woman who knows what it means to "keep calm and carry on," Lynda embodies all the qualities of a true friend.

CHAPTER ONE

STARING AT THE sheep dotting the basin below, Heather Stanhope shaded her eyes against the glare of the afternoon sun. This spring's lambs stayed close to their mothers as they grazed on the newly greened pasture. Heather guessed the total number of sheep as maybe three hundred. She found that puzzling—not because of how many sheep there were, but how few.

"Hey, you, you're slacking off. That herb field of mine isn't going to neaten its own rows."

Heather turned and smiled at Jen, her best friend's mother, who stood at the edge of the field with a farm cart mostly emptied of the chive seedlings she'd planted in her ever-expanding herb garden. "Busted. I guess I'm a little distracted. Sorry."

"Big surprise. You've been distracted from the minute you arrived on my doorstep on this spectacular morning, honey." Jen sighed happily as she swept her arm to encompass both her gardens and the view down the hill. "Did you ever see such a day in May?" She asked her rhetorical question as she walked down the row to Heather and put her arm around her shoulder. She gave her a quick squeeze before planting a kiss on top of her head. "My hands smell like bee balm and basil, and it won't be long before we'll detect lavender in the air. The scent of the dried oregano inside the shed made me daydream about whipping up a pasta sauce."

Heather closed her eyes and took a deep breath. "A Wyoming spring definitely is in the air. The sheep and lambs are my welcoming committee." She smiled at Jen. "And you, of course, with your garden cart and lots of chores I can do to earn my keep."

Jen shook her head. "Heather, I'll be frank. Seeing you gazing at those sheep hurts my heart. You know that dwelling on them or that land isn't going to—"

"Make those sheep mine. Or bring back what used to be mine," Heather blurted. She should be the one to acknowledge the truth. "Or change anything at all." No one, especially not the people closest to her, needed to point out the obvious. Heather stabbed the loose soil with the toe of her boot. She'd sworn she'd push down her sadness and keep her irrational longings to herself.

Heather looked into Jen's soft blue eyes. Beautiful eyes now full of concern. "Maybe I shouldn't have come back this early," Heather said. "Bethany's wedding is almost two months off. Better yet, I should have stayed away altogether." She winced. Now that was a thought better kept to herself.

"And leave Bethany without her maid of honor? *Unthinkable.* You know she wouldn't take one step down any aisle without you here." Giving Heather no time to respond, Jen nodded toward the newly tilled rows in her herb garden. Some seedlings were already in, and the perennials were poking through the soil. "Thanks for lending a hand with this, honey. We've got a lot to do before Spring Fling on Saturday."

"Yes, ma'am. I'm at your service." Maybe a few things had changed in her hometown of Adelaide Creek, but not Spring Fling. It was still the town's biggest festival of the year and drew visitors from all over the county and beyond. Spring Fling had started long before Heather was born, and judging from the billboards on the road into town, it had recently expanded what it offered. When Heather grew up here, the population had hovered around four hundred on its best day, but Bethany had said it was gaining a few new families every year.

"How 'bout you finish cleaning up the tarragon and thyme rows?" Jen said. "Then I'll show you some of the wool I'm offering."

Straightening and squaring her shoulders, Heather forced a smile. "Whatever you need, Jen."

Taking the cart with her, Jen headed back to her shed. Earlier, Heather had peeked inside to get a glimpse of the bins of last year's dried herbs Jen packaged for teas and sachets.

Thick gray clouds had formed rapidly and blocked the midafternoon sun. Heather glanced again at the gradual slope from where she stood on the ridge to the flat acres of the basin. Her Stanhope ancestors had once owned all of it and even more land outside her line of vision. Beyond it, foothills and more ridges and then the line of mountains, a constant presence for most of her life.

She hadn't been there to see the freak April blizzard, but Heather easily pictured the winter when three or four feet of snow covered the hills and pastures. She'd known that storm was on its way because she still checked the Wyoming weather almost daily. Force of habit, she supposed. Then the melt-off and rain had arrived. With a little luck, more rain would fall in May.

"Our land has a lot of energy now," her dad, a true sheepman if there ever was one, used to say when May brought buds to the crab apple and Hawthorn trees, the hardy dogwoods. The greening of the ground brought blankets of early flowers.

Heather had reveled in that energy and had been on intimate terms with every acre. In her mind's eye, she took a trip through that land and said hello to the admittedly ram-shackle house, the barn and hay bales, horses and stables, and the sheep shelters and water troughs in the pastures.

Along with her brother, Jeff, and their mom and dad, Heather had put in long days herding and otherwise tending their sheep in both bitter cold and blistering heat. She'd grown up witnessing the violent storms of spring and the snow runoff that made the actual Adelaide—Addie—Creek spill over its banks.

A few months later, every rancher and farmer begged for that water when stretches of rainless summer days opened cracks in the parched earth. The land in front of her had supported five generations of Stanhopes.

Until it didn't.

"Buck up. *No whining.* None of it matters anymore," Heather muttered to herself as she turned away from the sight of the sheep. She had work to do in Jen's herb garden. She had to laugh at herself, though. Who was she kidding? She could pretend she'd put her losses behind her, but some of the hurt burrowed deep in her being. The best she could do was learn how to make peace with it.

Four years ago, when she and her brother had been forced to abandon their old life, most everyone had wanted them to look on the so-called bright side. A phantom, she and Jeff agreed. Even the loan officers at the bank cheerfully pointed out that at least they'd walked away free of the debts that had burdened her family for decades.

And wasn't Heather lucky? She had the chance to take her skills as a pediatric nurse practitioner on the road. She could create a shiny new life anywhere she chose. Well-meaning words for sure, and from people she'd known all her life, but they had zero chance of accomplishing their mission. Back then, no balm in the world had had the power to soothe the pain of her losses.

Speaking of balm, Heather patted down the mulch, expanding the space devoted to these new bee balm plants that Jen added to her tea blends. The rest of this field was dominated by lavender plants tough enough to make it through the harsh weather and end up in Jen's sachets.

When she reached the end of the last row, she dusted off her jeans, took off her baseball cap and let her hair fly free. She headed back to the shed, taking in every sight and smell as she loped along. She calculated when the mock orange on the side of the house would bloom or the patches of prairie clover might cover the edges of the fields. The double doors of the shed were open, and she stepped inside and stood next to Jen, who was packaging and labeling herbs at the long table. "Reporting for duty, Jen."

Jen gave her a playful shove. "Nope, I've changed my mind. You've helped enough for your first afternoon home. You go on and get settled in at the bunkhouse. Bethany will be coming along soon, anyway. Then I'll see you both for dinner later."

Heather didn't protest. Excited to see Bethany—in person—for the first time in four years, she was ready to unpack. She also was a little worn out from the long hours in her SUV. She'd stretched the twelve-hundred-mile drive into a week-long trip from Red Wing, Minnesota, to Adelaide Creek. She'd played tourist and hiked and biked on trails and spent four days in South Dakota exploring the Badlands and Mount Rushmore. Everywhere she went in the Upper Midwest, she took in the landscape made magical by the onset of spring.

Finally, though, Heather's precious Wyoming cottonwoods welcomed her back home.

"Quit calling it that. It's *not* home anymore," she reminded herself.

She'd been gone four years now on nursing

assignments, two years in Red Wing, and the previous two years split between assignments on pediatric units in hospitals in Charleston and Savannah. Now, though, she was ready to stop roaming. Instead, she intended to build herself a full life.

Part of her newly formed resolve came from seeing Bethany so happy planning her future with Charlie Goodman. Before Heather had left Red Wing for this extended break, she'd noted places she could approach on her search for a permanent job. She'd even scanned real estate listings. If she bought a house in Red Wing, roots were sure to grow.

Heather navigated the twists and turns of the bumpy and slightly muddy path, a short-cut to Bethany's converted bunkhouse a quarter-mile walk from the sprawling build-ings and the farmhouse where Jen and Dan lived. In several weeks, perhaps by Bethany's Fourth of July wedding, the field around the shortcut would be splashed with sunflowers and primrose and blanket flower. They'd last until the path turned to dust in the fall.

Bethany's bunkhouse was the last place Heather had stayed before she'd driven away from Adelaide Creek for good. She'd always cherish her time living in what looked like a cozy cottage inside but was, and always would be, known as the bunkhouse. Heartbroken and angry, Heather had steered her car southeast and vowed never to come back to this town. *Ever*. It didn't matter that the creek snaking through the Stanhope ranch and well beyond was named after her great-great-grandmother Adelaide. So what if the once-scruffy outpost town then named itself after the same creek? Who cared about that Adelaide? No one.

When she was a kid, that historical tidbit about the Stanhope family had given her and Jeff bragging rights. And brag they had. Her face turned red even thinking about the way she and Jeff had acted like they owned the town. Now, with the Stanhopes gone, how the town got its name was only a bit of mostly forgotten local trivia.

Her gait changed from the heaviness setting in. Nothing new, though. It happened every time she thought of her brother. Like her, Jeff had slammed the door behind him when he'd left Adelaide Creek for points unknown. While she'd reported for duty on her first assignment in the pediatrics department at a hospital near Charleston, Jeff had headed west without giving her a way to reliably reach him, other than a cell phone number he rarely answered. He'd been clear enough when he'd declared himself done with everything from the past. Including her, apparently.

The last she knew, Jeff had signed on as crew on a commercial fishing boat out of Seattle. In her wildest imaginings, she'd never thought about a time when she and her brother wouldn't be involved in each other's lives.

Farther down the path, Heather left the herb field and the basin behind, but Jen's flock came into view. The two dozen or so sheep stood or lay in clusters, the picture of contentment in the sheared-down version of themselves. After the dip in her mood over the whereabouts of her brother, Heather's spirits lifted looking at the Shetland sheep with their finely crimped coats. They weren't pets, but somehow those prized wool producers sure seemed like it.

Bethany had sent videos of the Icelandic sheep her mom had more recently added. They weren't exactly exotic, but their small size and short legs made them look different.

Their mostly bare faces and heavy tan-and-brown coats weren't a regular sight in Wyoming sheep country. At least, they hadn't been when she was growing up.

At first look, Heather found the Icelanders, as Jen called them, amusing and a little out of place, like tourists who'd decided to stay but didn't know quite how to blend in. On the plus side, like Jen pointed out on her videos, these critters didn't mind the frozen, snowy winters and, best of all, her customers loved their wool.

Heather abruptly came to a stop, suddenly conscious of the tension building inside her. She shook her hands to loosen the muscles. Then she rubbed her palms as if she could massage away the cause of her frustration. She leaned forward, rested her hands on her thighs and emptied her lungs, making a deep guttural sound.

She loved the Hoovers—Bethany, Jen and Dan—with her whole heart. They were family, not of blood but forged in friendship, love and time—thirty-two years so far. But she'd never envied anyone with the same hot intensity that she envied them.

Unlike Heather's family, Dan and Jen had

kept their eyes open and read the flashing warning signs about diminishing wool and lamb markets. The old sheep-raising ways were vanishing and had left many behind, even some of the large landmark ranches built from next to nothing.

But her parents had held on, taking greater risks and adding to the debt her grandparents had left behind. Hadn't each generation of Stanhopes survived through these cycles many times before? Dips in markets were inevitably followed by rebounds.

Short-lived revivals, Jen had warned, which had led her to carve an early niche in the fiber market. Jen's struggle to adapt to change had morphed into a passion. Jen liked to say her sheep lived the good life, and because of these special creatures, so did she.

Heather straightened and forced herself to get moving. She'd been over and over the series of bad decisions her parents had perpetuated. Sometimes she even made peace with them. But this morning, as she'd driven into familiar territory, she'd found herself wrestling with all the memories, the light ones as well as the dark.

The sight of the "nothing fancy bunkhouse," as Bethany dubbed it, sent her mood on the upswing again. She lingered on the long porch with its stacked firewood at one end. Two rocking chairs sat side by side, the best welcome sign of all. During their breaks from nursing school, she and Bethany had whiled away many hours in the rockers listening to the buzzes, hoots and croaks of summer nights. In every season, this porch and the yard had been a premiere spot for stargazing. The two had sent wishes to the full moon, too, a ritual they'd believed they'd invented when they were still little girls with pigtails.

The bunkhouse was now a two-bedroom cottage with a fireplace and windows large enough to bring the outside in, especially the vistas of the mountains in the distance. At that moment, the angles and peaks were dark cutouts against a sky now turned purplish pink as the sun began its descent behind the range.

She got busy unpacking and was nearly finished piling sweaters and T-shirts into the dresser in the guest bedroom when she heard a car coming up the driveway. She was on the porch in time to see Bethany pull in.

Heather hurried to the driver's side and, two seconds later, Bethany was out of the car and hugging her so hard she could barely breathe.

Her best friend since babyhood threw her head back and let out a long wolf howl. "That's how happy I am to see you." She stepped back and held Heather at arm's length. "You're still a tiny dark-haired princess."

Stinging tears pooled in Heather's eyes, but she dammed them up fast with her index fingers. "And you're still a stunning blonde queen. Even in your scrubs, you're already a radiant bride."

Bethany waved her off. "Pfft…don't be silly. I'm radiant right now because *you're* here. *At last.* Video chats don't cut it." Bethany narrowed her blue eyes in mock reproach. "Hmm… I don't want to see tears, girlfriend. Let's just be happy."

"I'll try. I promise." Heather followed Bethany up the stairs. "I'm excited about staying in the bunkhouse while you're still living in it. I guess it's your last chance to enjoy this place."

"Right, *my* last chance, but not *yours*. You

can park yourself here anytime you feel like it for as long as you want." Inside the cottage, the fireplace and wide windows on three walls dominated the open space. "When we come back from dinner with Mom and Dad, we'll start a fire and break open a bottle of wine."

"Like old times," Heather said. "Everything I see brings back memories of all the things we did together here, even our moaning and groaning about having to wash those huge windows."

"I still gripe about that." Bethany flashed one of her amused, lopsided grins. Everything about her was a younger version of Jen. Mother-daughter matching blue eyes, blond hair and tall sturdy bodies they both periodically complained were too heavy. Not true. They were shapely and elegant. Queenly. Heather and her mom had dubbed them as royalty more than half a lifetime ago.

Heather sighed, long and loud. "Only you and your wedding pulled me back here, Bethany. You can read me like a book. You were certain I'd never pass up a chance to be your maid of honor."

Bethany crossed her arms and thrust out

a hip. "Well, we made that promise to each other when we were like…what, ten years old?" Out of nowhere, her eyes darkened and she turned away. She ran her hand down the back of her head and fluffed up her short wavy hair. Then she studied everything in the room, except Heather.

"Uh, was it something I said?" Heather joked, but she shivered as if a cold breeze had come through the windows.

Bethany raised her eyes but quickly dropped her gaze again. "There's been a… well, a *complication*."

"Complication? What does that mean? You didn't call off—"

"No, no." Bethany put her hands on her hips. "What I should have said is it *could* be a complication." She paused. "It's really up to you."

Heather stared at her friend as she tried and failed to figure out what Bethany was holding back. "Now you've confused me. Just spit it out."

"Okay, here goes. Two days ago, Jim, Charlie's original best man, was sent overseas on some kind of hush-hush mission for his company—kind of like what Charlie is doing now." Bethany's hands fluttered nervously. "Jim can't talk about it, so all we know is that he won't be back in time for the wedding. So Charlie had to ask someone else."

Heather shrugged. "Is that all? I didn't know Jim that well in the first place, so I'm neutral. But who's the stand-in? Someone from around here?"

"More or less. He moved here from Fortune, a town over in Saylor County." Bethany studied her shoes for a couple of seconds before lifting her head. "You know of him, but you don't know him."

"Okay." Bethany's tone left Heather even more puzzled.

"He's, uh, he's Mathis Burton."

Hearing that name knocked her off center. Her gut churned. The worst days of her life had had Mathis Burton's signature all over them.

GIVING BO A pat on his dark tan neck, Mathis Burton led the horse to the corral and turned him over to his hand, Kenny, to look after. "By my calculation, I've got about six minutes before the school bus pulls up and drops the twins off."

"Six minutes, huh? Not five. Or maybe seven?" Kenny teased.

"Nope. You know me. I like to be exact. Seems the bus driver and I share that trait." Managing all the details of his sheep ranch while raising six-year-old twins had a way of creating havoc with his tight schedule. But rain or shine, Daisy, the school bus driver, rolled to a stop in front of his mailbox on time.

Matt passed the house and then dense rows of pines and cedars and a healthy number of cottonwoods lining the long drive down to the mailbox. Lucy and Nick were the next-to-last drop-off for the driver, so they had plenty of time during their ride to wind down from school and wind up for their snacks.

"And here they come now," Matt said. The yellow bus rounded the curve and headed his way. On some days, like this one, Matt couldn't get his mind off of his twin sister. He blamed it on the cool spring day, the best kind of day for working outside—and for riding. When the weather was fine, Susannah was always taking off for the stable where she'd boarded Pebbles, her black-and-white Appaloosa.

His sister still sometimes hovered around him like a ghost. She was the voice he heard in his head, speaking to him, usually reminding him of things he needed to do for the twins—her twins. As if he would forget. He'd never brag about it out loud, but in his mind he liked reassuring her that he knew what he was doing. *I know how to read a calendar and watch for the dentist appointments coming up. That's why I write them in red and add reminders on my phone, Susy.*

Even after four years of being their permanent guardian-uncle, the weight of the responsibility would occasionally drop like a boulder on his shoulders—mostly because of challenges with the ranch he counted on to support them. Lately, the figures on his spreadsheets weren't what he'd hoped and sometimes taunted him at night when he tried to sleep. More than anything, security was his goal. Not so much for himself but for the twins. They were the true center of his life now and that wasn't going to change.

The worrying thoughts and doubts he harbored immediately lifted when the school bus pulled up. Lucy and Nick waved goodbye to Daisy before hurling themselves against him and giving him hugs. Just by being buoyant little kids, his two charges chased away his fears. Today, life was good.

"Tell me the truth. Are you smarter now than when you left this morning?" Matt grinned at the two, one on each side of him as they started up the drive.

"Are you going to ask that *every* day, Uncle Matt?" Nick's shoulders slumped as usual. Nick liked to pretend to be burdened by the question.

Matt chuckled. "That's the plan."

"I can find China on a map," Lucy announced. "That was fun. Do you know how big it is?"

"Hmm… I might need a reminder. We'll spin our big globe tonight and you can show me."

Lucy yanked the stretchy yellow bands off her two ponytails and combed her fingers through her auburn hair to let it fall free. Her daily ritual. "Where's Gram? I don't see her car."

"She had another one of her committee meetings to get ready for Spring Fling this weekend. You know your gram. She's doing her part to make this year's fair a huge success. Even better than last year."

"Are we going to ride on the Ferris wheel?" Nick asked.

"I expect so," Matt said, "unless it rains on us. Or snows. You never know."

"I'm going to stuff myself with hot dogs again," Nick said, "but I'm not getting sick this year."

"Please don't," Matt warned, trying to wipe away that particular image from his memory bank.

Matt wasn't alone. The withering look Lucy sent her brother's way was one for the record books. "You can stuff yourself while Gram takes *me* to the spinning tent. We're going to the grown-up dance, too, aren't we, Uncle Matt? Gram, too? You know Gram, she loves dancing."

Apparently assuming his answer to all of her questions was yes, Lucy ran ahead, hair flying and backpack bouncing as she passed Nick. He also took off, but Matt noted him struggle to catch up.

With his tail wagging wildly, Scrambler was in the mudroom waiting for the kids to fuss over him. Scrambler was a rescue and although speculating about the dog's parentage was fun, it was never definitive. Mom called him a terrier-beagle with maybe some spaniel, and she'd claimed him years ago for no reason other than his cuteness and need for a new home. They'd all lucked out because Scrambler adored kids. Lucy and Nick were indulging Scrambler with endless hugs and pats and sweet talk when Matt caught up with them on the porch. He reminded the twins about the next steps in their routine, and looked on as they kicked off their shoes and hung their jackets on the designated hooks—red for Nick, yellow for Lucy.

By the time he'd shed his own boots and jacket, the two had dragged the three-legged step stools to the sink. Those stools meant the kids never had an excuse to miss washing their hands. Splashing each other was more like it, and more fun. "Hey, you two, let's work on the grime." He snickered at his foolish attempt to sound stern.

With a little mild intervention, the hand-washing routine was more or less accomplished, and he sent them off to their rooms upstairs to change their clothes. He might have let that go, but their gram was old school and made changing into play clothes nonnegotiable. No messing up new school jeans when the old ones were worn at the seams and only fit for play.

It didn't take Matt long to smear peanut butter on crackers and add apple slices to the plates. In absolutely equal numbers and amounts, of course, because the twins had an eagle eye for that sort of thing. Anything deviating from identical servings would be duly noted. He didn't complain, though. He and Susannah had been like that, too.

Matt smiled at his favorite sound; the *clomp, clomp, clomp* on the stairs when the kids hurried back to the kitchen. He could measure their growth by the change in the noise they made, and not just in their speed zipping down the stairs and the race to the table, but in their chatter. History repeated itself. Fraternal twins, Matt and Susannah had resembled each other like non-twin siblings, but they'd moved in sync, like Lucy and Nick now.

The pair slid into their chairs and exchanged a grin before licking the peanut butter off the first cracker. Then they gave each other a pointed look, their signal to break off tiny pieces from the edge of the cracker and let the crumbs fall to the floor, little gifts for Scrambler.

Matt leaned back against the counter and studied the two. Nick with dark hair and light brown eyes, and Lucy, who'd inherited Susannah's and his mom's auburn hair and dark eyes. He listened to their plan to ride their bikes around the front yard and play with the dog. Good. They'd been cooped up during a long winter and a cold spring so far. A couple of storms had brought snow and icy rain, along with high winds whipping through the basin.

By the time Mom's car came up the driveway, the kids were outside and Matt had cleaned up the snacks and got potatoes wrapped and ready for the grill. He looked out the window to watch the kids run to greet their gram.

Lucy and Nick had only been two when they'd come to stay with Matt for what was supposed to be the duration of Susannah's overseas deployment. They'd considered the possibility remote, but if anything happened to her, of course Matt would become their permanent guardian. He remembered the trip to the lawyer's office to sign the papers. They hadn't dwelled on the risks that were an undeniable part of war and Susannah's part in it as a helicopter pilot. But not dwelling on the risks wasn't the same as not worrying. He and his mom had barely adjusted to taking care of a couple of toddlers when the worst possible news came only two months into Susannah's tour.

In an instant, they'd become the twins' forever family, and their only family. What they knew about the twins' birth was limited to what Susannah had told them, which amounted to her writing off the kids' dad as a mistake. A big one. No details. The way she'd told the story, she hadn't been with him long, but by the time she'd known he was 100 percent wrong for her, it was too late. She was pregnant. She'd been working up the courage to break the news to him, but before she'd had a chance, he'd been killed in a training exercise on base. But she'd been unequivocal about one thing. She would never have taken up with him again.

From the moment he and his mother got the shattering news of Susannah's death,

Matt had diverted his grief into doing whatever was best for Lucy and Nick. First, he'd pulled back his role in Finer Rides, the successful pack trip company he owned with his friend Ruben Stiles. Then, in a quest for stability—meaning an environment where he'd be home all the time—he'd bought the ranch. He'd been mulling over that decision even before Susannah had left, but with her gone, he'd jumped at it as a first step in creating the kind of childhood his sister would have wanted for her kids.

Mom had changed her life, too, when she'd given up her job as a history teacher at a high school in their home county over one hundred miles away. Still in her fifties, she'd sacrificed the work she loved to be his partner in raising her grandkids. Standing at the window and watching her shower all her attention on the two, he doubted she regretted her choice.

Bouts of sadness over losing his twin could slam into Matt without warning and knock him off balance. Every now and then he'd catch himself letting out a little moan, as if suddenly remembering Susannah was gone. Then he'd hurt like he'd lost her only yesterday. Sometimes he'd see his mom staring off into space. He didn't want to invade her privacy, but he'd bet something had come over her and she'd slipped into that pocket of her mind reserved for Susannah. Maybe she had random thoughts, too, like he did, fleeting memories and images that arrived like a gift to boost her spirit. But on other days a memory could slash him open.

He and his mom didn't talk much about any of this. At first, their lives were all about the twins, and over the past few years he'd followed Mom's lead as they'd drifted into a pattern of leaving each other to handle their grief alone.

Matt supposed that was okay, but there were times when he wouldn't have minded sharing a heart-to-heart about missing Susannah.

"Don't you need to be at the shelters or out in the fields? How are our babies coming along?" Mom asked when she came inside and joined him at the counter. "I can get the burgers ready for the grill."

"I don't need to be anywhere but here helping with dinner. To answer your question, we moved some moms and their lambs down to the pasture by the creek. Kenny looked after the horses so I could be on time to meet the bus. Fence repairs are on the agenda for tomorrow."

He'd been waiting all winter for mild weather like this to make a dent in the long list of chores that never seemed to stop. He didn't complain. Staying on the move kept worry from putting a dent in his upbeat attitude about the future of the ranch. He called it optimism that came naturally to him. Mom labeled it bravado—in a skeptical tone to go with an arched eyebrow.

Matt would much rather focus on recent projections that lamb prices would be up this year than dwell on their drop last fall. Same with the wool. Disheartening markets today could turn into promising ones by next shearing season. He wouldn't let his natural optimism waver because of a couple of lean years. Risky business being a sheepman these days, but weren't most optimists risk-takers?

His mom's wistful smile brought him out of his jumble of thoughts. "The twins are so full of life, Matt. They remind me so much of you and Susannah at the same age. You should be proud. Maybe I don't say it often enough, but you're doing a great job with those two."

Matt puffed out his chest and forgot his challenges whenever his mom said things like that about the twins. But he couldn't take all the credit, only his rightful share. "*We're* doing great. And the ranch is holding its own."

Not a ringing endorsement, but it was true nonetheless. The way Matt sized up the situation, he owned this ranch only because the Stanhopes hadn't changed with the times. For many ranching families, shrinking the herd, selling off some acres and pocketing the profit had been the wisest choice.

What had once been grazing acres around Adelaide Creek were now sites of private vacation homes. For people who craved space and a rugged landscape, the whole of Adams County was a little more remote, less commercial, than Jackson and the Yellowstone region to the north, so vacation homes were dotting the landscape everywhere. Matt called those places mansions since they were almost as big as some of the new lodge-style hotels sprouting up all over the place. Tourist ranches were on the rise, too.

Matt's independent streak led him to try to buck the odds in the only way that made sense. Go small, but go premium, both on the wool and the meat. That was why his sheep were numbered in the low hundreds, not the thousands that the Stanhopes had once raised.

"Bethany Hoover's wedding was the main topic at the meeting today," Mom said.

That brought his attention back to the here and now. "How so? It's still weeks away." Since he'd recently agreed to be Charlie Goodman's best man, he supposed he ought to pay attention. He was the groom's second choice, but that was okay. Charlie had known Jim, the intended best man, all his life, but he and Matt had met during their college days in Laramie. Charlie had done a couple of tours in the army before going to work as a civilian in intelligence, operating from remote locations. Who he actually worked for was part of the mystery surrounding his job. Matt had reconnected with Charlie when buying the ranch had put them in the same town.

"The buzz wasn't about the wedding

plans," Mom said. "Your counterpart, the maid of honor, was the big topic of conversation."

"Oh? How so?"

"Well, she's Heather Stanhope, Matt. She's back from wherever she's been living these last years. Minnesota, I think." She pulled cucumbers and greens out of the fridge and put them on the counter. "From what I heard, Heather might be here for most of the summer. She's staying in Bethany's place on the Hoover ranch."

Hearing her name made him jolt to attention. Charlie hadn't mentioned the maid of honor and Matt hadn't asked. But so what? It was probably best not to make too much of this development. "Well, that's good. I'll enjoy getting to know her."

That arched eyebrow made another appearance. Mom's way of telling him how ridiculous he sounded.

"No, no, I mean it, Mom. I wanted to meet her back when we closed on this place. This house and the land are special." He glanced around the kitchen, doing a quick inventory of all the repairs and updates he and Mom had done over the years on a house that had started as a crude two-room cabin more than a century ago. He was standing a few feet away from what had been the sleeping corner for the first owners. He'd seen an old drawing of it.

Matt had been disappointed when Heather had left town around the time he'd bought the ranch from the bank. After the bank foreclosed on the land and everything on it. He'd have welcomed the chance to ask Heather about growing up on the ranch. She probably had a few good stories to tell. Over the years, Matt had heard a little talk about Heather now and again. Most of it positive.

Matt and his mom had met her brother, Jeff, once, and that was on the porch of the nearly hollowed-out house. The word *forlorn* came to mind to describe both the house and Jeff, who'd stopped by only to pick up tools from the barn. His eyes had flashed with anger, and he'd spoken in short, terse phrases. The last image wasn't of Jeff himself, but of the clouds of dust the tires had kicked up as he'd floored the accelerator and sped away.

"Don't get your hopes up," Mom warned. "I doubt you'll have much chance to spend time with Heather. Really, Matt, what makes you think she's changed her attitude about you? Remember what the loan officer at the bank said? Heather was devastated, not only because she and her brother lost the land, but they'd lost their mother, too. A double hit. That's why she didn't come to the closing."

"What happened to the Stanhopes was terrible. I get it," Matt said. "But that was four years ago. Besides, lots of folks around here have been through the same thing, even Dad's parents."

Restless, he walked to the window, braced his arm on the frame and watched Scrambler dutifully going after the sticks Lucy and Nick tossed his way. A little too old to turn the game into a competition, Scrambler was inclined to take his time and slow-trot the stick back to the twins.

"C'mon, Matt," Mom chided. "Your grandparents *sold* their ranch before their troubles got so bad they risked losing it. Heather Stanhope and her brother must have felt a great sense of loss."

Matt winced. That part of the story hadn't resonated back then quite the way it did now. He'd been cavalier about the Stanhopes, more or less blaming them for their bad luck. Since

Finer Rides had done so well, he'd been pretty cocky about turning the ranch into a profitable venture.

He turned back to his mom. "Okay, I get that history and the hardships. But it's not like we don't know what it's like to lose people we love." First, his dad had died way too young. Then Susannah. Nothing could ever compare to losing his twin.

"Maybe Heather's still bitter, but I can't do a thing about that," he said. "Anyway, from what Charlie told me, this is a really small wedding for family and a few close friends. A no-gift policy, too. They're telling people to donate to the food pantry and shelter in Landrum instead."

"I like that," his mom said. "It must be hard for Bethany to plan a wedding with Charlie gone for such long stretches."

"I have no idea where Charlie is right now. But he was scheduled to get a week away for the Fourth of July. The date chose them, not the other way around."

"It seemed like an odd day for a wedding, but now it makes sense."

"It also makes sense that Heather and I be

civil, at the very least." He shrugged. "Besides, we're adults, not kids."

Mom chuckled. "My, my, don't you sound reasonable."

"As always," he kidded. "Reasonable is my middle name."

"You could be right—maybe the pair of you will be two peas in a pod. But I'm not betting on it." She flicked her hand. "Shoo, shoo. Go on, get the grill ready. I'll finish the salad."

"Yes, ma'am." Matt tipped a pretend hat and went out to the gas grill on the concrete patio. Late afternoons and evenings were still too cold to eat outside at the picnic table, but it was warm enough to use the grill.

Matt waved to the kids. They were sitting on top of a pyramid of crates he'd stacked, fastened together, and secured to the ground. He'd named his invention the Twins Topper. It gave the kids a hill to climb with a safe perch on top they could call their own. Scrambler sat between them. They'd taken their arms out of their unzipped sweatshirts but kept the hoods hanging on their heads. Their gram would fuss about the cold air, but he let it go. They had the good sense to put their arms in the sleeves if they needed to. He slipped his phone out of his pocket and got a shot of the twins and Scrambler before something else caught their attention and they ran off.

Maybe Heather Stanhope would feel a little better about him once she knew these two irresistible kids were being raised here. Matt hoped the kids would want to be shepherds one day.

When he walked toward the twins, he couldn't miss the contrast between the two. It nagged at him a little because it wasn't the first time he'd noticed subtle differences appearing, especially in Nick, over the last few months. At the moment, Lucy sat straight and was talking to Scrambler as she scratched behind his ears. Nick was slumped and leaning against the dog's back. His eyes were half closed.

A few weeks ago, he'd questioned their doctor about Lucy's vitality and Nick's tendency to run out of gas. "Nothing to worry about," the doc had said without hesitation. "At this age, girls develop a little faster than boys. But I understand. You and your mom took these kids in under tragic circumstances, so it's only natural you'd be nervous."

Matt had left the doctor's office relieved to know that nothing unusual was going on with Nick. But he didn't like labels and he took issue with being dismissed as a so-called nervous parent. Now, though, when he looked at Nick cuddled up with Scrambler, the doc's words came back to Matt. He could relax, right? Nick was fine. They were all fine.

CHAPTER TWO

Jen peered over Heather's shoulder, where the screen on her tablet showed the figures from the last sale. "Yikes, I should be paying you a hefty hourly wage—and a bonus." With Spring Fling in full swing, they stood inside the tent at the folding tables that served as a makeshift shop counter.

Heather responded with a proud smile. "I had a feeling you'd be happy about that." She'd sent a woman off with three drawstring muslin bags filled with Icelandic wool destined to become a rug. The bags were imprinted with Jen's company name, Cold Country Wool, and her logo, an outline of mountain peaks behind a pair of pure-white sheep. Who could resist sheep decked out in their full wool coats?

The impressive Cold Country Wool tent had been like a magnet for visitors since the fair launched that morning. Almost every available space in the tent was filled with baskets of wool and spun yarn. Large fleeces sat on Jen's folding shelves, which Heather had helped her set up earlier. On the other side of the tent, similar baskets and shelving were filled with tea and herbs and jars of Jen's popular chokecherry jam. All her products were popular with tourists and locals.

"Or maybe a commission is in order," Jen added. "I saw you sell a bagful of that Shetland yarn I dyed with turmeric."

"An eye-popping yellow." Heather picked up a skein of the wavy Shetland wool transformed by the dye. "You've almost sold out."

"That's the idea. I don't do much dying myself anymore," Jen explained. "It eats up time, so I leave that to the hand spinners who like to do their own thing. But I do get a kick out of experimenting now and again."

Heather smiled at Jen. "I'll work for free. Why not? You offer great benefits. I get to hang out in my own room in Bethany's comfy bunkhouse, complete with satellite TV and the internet. You throw in a spectacular view, and what more does a girl need? It's fun selling fleeces and yarn to your throngs of admirers while inhaling the heavenly aroma of your lavender."

"I'm happy if you're happy." Jen gave her shoulder a quick squeeze. "We're almost done for the day. Bethany should be coming along, and we'll close up and get some dinner at one of the food tents. Meanwhile, I need to get back to the spinning tent. I promised to do another demonstration."

Heather got to work straightening out the baskets of soft wool, but started when a familiar voice called out to her. "Heather?" Her name had been spoken as a question a couple of times that day by people surprised to see her in town.

Recognizing this voice, she turned around quickly. "Hi, Cookie."

Cookie had been one of her mom's closest friends and a constant presence during the hard years of cancer treatments and the rise and fall of hope. Cookie also happened to be the last person Heather had called before leaving town. Seeing her approach slowly and using a cane was a shocker. That was quickly replaced by a sinking mix of regret and shame over her broken promise to Cookie to stay in touch.

"What brings you back to town?" Cookie asked.

"Bethany Hoover's wedding. My last nursing contract ended a couple of weeks ago, so I came early." Heather forced a smile and breezy tone. "Then I'll head back to Minnesota. Uh, probably."

"And here I thought you'd be smart enough to put yourself in a warmer place," Cookie teased.

"As it turns out, I get along quite well with snow." Heather glanced at Cookie's cane, not meaning to stare.

Cookie patted her left hip with her free hand. "As for me, I have a new hip, but she still hasn't learned how to keep up with me. The two of us are training for the day I can toss this cane in the back of the closet where it belongs."

The nurse in Heather was amused. She'd never heard anyone turn a replaced hip into a pal to train with, but that was Cookie.

"Any chance you'll stay?" Cookie whispered.

Heather shook her head. "I don't see how… It's hard. And it's time for me to settle down in one place. You know, get a permanent job."

And a house. A man to share her life with would be some icing on her sometimes lonely cake. Heather chased all those distracting thoughts away by gesturing around the tent. "I've been hiding out in here all day, but it seems almost everyone I ever knew has wandered in to see what Jen is up to."

"Like me," Cookie said. "I never leave any of these events without a bag of Jen's lavender sachets and a package or two of tea."

"It's been fun helping her get ready for Spring Fling. It's so different from the work I usually do. And Jen manages to make everything look easy." She took a couple of steps toward the tea and herbs and picked up a shopping basket to hold for Cookie. "Everything you want is right here."

"Ah, yes, here's the nettle tea." Cookie dropped two packages in the basket followed by half a dozen sachets. "Little gifts for special people."

When another customer came in, Heather excused herself and helped her pick out an assortment of the Shetland wool. By the time she'd bagged the shopper's items, Cookie was ready to leave.

Heather took in a breath. It was now or never.

"You know, I was planning to call when I—"

"Don't." Cookie reached over to touch her hand. "Don't say a word. I'd hoped to hear from you after you took off, honey, but I understood. You needed to leave everything and everyone behind. All you ever need to know is that I loved your mom like a sister."

Heather fought the pressure building behind her eyes. She simply nodded as she ran Cookie's credit card and bagged her purchases. Cookie's smile was a little sad when she spoke. "Have a good time fussing with the wedding. Bethany must be thrilled you're here. The best man's mother, Stacey Burton, is a good friend of mine. I imagine you'll meet her at some point." She waved her cane. "Maybe I'll see you later at the dance. I'll have to settle for watching." Then she was gone.

With the subject of Bethany's wedding still in mind, unfortunately, it also made her think of Mathis Burton. As the initial jolt at Bethany's best man news had worn off, Heather had tried her best to cover up her dismay. She'd assured Bethany she was fine—or would be. She needed a little time to get used to the idea, that's all. A little lie. Maybe it didn't make sense to other people, but Heather had assumed there'd never be a need to cross paths with Mathis Burton.

Heather couldn't deny Mathis sounded like an okay guy. More than okay. When Bethany described him, she led with his great looks. Tall, with broad shoulders, dark reddish-brown hair, blue-green eyes and, what Bethany prized most of all, a sweet smile. Bethany didn't know him well, but he—and his mother—had made quite an impression in Adelaide Creek. It hadn't taken long for everybody in town to learn Mathis, with Stacey's help, was raising his sister's twins. She'd been a helicopter pilot killed in Afghanistan when her twins were only two years old.

Heather listened and nodded along, but she hadn't needed a rundown of the man's virtues. They were beside the point. She understood that Mathis wasn't a criminal, after all. He bought a ranch that was up for sale. It wasn't his fault it happened to be the ranch she loved.

But tell that to her heart.

The afternoon passed quickly. Heather's job was done once she and Jen finished cleaning up the tent and straightening the shelves. Jen almost shoved Heather out of the tent. "Wander around. Take a good look. You'll be surprised by all the changes to our famous Spring Fling. It's a lot bigger these days."

The Cold Country Wool tent was one of a couple dozen set up for the weekend event, which was always held in mid-May. Other than a few exceptions like Jen, the people selling wares came from all over their part of Wyoming. Adelaide Creek had one main street, Merchant Street, which had a small town hall at one end. Behind that building, the town had a cemetery and a war memorial, a small playground and a makeshift diamond for baseball games. It wore a decidedly different look during Spring Fling weekend.

She took a photo of a banner with whimsical curlicue writing that marked the start of an area designated as "Adelaide Creek's Hall of Tents." It was late in the day, but a fair number of people were still milling around. She visited potters and photographers with names she didn't recognize. One man sold felt cowboy hats and another displayed hand-tooled leather bags and belts.

One artist immediately captured Heather's interest. A young woman, early twenties tops, sold jewelry made with Wyoming jade. Heather found long earrings with dangling dark green jade ovals and shiny silver beads. A bit much for her own small face, but the added panache was perfect for the look Bethany and Jen pulled off. She bought a pair for each and tucked them in her backpack.

Tinny carnival music blared from the carousel as Heather strolled beyond the tents and past the food trucks, where the smell of popcorn and fried dough competed for top billing. Tempting aromas, but she had dinner on her mind, specifically barbecued chicken and ribs in the tent where she was to meet Bethany and her folks. The largest tent by far sat like a centerpiece of the festival. Heather stopped to watch two guys rolling a piano up a ramp to the stage inside. A half dozen men and women with guitars and fiddles followed.

The musicians and the tent triggered precious little-girl memories Heather wouldn't trade for anything. Her mom and dad had never missed Spring Fling or the Christmas Village on Merchant Street in December.

The dances were always the best part. Her dad had taught her the beauty of a country waltz; how to let her heart feel the melodies and rhythms of the fiddles and guitars. She'd felt wonderfully grown up when Dad had danced with her at the summer fairs in their region. When they were teens, she and Bethany had never wanted for dance partners, at least not for long. If their dads saw either one of them sidelined, they'd swoop in and get them dancing again.

Heather stared inside the tent where the musicians were setting up. If she was going to make it out to the dance floor that night, she'd likely need to count on Bethany's dad one more time.

MATT TOOK HIS mom's elbow as they left the floor after a good run of "Boot Scootin' Boogie," a line dance his dad used to enjoy. They went back to the table where his mom's friend, Cookie Rogers, kept her eye on the twins.

So far, they'd all had a good day. Better than good. For one thing, Nick's eyes and his stomach had synced this year, so the hot dogs he'd drowned in mustard and ketchup stayed put in his little tummy. They all rode the carousel a couple of times, but the highlight for Matt was waving goodbye to the two as the kiddie train left the station and circled the grounds. This was the first time they'd been old enough to take that trip without their gram squeezing in with them.

"Come on, Lucy girl, your turn." He lifted her out of her seat and raised her in the air. "We're going to have ourselves a dance."

His mom appeared and grabbed Nick's hand. "And I need a new partner. Follow me."

Matt lowered Lucy to the floor, took both her hands in his and stepped side to side to a lively country-western beat that made it easy to circle the outer edges of the floor. Nick and Mom followed them.

Matt chuckled when he twirled Lucy under his arm. "Isn't that fun? You're already a fine dancer, Lucy." One day he'd tell her about her mom and how she'd won a couple line dance contests back in the day.

Lucy's big smile hadn't left her face since the music started. "This is so fun, Uncle Matt."

"It's not over yet." Matt didn't have words to describe what Lucy's shining face did to his heart. "Let's make another trip around, sweetie. Want me to pick you up? You'll like the view from up here."

When Lucy nodded, he hoisted her up to rest against his hip and held her arm out like a real dance hold. "Now you can see everything." He turned this way and that as he danced past couples Matt knew from the ranchers' association.

Then the librarian who ran the story hour for the kids smiled at him as she and her husband danced by. All evening, he'd said hello to people he hoped finally no longer thought of him as the stranger who'd bought the Stanhope place.

Halfway around the room, he spun twice with Lucy and, when he stopped, a pretty woman he'd never met was smiling at Lucy.

It was her. Heather Stanhope. He was sure of it. She glanced at him before her partner, Dan Hoover, pivoted away and her back was to Matt. Dark wavy hair hung past her shoulders. A petite woman, the top of her head barely came to Dan's shoulder.

Matt recognized Heather from a photograph in the *Adams County Register*. The newspaper had published a series of stories discussing the dramatic changes to ranching and farming in the area over several generations. The history of the Stanhope family intrigued him, especially the women. From the articles and photographs, the women had been full partners in this rough and rugged business of sheep ranching. The Stanhope family also had produced a number of beauties. The first Adelaide was also petite and pretty with thick dark hair.

When the music stopped, Matt put Lucy down and did a little bow. "Thank you, Miss Lucy. A gentleman always thanks the lady for the honor of allowing him to dance with her."

Lucy giggled. "You're so funny, Uncle Matt."

"I try, kiddo," Matt said in a serious tone. "Let's go see if Nick and Gram had as much fun as we did."

Lucy ran ahead of him and was soon comparing notes with Nick, who was drawing on a napkin now. Matt glanced around him at the tent packed to capacity, and with a lull in the music, the space filled with the buzz of people talking and laughing. He inhaled the aromas coming from the popcorn machine and the hot pretzel cart, the only food served in the tent.

Matt sat next to Nick and listened with one ear to the kids' conversation and with the other ear to Mom and Cookie's. Mostly, he tried not to be obvious about keeping an eye out for Heather. This evening offered a chance to meet her before the wedding hoopla started. He wasn't sure why, but he needed her to know how much he respected her family's history. Even more so now that he knew firsthand what it took to make sure the sheep earned their keep.

When the music came up it was a mellow waltz, and Heather and Dan Hoover were almost the first on the dance floor. Opportunity knocked.

He got to his feet. "Can you keep an eye on the twins for me, Mom?"

"Sure. Are you finally going to ask someone to dance?"

"Sort of." He kept his eye on Dan and Heather and made his way to the other end of the floor. He was self-conscious enough without making his move right in front of Mom and Cookie and the twins.

As Dan and Heather passed, Matt saw his chance. He dodged one couple dancing by and slipped in beside Dan and Heather before they moved away. He tapped Dan on the shoulder. "Mind if I cut in?"

Heather frowned and she opened her mouth as if to say something. Matt braced to hear whatever it was, but Dan spoke up first.

"Well now, Mathis, seeing as how it's the twenty-first century, it's really up to the lady." Dan kept one hand on Heather's waist and the other still held her hand.

Even in the dim light, he saw her eyes flash with sudden emotion. Anger? He didn't think so. A touch of apprehension was more like it.

"This particular lady isn't into public scenes." She nodded to Dan and turned to Matt. "I suppose we had to meet sometime. I'm Heather Stanhope."

Dan gave Matt a friendly pat on the shoulder and backed away.

Matt made a quick decision not to waste time responding to her comment and instead picked up on the mood the music created. "As it happens, I'm not a half-bad dancer. I can waltz us around this floor pretty good." He bit the inside of his cheek. Great. He'd managed to sound like a braggart with an exaggerated cowboy drawl.

She offered a crooked smile and raised her arms. "Okay then, mister, show me what you've got."

Grinning at her challenge, he promptly stepped forward and put his hand on the small of her back. When her warm fingers disappeared in his other hand, Matt picked up the three-quarter time and they easily fell in sync with the other dancers moving as one around the floor. She was light in his arms as she took sure, confident steps.

As they rounded a corner, he saw his mom waltzing with Grey Murtagh. He checked his table and saw that Cookie was gone and now Jen Hoover had one twin on each knee.

"Jen Hoover and my mom are friends," Matt said. "I see the mother of the bride is looking after my twins right now."

Heather tilted her head and looked into his eyes. "Then they're in good hands."

"Yes. And so am I." The words slipped out before he could think about them, which would have been more like his usual self. But then he'd have missed her pretend disapproving eye roll.

"How's the Mr. Charming Cowboy act working for you?"

"Don't know. I never tried it before." He smiled and lightly squeezed her hand. "At least I'm not shy and tongue-tied around the pretty bridesmaid."

She shook her head but offered no comeback. Emboldened now as the music got slower and the volume lowered, he added a little flourish and a couple of twirls. "You dance like you really enjoy it," he said.

"Like you." She tilted her head back to look at him. "I saw you with your little niece. She looked so thrilled to be with you. You looked pretty happy yourself."

He'd have liked to tell her making Lucy happy made him happy, but now he really was tongue-tied. Of course, Bethany and Jen would have told her his family's story. Luckily, he didn't have to respond because the music was winding down. One last twirl and they came to a stop exactly on the final note. Perfect timing. Couldn't have been better if he'd choreographed it himself.

Heather gave him a quick smile as she stepped back. "Not bad."

Matt jumped in and pointed to the cash bar

set up in the corner. "Can I get you a drink? Beer? Wine? A little bourbon?"

She twisted around and looked in Bethany's direction. Her friend was chatting with Dan but gave her a wave. "Um, okay. One beer before I go home."

"Great. I'll get our drinks and meet you at your table."

Giving him a frankly curious look, she nodded and walked away.

As he navigated around the tables, he checked on the twins. They were safe with Mom, Grey and Jen. He waved, and his mom got to her feet and, with Grey trailing behind, hurried to him. Her face was a little flushed when she said, "Grey is going to drive the twins and me home."

Matt shook his head. "No, no need for that. I'll take you and the twins now." He'd ask Heather for a rain check on that drink. Grey was a good guy and all, but Matt didn't want to impose.

"It's all decided. You stay here," Mom said, backing away. "Don't worry about anything. Enjoy yourself. It's about time, honey."

"The pleasure is all mine, Matt." Grey

cupped Stacey's elbow and the two were off before he could protest.

Looking over her shoulder, his mom lifted her hand and fluttered her fingers. He knew that little gesture well. It was her all-purpose "the subject is closed" wave, usually delivered when she left a room.

"Thanks," he called out. From his place in line at the bar, he watched Grey and Mom laughing as they helped the twins into their jackets. The foursome left through the tent's side entrance. Well, well, look at that. Mom and Murtagh? Really? Nah, she'd never mentioned him in any special way before.

By the time he got to Heather's table, Dan had gone to join Jen. That left Bethany, who greeted Matt but quickly stood. "I see Millie from the hospital. Her dad's been sick. I need to go say hello." She took off in a shot.

Matt put down the two bottles of Jadestone local brew and pulled out the chair next to Heather's, thinking that she had such poise and such big brown eyes. From what he'd heard, she'd inherited her share of Stanhope steel. He lifted his bottle of beer and didn't wait for a formal toast but tapped his bottle against hers. "It's true my name is Mathis, but I go by Matt. I think it's a good idea for us to get to know each other."

She took a quick swig of her beer. When she leaned back in her chair, she looked at him through penetrating eyes. "And why is that?"

Her icy tone threw him. "Since I'm the best man and you're the maid of honor at the same wedding. Seems to me being on friendly terms is a good thing all around. Especially for Charlie and Bethany's sake." He puffed his cheeks and blew out the air. He was suddenly tired of tiptoeing around. "Look, the wedding aside, I understand why you might not think too much of me, but I've got to say people around here have only good things to say about you."

Heather's expression softened. "You exaggerate." She paused, but not for long. "I was surprised by how many old acquaintances I ran into while I was helping out in Jen's tent today." She bit the corner of her lower lip and stared at the dancers. "But most people have either already forgotten about me and my family, or they will soon enough. The Wyoming Stanhopes are history."

How could she believe her family would

ever be forgotten? Astounding. "I've seen proof of your family's hard work in this community. They made a big difference over the years. I saw photos of the Stanhopes in a newspaper series about sheep ranching in the county." He paused and sipped his beer. "The articles were published to help launch the ranching retrospective display at the Adams County Gallery over in Landrum. I hope you're not touchy about being compared to Adelaide. Truth is, you look an awful lot like her."

Heather smiled. "It's never an insult to be compared to my great-great-grandma Adelaide."

"Have you kept a lot of family memorabilia?"

Her mouth turned down when she said, "Not really."

"Take it from me, it's hard but worth it to visit memory lane once in a while."

She took a gulp of her beer and then nervously drummed her fingers on the side of the bottle. "When our mother got sick, my brother and I helped her go through boxes and boxes of family history in the attic. We hadn't ventured up there in years."

It wasn't difficult for Matt to picture what a huge job that must have been.

"By that time, we'd run through all our options, so we knew we were losing everything." She averted her gaze but lifted her chin a tiny notch. "But Mom insisted we organize the old ranch logs and the account books and get them ready for the county library's archives. Our records went all the way back to the starting days of the ranch."

"Must have been a huge job, but interesting, not to mention a benefit to the county."

"I guess." Her tone was as weak as the words. "For weeks, I'd come home from work and we'd sort and label all the papers and the photos. Mom was a stickler for detail and left nothing to chance."

A mind-boggling undertaking, Matt thought as the music dropped off and the tent quieted. He'd recalled the write-up mentioning the records her family had preserved. Handwritten logs of herd numbers, shearing stats, annual lambing, wages, bank loans and sales. "The work was worth it, and the retrospective at the gallery does your family proud."

Finally, she looked him directly in the eye. "I'll be sure to get to the gallery before

I leave again." She shifted her gaze to the dancers coming off the floor now.

"I'd be pleased to take…" He stopped himself before he made an offer she'd be sure to refuse. He could see from her stiffened jaw she'd mentally finished his sentence and quickly rejected the idea.

A faint smile appeared when she said, "Thanks, but that's something I need to do alone."

"Of course," he said quickly. "I'm sorry. I shouldn't have presumed…"

"Don't apologize," she said kindly. "No need. I just don't want to talk about my family anymore." The band started again, and she popped up from the chair and held out her hand. "So, Mathis-who-goes-by-Matt, I can't do the two-step alone. You game?"

What a question. He got to his feet and took her hand. "Oh, yeah."

CHAPTER THREE

HEATHER SHOVED HER hands in her jacket pockets and detoured off the path, ambling up the rise where the Icelanders and Shetlands were hanging out on the chilly, cloudy day. With their recently sheared wool growing back, they were just full enough not to look bare. Their heads lowered, they were focused on finding enticing morsels in the pasture. She skirted the edge of the field and passed the water troughs she'd helped Jen fill yesterday. Taking care not to get too close and risk scaring the sheep off, she moved slowly but purposefully.

"With Jen looking out for you, I promise you'll never go hungry," she said aloud to the sheep out of long habit. It was in her blood to talk to these creatures, even if they paid absolutely no attention. Maybe because she sold their wool in person to eager buyers well versed in the lingo of fiber art, Heather understood what all the fuss over wool was about.

Her mother would have called Icelanders charming, even whimsical. Then her dad would have groaned and teased about romanticizing these four-legged cash-producing creatures. Her father had been the extrovert in that pair, but her mom had brought a brand of humor that had kept her dad entertained.

Even with the small scale of Jen's operation, tending the gardens and doing something as familiar as filling the water troughs triggered waves of nostalgia for the kind of physical work Heather relished. She didn't even mind her achy back.

The sheep her parents raised were bigger, the common breeds meant to produce meat—and lots of it. She hadn't asked Matt what kind of sheep he was raising, but most likely they were Rambouillet or Merino. Mom and Dad used to talk about their fleeces being sent to commercial mills and coming out as blankets and sweaters. She'd liked that story, especially the way it fed her imagination about Stanhope sheep providing both warmth and dinner.

Matt, again. She'd had a hard time shaking off the memory of him holding her hand or his light touch on her back. Bethany's description hadn't done the guy justice. His thick wavy hair was a little wild and unruly, enough to draw her eye, but not scruffy. A killer smile and smooth on the dance floor were two items on a list describing a nearly irresistible guy.

Heather stopped, bent over and grabbed her ankles, and stretched her back. Maybe it ached a little more than she cared to admit. Pediatric nursing was plenty taxing, but it didn't call on her ranching muscles.

Straightening again, she admired Jen's pastures, various shades of green and tan under the morning sun. The slabs and outcroppings on the nearby rocky hills sparkled almost as brightly as Matt's niece. She nearly laughed out loud remembering the adorable little girl circling the dance floor in her uncle's arms. Lucy. She could have been Heather herself as a child growing up on the same ranch and happily dancing with Daddy at Spring Fling.

After Saturday's fair, she no longer feared feeling like a stranger in town. She'd seen too many familiar faces for that. She wasn't the first Stanhope who dug up roots and planted them elsewhere, but with Jeff gone, too, hers would be the last.

Heather picked up speed when she passed the cedar fence and the fresh rails on the gate she'd helped Jen repair yesterday. Jen stood on the porch and gestured her to the house, not the shed or greenhouse. She held up a giant mug. Hot green tea. Heather was certain of that, because anyone who entered Jen's kitchen was welcomed with a cup of green tea with lemon.

Heather left her work boots on the porch before she went into the kitchen and settled at the table. Jen pushed a plate bearing a warm cinnamon muffin in front of her.

"Tea and muffins," Heather said. "Some things don't change with the times."

"There's plenty more of everything," Jen said, nodding at the plate.

"You'll be happy to hear your sheep friends are depleting your pasture," Heather reported with a smile, "which is as it should be in May." This was as good a time as any to mention something else on her mind. "Are my mom's paintings still up in your attic?"

"Still snug in their crates up there, except for the ones she gave me." Jen pointed into the dining room at the familiar oil painting of the sun setting behind the mountain range in the distance. "The attic is the safest place for them until you settle somewhere. And Jeff, too. One day, you'll proudly hang those treasures in your own homes."

"Yes, and maybe sooner rather than later." Heather stared at the painting, as she had the other night at dinner with Jen and Dan. A self-taught painter, her mother had captured a moment when the sun had turned the sky pink and red, but the peaks and rocks and even the pastures below were graduated shades of violet turning to lavender and finally transforming to a vivid purple. Morning and evening light had a way of creating for real what her mother immortalized in watercolors and oils.

"I see that picture on my wall every day and think of Noreen," Jen said in a wistful tone. "I've got the watercolor she did of you and Bethany up in our bedroom."

Heather swallowed a mouthful of tea and struggled with the push-pull of her thoughts. Her eagerness to see a few of her mom's pieces was disrupted by a twinge of fear that seeing the paintings would plunge her into a bout of sadness—with self-pity stabbing at her heart, too. Finally, though, the longing to see her mom's work won out. "Would you mind if I went up to the attic and had a look at them? Not all, but maybe a few. The other night at the dance Mathis—Matt—was telling me there's a ranching exhibit at the county gallery. It made me think about her work."

"I haven't been over to the gallery lately, but I heard a couple of the paintings you donated are part of the retrospective." Jen got to her feet and lifted her gaze to the ceiling. "I'd enjoy a little art show myself." She grabbed a claw hammer from a kitchen drawer and gestured for Heather to follow her. They went up the curved staircase to the second floor and then navigated the narrow creaky flight to the attic.

Jen and Dan's attic was stuffed full of dusty trunks, stacks of cartons and mismatched chairs. In one corner, an old rocking horse sat next to a wooden cradle. "I'm going to rub those down with lemon oil one day and see if I can bring them back," Jen said, pointing to the items meant for babies and toddlers. "I'm hoping I'll have use for them sooner or later." She flashed a sly smile. "Preferably sooner."

Heather scoffed. "Now, now, give Bethany and Charlie a little time."

"C'mon. You can't blame me for yearning for a grandchild scampering around here before too long." She led the way to the opposite corner where the paintings were stored in protective coverings Dan and Jeff had made from strips of pine. "There they are, safe and sound."

Heather followed and pulled out the first in the row of paintings. More than any other memory of that day, it was their silence as they had worked that stuck with her. She and Bethany hadn't spoken as they'd wrapped the framed paintings and placed each in its own newly built snug box. Dan and Jeff had used a staple gun to secure the top cover. Then, frozen in numb silence, Jen had added the label and they'd moved on to the next one.

Heather patted one of the labels she had printed. "I remember this. It's a landscape, but not the one I was thinking of for Bethany and Charlie." Heather searched for a smaller box. "Bethany's favorite spot was down by the willows at Addie Creek."

"I'm positive she and Charlie would be thrilled to have one of Noreen's landscapes," Jen said, raising her eyebrows and curling her mouth into a lopsided smile. "As you know, Charlie and Bethany declared a no-gift rule for their wedding. Between the two of them, they've got all the dishes and coffeepots and toasters they need. But they don't have a Noreen Stanhope original to put a special stamp on their first house."

"I only met Charlie a couple of times before I left town, but I think having a small, no-fuss wedding here at the house is a perfect fit for Bethany," Heather said. "She never was a girl to get dreamy about fluffy white dresses and a guest list of hundreds." She leaned toward Jen. "Going to be an interesting wedding shower without gifts to open, but I'll do my best."

"My girl is one of a kind," Jen said, with a pride in her voice. "It's no surprise the two of you have been friends forever."

Heather searched the labels until she found the one she wanted for Bethany and set it aside. She also set aside another one of Wyoming sheep country under a cover of white snow. "Bethany always had a soft spot for quiet winter nights when everything is blanketed in snow. I'll give them both paintings. Mom would approve."

The last piece in the row was the one she'd had on her mind and wanted to look at now. "I was thinking about this painting the day I drove into town. I like to remember the way Mom captured the two of us and the horses."

Jen sighed. "You two and your classic brown Morgans. Noreen started sketching you and Jeff when you were toddlers. She practiced on you." Jen placed the hammer close to the crate. "Enough reminiscing. Shall I start pulling these staples?"

Heather paused to reconsider disturbing what had been a big undertaking to secure the paintings. "How about just this one? I don't want to pull them all apart. Besides, if I get a yen to see more, I can go through the unframed canvases we rolled up for storage." Heather pointed with her chin at the collection of cardboard tubes standing upright in the corner.

"Got it." Jen carried the crate to the window to catch the natural light. With Heather steadying the crate, Jen freed the staples with the claw and, in a matter of minutes, lifted the front cover off and set it aside.

Heather knelt on the floor and loosened the thick plastic covering. She didn't need to take it completely out of the box to stare at it and satisfy her longing to connect with her mother—and Jeff.

Jen smiled. "Don't you love its name? *J & H with Pals.* Short and sweet."

Their four-legged pals, her dad had called the horses. "We were teenagers when she painted this." Heather inhaled the faint scent of the oil paint. Or thought she did. Was that possible? This painting was over fifteen years old. It had to be her imagination. "She used to paint at the dining room window, and my mind is conjuring up the scent of the room."

"At first, Noreen balked at trying oils," Jen said. "She protested about spending so much money on a hobby."

Heather scoffed. "Hobby. Ha! Such modesty. She still considered herself an amateur, a dabbler, even after we persuaded her to display her work at the local fairs." Heather ran her hand across the top of the smooth pine frame. "This one took second place in a show. It seemed to embarrass her to be noticed."

"I remember that." Without touching the canvas, Jen swept her index finger across the head of Velvet, Heather's horse. "Noreen captured her brown coat and tan mane and tail." Heather had named her Velvet after she'd first stroked the horse's face and neck. No other name fit. "Your mom was thrilled to place in the show because it meant she did justice to you and Jeff, and to the creek behind you."

"I never knew that," Heather whispered, "but it doesn't surprise me."

Heather turned away from the painting. "I'm glad my middle name is Adelaide, but I usually think of it as Addie, like Addie Creek." A touchstone. Every year her dad had called it a miracle when the cottonwoods and willows lining the creek survived the winter blizzards and the lightning strikes during thunderstorms.

"Well, Miss Heather Addie, you're sure to be surprised by how much our dot on the map has changed. Lots of newcomers in town. They've given our little Merchant Street

Diner a new lease on life. So has G & G, the combo market, groceries and gifts."

"And there's even a caterer," Heather added with a chuckle. "Lucky for us, Donna Kay does simple food for simple wedding showers."

Jen paused. "We don't like seeing so many ranches selling out to the big guys or closing down altogether, but I figure most people think the changes aren't so bad."

Heather didn't offer a counterpoint. She intended to stay far away from discussions about what was good or bad for Adelaide Creek. "Interesting, but I'm not here to reminisce. I came with weeks to spare so you can boss me around and let me be useful. Same with Bethany, but so far, she's been a thoroughly undemanding bride." She put the cover back on the painting. "If you have a staple gun handy, I'll put this together."

"Nah, I'll do it later," Jen said. "You're sure you don't want to look at some of the others?"

Heather whispered no and glanced at Jen as her heart turned mushy for the woman who'd been her second mom. "I'm satisfied for now. It makes me think of Jeff, but also of Velvet and Corkie, a couple of great horses."

As heartbreaking as it had been to part with the two Morgans, it had comforted Heather to know that they would be together and well cared for at a tourist ranch in Utah. She had the annual photo sent with a Christmas card to let her know all was well.

Jen's voice dropped to nearly a whisper when she asked, "Do you think Jeff will come back one day?"

"Hard to say." Or even imagine. "But if he does, he'll find himself another Corkie. Horses, Jen. The one thing your spread is missing," Heather teased. She'd done a little riding in the last four years, but she'd been too mobile to buy and board a horse. But when she settled down in Minnesota, she'd buy both a house and a horse. Who knows, maybe she'd even meet a man who owned horses and liked to dance. Now that would be a piece of good luck. Mathis Burton immediately came to mind. Ridiculous. He was not even in the running.

"We have lots of stables around here, honey. Since we've got weeks before the wedding," Jen said, "maybe you could get out for a trail ride. Bethany doesn't have the same passion for horses as you, but maybe you could kidnap her and take her along."

"Now there's an idea." Heather sighed. "Like old times."

THEY STOPPED THE horses at the crest of a hill above the pasture. "See? If you hadn't taken me up on my offer," Matt said, "you'd have missed your chance to enjoy all this."

Heather offered a small smile, her expression thoughtful as she took in the scene in front of them. Likely, she was caught up in the moment, like him—everything seemed perfect.

She leaned forward and stroked Pebbles, a classic white Appaloosa spotted in black. "You took me by surprise," Heather said. "One minute I was with Jen up in her attic. We were talking about the horses my brother and I owned, and I no sooner left her house than you called. And here I am on a dazzling horse on this gorgeous day." Her smile widened. "Your Pebbles is the perfect size for me."

"That she is." Matt heard a hint of sadness in his voice, not something he wanted interjected into their ride. "My sister, Susannah, searched a long time and tried out at least a dozen horses before she met her pretty Appaloosa. She said her spots were like black stones tossed onto white sand. And in an instant, it was decided. Pebbles had trotted straight to her heart. She boarded her at a stable but spent most of her time riding when she was home on leave."

"And you decided to keep Pebbles in the family when you moved out this way from Saylor County."

"Oh, yeah, we couldn't sell her," Matt said, shaking his head. "Not the horse my sister adored. Mom and I both ride her now and again to keep her in shape." He chuckled when he added, "I get the feeling Pebbles is kinda partial to girls. She perks up when Mom comes around. She lowered her head and started that happy nickering the minute you said her name and gave her a friendly pat."

"Is that so?" Heather smoothed her hand over the horse's neck. "That's because she's a smart girl. She knows a kindred spirit when she sees one—or maybe smells one."

"It's clear Pebbles has good instincts." And

with Heather riding her, the two made an especially pretty picture.

The ride, the easy talk and covering this familiar terrain struck Matt as the ideal first date. Not that he'd call it that or say it out loud and watch her gallop off the ranch. But he couldn't deny wanting to show Heather a good time while he tried to get to know her better. Sweet as this afternoon ride was turning out to be, it had a whiff of danger about it, too. From what everyone had told him about Heather, the life she'd once expected—and longed for—was the one he was living now.

He pushed those thoughts aside and focused on the moment. "Want to keep going?"

Her face lit up with enthusiasm. "You bet I do."

Matt led them down the farm road past grazing sheep and lambs who barely noticed their presence. The random stands of cottonwoods splashed the landscape with light greens and flowering trees were dabs of white and magenta.

"I remember every dip and rocky patch ahead," she remarked as they crossed the ridge.

"Then you'll guess where we're headed," Matt said.

"Hmm...we'll see. You have a lot of choices ahead."

Matt breathed in the cool moist air that carried the smells of sheep and horses. Every now and then, he stole a look at Heather in a wide-brimmed hat protecting her face from the sun.

As if she sensed being watched, she turned her head before he could quickly look elsewhere. He covered by pointing over her shoulder, pretending to study the half acre or so of boulders and scruffy sagebrush and random shrubs pushing into any available crevice. Even the sheep, who rarely gave up on anything with roots in the ground, had abandoned the barren site.

Heather turned to look where he was pointing. "Jeff and I rescued more than a few lambs wandering among those boulders. The ewe moms weren't pleased with their offspring when that happened."

Matt chuckled. "Most folks have never seen what sheep are capable of when their babies disappear from their sight. Talk about frantic."

"They don't mind scolding those way-ward lambs, either," she agreed with a nod. "Granted, not all ewes are equally fierce. But that only proves that, like every other animal, each sheep is unique even if they all wear the same uniform."

"You're right," Matt said. "They may be shy with us most of the time, but they like to hang out in their groups. A lot like horses that way. And people, too, I suppose." Matt veered Bo slightly to the left and Pebbles followed without Heather's coaxing.

Heather flashed a challenging smile. "We're going to the creek, aren't we?"

Matt grinned. "I assumed you'd want to have a look at Addie Creek while it's still running high. I don't have to tell you that only lasts so long."

Matt picked up the pace to an easy lope in the direction of the creek a couple of miles off.

Minutes later, they came to a stop and dismounted. "You like to move with a little spring, don't you?" Heather asked Pebbles as if expecting an answer. "Loping along wasn't cutting it, huh?"

"She's okay with loping," Matt said, "but

she has a need for speed. Just like us." He led the way through the stubby pines and the cottonwoods to the willows growing along the banks of the creek. The water tumbled over rocks and formed swirling pools that overflowed and sent the water rushing downstream. Music to his ears, that sound—a gift left behind by the recent rains.

A commotion in the sky suddenly caught his attention. Heather's, too. They watched a half dozen or so V formations filling the sky with geese. Matt glanced her way, but she stood motionless, watching the birds put on their show. And listening. These were a noisy bunch and likely headed farther north to their summer home.

"I saw the same spectacle in Minnesota," Heather said. "It never grows old."

"No, it sure doesn't," Matt said. "As young as they are, even Lucy and Nick stop what they're doing and watch the sky."

Standing side by side, he was again struck by how she had to tilt her head way back to look him in the eye. She raised her chin and glanced away. "Can I ask you something?"

Matt smiled and touched the brim of his hat as he nodded. "Be my guest."

"When I was in Jen's herb field the other day, I saw your sheep grazing in the basin." She paused and scrunched up her mouth. Then she gave the air an energetic swat. "Oh, never mind. It's not really any of my business."

"Don't stop now," he insisted. "What's on your mind? Tell me."

She scoffed but raised her head. "Okay. I was struck by how few sheep are grazing there." She twisted around and gestured back at the ridge. "We had many hundreds of sheep rotating on that pasture alone. I know you don't have the acreage my grandparents owned, but still…"

"Markets dictate the size of what I do here." He spoke flatly and purposefully. "Maybe at one time the ranchers had to go big or go home, as the saying goes, but not now."

Seeing he had her attention, he put his realities on the table, so to speak. "I got into this knowing the only way I could compete and survive was to aim for high quality— lamb is almost a high-end specialty market now. Quantity won't get me what I need anymore." His buyers were the smaller independent processors that sold to limited markets. Same with the wool buyers.

He'd answered without judgment or criticism she'd see as directed at her family. Maybe there was nothing that could've saved their ranch, but they'd struggled to hold on past the point of no return.

"I get it. And it's hard to argue with you," Heather said with a sigh. "Not after what... well, you know the rest." She kicked at the ground with her boot. "It just seemed odd, that's all."

Matt pointed to the creek. "Your answers are right here." He spoke more sharply than intended, but these were tough times in an already difficult market. "I can grow enough hay on the land to get through the winter and when the pastures go sparse late in fall. I seed the pasture to add plants that are good for these sheep. But I can't control—or predict—the water supply." His jaw tightened. "Not enough rain, not enough snow, adds up to drought." He extended his arm toward her. "But you know that."

"Yeah, well, I've experienced that a season or two," she responded in a clipped tone. "I suspect you're curious why my family was so slow to accept what everyone else saw coming."

Surprised, he was unsure about directly responding. How could she know that question had been on the tip of his tongue from the minute he'd seen the ranch listed for sale?

"You don't have to say a thing, Matt. I know what you're thinking."

"You do?" he said with a smirk. "I heard you were quite a lady, but little did I know you're a mind reader, too."

She let out a quick snort. "No, I don't need to possess special powers to know you have questions. It's just that the answers aren't very original." She turned away, stepped to Pebbles's side and stroked her face, and the horse's ears pointed to Heather in response. "Uh, I'm sorry about your sister. You must miss her terribly. And believe me, I understand why you couldn't leave this Appaloosa behind."

He was about to respond when the trilling of her phone broke into the peaceful aura of the creek. Any possibility of changing the mood faded.

Heather frowned as she pulled the phone out of her pocket. But when she checked the screen, she relaxed and broke into a radiant smile. Her thumbs got busy for a few seconds on the keyboard. "Sorry for the interruption," she said. "Fortunately, it's nothing I need to handle right now."

Matt frowned. Who had made her face light up so fast? None of his business, and he shouldn't care anyway.

Heather went back to giving Pebbles some attention.

Matt followed her lead and took up his favorite topic. "Did you know Susannah and I were twins, like Lucy and Nick?"

Heather shook her head. "Bethany didn't mention that."

"Being someone who works with kids," he said thoughtfully, "you must be familiar with what that's like. The twin bond, I mean."

Heather's light brown eyes revealed empathy. "There's research, but twins themselves are the best evidence. They say it's unique, unlike any other bond."

"Then you'll understand why I lost a chunk of myself when Susannah was killed. It's like a piece of my heart broke off and was carried away with her." He put his hand over his mouth, surprised by the strength of his words. He hadn't even said that out loud to Mom. He cleared his throat and nodded to Pebbles. "Having that good-tempered horse is like keeping a little something extra of her here." That was the best he could do for an explanation, though words never quite did the job.

Heather's eyes became suspiciously red and watery. She stayed silent but nodded in acknowledgement.

"And, uh, speaking of twins, I like to be there to greet my tykes when they get off the school bus," Matt said. "Fortunately, my mom is there if I can't be."

Heather quickly mounted the horse. "I get it. You're a parent with a schedule. Let's go."

Matt picked up the pace on the long clear stretches of the farm road. Bo's steady, rhythmic gait told him his horse was happy and even reluctant to slow down when the stable came into view.

"We'll leave the horses for Kenny to look after. I'll come out to check on them later." Matt dismounted. "As long as you're here, you can meet my twins."

"I'd like that." She rubbed Pebbles's forehead and said goodbye, and got a soft nicker in return. "What a great horse, Matt. Riding her was like being with an old friend." Heather's smile was intimate, warm. He knew the ride had been a success.

"I had a gut feeling you'd like riding our Pebbles."

When they turned the corner toward the house and the yard, the twins started shouting "Uncle Matt, Uncle Matt" in unison as they ran to him.

They hugged his hips and he scooped them up, one in each arm. "You must have had a fun day, little cubs. In a minute, you can tell me how much smarter you are. First, though, there's someone here I want you to meet."

Lucy giggled and pointed at Heather. "It's the lady you danced with in the tent."

"The lady's name is Heather Stanhope," Matt said.

"And I'm pleased to meet you, Miss Lucy," Heather said before turning to Nick. "Both of you."

Nick's forehead was marked with a few worried creases. "Were you riding one of *our* horses?"

What? Matt had a six-year-old detective on

his hands. "I *invited* Heather to ride Pebbles. Where are your manners, buddy?"

"She's a lovely Appaloosa. Her polka-dot socks are very fancy, don't you think?" Heather asked, smiling at Nick. "I could tell she likes to ride around the ranch."

"She's sorta mine," Lucy said, "but I'm not *quite* old enough to ride her yet, so it's okay if you do."

"Why, thank you," Heather said. "That's very generous of you, Lucy."

Matt let both kids slide down to the ground. "Okay, you're too big for your old uncle to haul around for very long."

That set off a bout of giggles as the twins ran past his mother, who was approaching. They were soon chasing Scrambler, whose little jumps and barks showed how happy he was to see them.

"I'm Stacey," Matt's mom said as she approached Heather with her hand outstretched, "but you need no introduction. I would have said hello when I saw you in Jen's tent at Spring Fling, but you had your hands full."

Matt stood back while Heather shook his mom's hand. "Nonstop traffic. Those spinners and knitters know what they want and where to come for it."

Heather spoke to both of them when she said, "They're adorable kids, those two. Liking school, are they?"

"So far," Matt said, holding up a hand with crossed fingers.

The three of them walked along until they reached Heather's car and she raised her hand over her head so the kids could see her wave goodbye from the other side of the yard.

"We'll stay in touch," Matt said. "No telling what might come up with the wedding."

Heather grinned. "Jen and I are arranging a shower. Charlie keeps in contact when he can, meanwhile Bethany's working extra shifts, including Memorial Day, so she can get a whole week off in July."

His mother's eyes immediately lit up. "Speaking of weekends, don't forget about our newest event in town. Steak Fry Saturday. I assume you heard about it."

"Jen may have mentioned something about a new event."

"You'll probably see the flyer posted around town," Matt said. "It's a fundraiser for the volunteer fire department and the library."

"Having it in the evening makes it more or less adults only," Stacey said. "It gives us a great excuse to hire a band and dance the night away."

"And to dress up in costumes," Matt added. "We take that part very seriously."

"Sounds like fun," Heather said, although Matt detected a puzzled look in her eye.

"It's right after Memorial Day, and for now, we hold it here at the ranch," his mom explained.

Heather's expression darkened in an instant. That was clearly not happy news to her.

"The Hoovers will be here, of course," his mom said, seemingly oblivious to the drop in temperature, "and I hope you'll join us. Nice to meet you, Heather. See you soon." She turned and headed toward the house.

Matt offered a crooked smile. "Yes, please come. Like she said, there will be live music."

"Well, how can I refuse?"

Was that sarcasm? He wasn't going to have a chance to find out because without giving him a glance, she muttered a quick, "Thanks again," while she climbed into her SUV and took off as if she couldn't leave fast enough.

He stood in place and watched her nose her vehicle down the bumpy drive at a fair clip. Then, before she reached the road, she came to a sudden stop. Her hand came into view, and she gave him a long wave. In a few seconds, she'd transformed from cheerful to icy and back again. Puzzling.

But naturally, he waved back.

CHAPTER FOUR

INSTEAD OF HEADING inside the bunkhouse, Heather flopped into a rocker on the porch to get her bearings. On the drive home, she'd replayed her flip remark over the invitation. If she'd waited a second or two longer to respond, she might have softened the edges of her cynical tone. But she'd let down her guard and now she'd been railroaded somehow, expected to be a guest at a party at *her* house.

She let her head drop to the back of the chair and rocked with a steady rhythm. Not her house. That was the point. When were Jen and Bethany planning to mention this new fundraiser? What did they call it? Steak Fry Saturday. She had to admit it was a good way to raise money for the town.

She'd made a quick escape from Matt's house, but in the rearview mirror, she'd seen his frown. She wasn't sure what that was all about. How had he thought she'd react?

She should have said that to Matt's face and maybe he'd have backed off.

Another voice in her head sang a different tune, one lulling her into accepting that Stacey and Matt hadn't meant to stir up bad feelings. It was the same voice telling her she shouldn't be impolite. Something about the guy—way beyond the sweet smile and penetrating gaze—touched her heart. She couldn't quite describe it, but she'd put aside her quick negative reaction and hit the brakes. A friendly wave wouldn't hurt her.

Underneath all her fretting, she'd surprised herself by how easy it had been to put her feet on the familiar ground of her former home. She'd been a little shaky earlier when she'd made the turn up the drive. After giving the house only a passing glance, she'd focused on the walk around the barn to the stables. She'd take that walk again for another chance to ride Pebbles, but lingering and socializing with other people in the large grassy front yard held no appeal at all.

Heather checked the time on her phone. She had exactly thirty minutes before the on-line meet-up she'd arranged with Jillian with a quick text sent while down at the creek. She missed her former patient, a hard-fighting ten-year-old who'd managed to beat leukemia and grasp a future.

Heather got to her feet, stretched her arms over her head and then bent side to side to work the kinks out her body. Like her ranching muscles, her riding skills hadn't been taken for a test drive in a long while. The last time she'd been on a horse was over three years ago in Charleston, when another nurse had invited her for a Sunday ride with her and her two teenage daughters.

Heather needed a few minutes to clear the jumble of thoughts competing for attention. Too much was happening too fast, especially because already this trip wasn't what she'd expected. She'd envisioned sticking close to the bunkhouse, helping Jen, reading novels and catching up on nursing journals. She'd hike alone or with Bethany on the Hoovers' land and the local trails. Riding special horses to her beloved Addie Creek hadn't been in her vision. She snickered. Costume parties held at her old house hadn't been an agenda item, either.

Early in the ride, her curiosity about the reasons he'd offered her this chance had given way to the simple pleasure of it. Deep inside she'd still been a teenager, riding Velvet across the same hills in search of her dad. She'd loved her mom, but she'd always been freer, happier, when she was in the pastures and fields with her dad—and the dogs.

Stop! Losing herself in memories so intense scared her.

Then, there was the man himself, maybe not movie-star handsome, but with a warm, welcoming smile that made him appealing, even magnetic. Lacking pretension, he didn't try to be cool and distant. When she'd seen him in the full light of day, she'd realized his deep-set eyes were more green than blue.

Kicking off her boots, she went inside and washed the outdoor grime off her face and hands. She ate a couple of Jen's oatmeal cookies and washed them down with lemon sparkling water. Ready to switch gears and talk with the girl who'd dominated her life in Red Wing, Heather settled at Bethany's table, and a couple of clicks later, Jillian's smiling face appeared, along with a windshield-wiper wave.

"Here's my girl," Heather said, exhaling and letting go of the emotional background noise of the day. "Look at your red hair, you cute pixie."

Jillian patted the top of her head. "It's my same color, but the doctor said it might not be as curly." She held up a book, the latest in a mystery series Heather had started reading to her when Jillian was weakened by the worst of her leukemia treatments.

In the girl's other hand, she was cradling Tulip, a prima donna kitten who persisted in her demands for nonstop attention. "I can go to the library now, so I stocked up on mysteries." She patted her head again. "And I only wear a hat or a scarf now if I'm cold."

"That's so good to hear, honey," Heather said, remembering the way she'd tucked more blankets around Jillian to keep her warm. On one especially bad day, Heather had pulled two knit hats down over Jillian's ears. "How about school?"

Another wide smile appeared. "I did well enough to be in sixth grade in the fall. Mom said for sure I can go in person and be with my friends."

"That's a relief," Heather said, giving a little cheer. "I guess we did a good job, didn't we?" She'd helped supervise Jillian's homeschooling, and weeks would go by when her young patient wasn't up to anything more demanding than an art lesson. Anime had been the girl's favorite and always brought a smile to her face.

"I miss you," Jillian said. "Mom says the house isn't the same without you." She turned the cat's face closer to the screen. "Tulip misses you, too."

"I miss you and your mom… I'm not sure about Tulip." Sadly, Tulip hadn't been her favorite part of the job of being Jillian's nurse-caregiver for the past year. The cat had a pretty powerful jealous streak and from day one had viewed Heather as an interloper. "You know how she snubbed me." To put it mildly. The cat was clever and had only hissed at Heather when no one else was around. "Little Tulip was probably glad to see me go and have you all to herself again."

Jillian nodded, conceding the point, at least for now.

"Hey, guess what? I was out for ride on a really nice horse when you called."

"*Cool.* How did that happen?"

"A friend of a friend, sort of, has lots of

horses, and let me ride one." No need for other details. "I had so much fun."

Suddenly, Olivia's face appeared from the side of the screen. "What sort of a friend? You reacquainting with anyone special?"

"The guy who owns Pebbles, a black-and-white Appaloosa, is going to be the best man at Bethany's wedding," Heather explained. "That's why we happened to meet."

Olivia, her employer for the past year, was now Heather's closest friend in Minnesota. The only close friend she'd made in the last four years. Over the time they'd known each other, they'd exchanged stories, so Jillian's mother knew why Heather had signed on with a service for traveling nurses. After stints in Charleston and Savannah, she'd headed north to a Minnesota hospital. From there, she had taken on a private case—the care of nine-year-old Jillian. Even better than the girl's tenth birthday was her recent celebration of being declared in remission.

"Appaloosa," Olivia repeated, glancing down at Jillian. "Now that's a word that's fun to say."

"So it is, and she's a beauty." Heather ended up telling Jillian and Olivia about selling wool at the fair and helping Jen plant her herbs. Almost as an afterthought, she mentioned Matt and the ranch. "Adelaide Creek was noisy and bubbling along today. It reminded me of the times Mom put Jeff in charge of me and he'd put me on his horse and take me down to the creek to play."

"Sounds like nothing's changed much around your old stomping grounds," Olivia said.

"I didn't mean to imply that," Heather said more sharply than she intended. "Everything's changed." She softened her tone when she added, "It's kind of hard to explain what it's like being back here."

Not to be forgotten, Jillian put her face close to the screen. "Tell me more about Pebbles. And the Icelanders. Can you send more pictures of them?"

Of course Jillian would want details. She'd always been like that. Sharp and analytical, like her radiologist mom, when it came to her cancer, Jillian wouldn't stand for people talking in code around her. She wanted to understand what was going on in her body. She kept her own calendar and marked off days between treatments. Even at nine years old, she'd declared herself part of the treatment team.

"Oh, sweetie, I doubt I'll get a chance to ride her again," Heather said, taking her questions one at a time. "The horse belongs to the man's little girl, but Lucy is still too young to ride her. I wish I'd thought to take a picture of Pebbles, though." And the creek and the pasture. "If I ever see her again, I'll definitely ask Lucy if she minds if I take a picture or two."

Heather knew Olivia would prefer the subject of horses to go away. She'd promised Jillian she could learn to ride, but that was before she got sick. After what her daughter's body had been through, Olivia wasn't ready to risk putting her on a horse just yet. As a doctor who read X-rays and MRIs and scans all day long, injuries were never far from Olivia's mind.

"But I am going to a special kind of party in a couple of weeks," Heather said, jumping at the logical place to change the subject. "It's like Halloween, so I'll need a costume. Any ideas?"

"You could be Annie Oakley. She liked

horses," Jillian said, still stroking the purring cat. "She had a holster and a gun, too."

Heather chuckled at the image of herself sporting a low slung holster, or maybe with a rifle hanging over her shoulder. "I don't think so. I never was much of a hunter, not like my brother. But I need to find a cool outfit." Heather heard herself talk about Steak Fry Saturday as if she'd made up her mind to be there. Her earlier indignation had morphed into a fun story to tell Jillian. "I have no idea where to get a costume, but I'll ask Bethany and her mom. They know where to find everything."

She smiled at Jillian. "You know how everybody says you look like your grandma Alice?"

"Uh-huh. We have the same red hair and gray eyes."

"That's what people say about me and my great-great-grandma Adelaide. So maybe I could dress up in clothes like she wore. Then I'll look even more like her."

"Mom and I want details and lots of photos of your party," Jillian said. "Right, Mom?"

"Absolutely," Olivia said, wrapping one arm around Jillian's shoulders. "But we should probably go for now." Giving Jillian a quick squeeze, she added, "You can talk to Heather again in a couple of days."

"Okay," Heather said. "We'll do more catching up soon."

"*Very* soon," Jillian said, as if issuing a warning. "And remember, I want photos of everything. I liked the picture of the tents in a row at the fair."

"You bet. I love our chats, sweetie." Heather blew a kiss to Jillian.

As soon as the screen was dark, she leaned back in her chair and rubbed her upper arms to get warm in the chilly air. Jillian usually had a way of wiping away Heather's anger about the past and fears for her future. Nursing a desperately ill child had taught her a lesson in endurance.

She was reminded that when she went back to Red Wing, finding a house—a big house—she could turn into a home sat at the top of her list.

Heather went into the kitchen intending to brew a cup of tea, but instead, a spot on the counter led to grabbing the sponge and spray cleaner. In a matter of minutes, Heather had burned off her restless energy and every flat surface in the kitchen gleamed. When Bethany called her name, she was on a stepladder making the glossy white cabinet doors shine.

"What's gotten into you?" Bethany asked.

"Oh, the cleaning elves took over my body." She made Bethany smile by sending a silly grin her way. "But don't worry, it doesn't happen very often."

"I remember," Bethany said dryly. "We've lived here together before."

"I'm calling the job done." Heather climbed down off the stepladder and moved it out of the way.

"And I'm done for two whole days, my friend. You up for a trip to Landrum tomorrow? Then on the way home, I thought we could drive by my new house. The couple hasn't moved out yet, but we can still have a look at the outside."

Speaking of turning houses into homes… "Perfect. Spending a day with you is just what the nurse ordered."

"That's what I hoped you'd say. First, a fitting for our dresses, and then a little frivolous shopping. We can eat at one of Landrum's new hot spots." A smile tugged at the corners of Bethany's mouth.

Heather chuckled. Landrum, known to Adelaide Creekers as the "big town," had a population in four figures, not three. They'd gone to high school in Landrum and Bethany's hospital was on the edge of town. *Hot spot* was not a term usually associated with the town's fast-food places and burger bars. "I'm up for anything you want to do. I'm the maid of honor, so your wish is supposed to be my command."

"Ha! That will be the day," Bethany said, glancing at her watch. "Mom called as I was leaving the hospital. Would you like a plate of her beef stew?"

"Of course. You know I never pass up a chance to spend time with your folks."

After a quick change of clothes, Heather and Bethany started along the path through the fields.

"What have you been up to today?" Bethany asked.

"Well, before I got the cleaning bug, I was online with Jillian and Olivia. It was good to catch-up. Jillian got used to having me around."

"Yeah, well, she's got competition," Bethany said. "I'm getting used to having you around again. Mom and Dad, too."

"Stop right there," Heather warned, determined not to be drawn into a conversation about her future plans.

"In case you missed my tone, I was teasing," Bethany chided.

If only that were true. In Bethany's mind, since Heather could stay on at the bunkhouse indefinitely, why move? Why go back to Red Wing? But whether her best friend understood or not, staying wasn't a good choice for Heather. Living vicariously, including riding someone else's horse, wasn't enough. She wanted a life she created by herself, for herself.

"What about the rest of your day?" Bethany flashed a teasing grin. "I hope it wasn't hugely dull without me."

Heather suppressed a smile. "It wasn't too bad. I muddled through."

"WHY DID YOU WAIT until I was nearly out the door before you brought up Heather?" Fair or not, Matt let every scrap of impatience show in his voice. He wasn't running late, at least not yet. But he was due to pick up the twins at school and head over to Landrum.

His mom stood with her back against the kitchen counter, her arms crossed over her chest. "It's just that having a 'let's get acquainted' dance at the fair last week was one thing. But inviting her for an afternoon ride?" Demonstrating her conviction, she jabbed her index finger in the air. "Was that really necessary?"

"Necessary? No. But enjoyable? Even fun? *Absolutely.*" He hadn't stopped thinking about her, a pleasant way to pass the time. Dangerous, too. Matt prided himself on his equilibrium, but Heather had threatened that, if only because she kept intruding into his thoughts. Now Mom was reading his mind. "And if I recall, you were the one who insisted she'd love Steak Fry Saturday. No matter that we hold it here at *our* ranch."

"What? Like she wouldn't see the flyer around town? She's staying at the Hoover bunkhouse," Stacey said, "so I'm sure Jen and Bethany would mention the event. She'd have come along with their family whether I invited her or not."

Matt wasn't as sure about that as his mom. "Or maybe she'd have begged off."

His mother sighed. "I'm only warning you not to go asking for trouble, Mathis."

"Uh-oh, you called me Mathis, so I know you mean business." His teasing was meant to lighten the mood. She had no need to worry about him—or the twins. But trying to convince her otherwise would be the same as telling her not to breathe.

"Jen Hoover isn't a gossip, Matt, but she told me a while ago what the Stanhopes' last few years here were like." Mom gestured around the room. "It all slipped away one piece at a time, starting with small sell-offs of acres, then the sheep. They lost Heather's dad first and then her mom." She turned away and stared out the window over the sink. "I don't imagine I'd want to head off to party in Susannah's old house. I expect Heather might feel the same about being here."

The flip-flop in his gut at hearing Susannah's name never changed. Especially when it came out of the blue, like now. His mother's point wasn't lost on him. "I get it, Mom, but we stepped up to volunteer our place."

Mom's expression softened now. "True

enough. I'm not sure what these anxious feelings are all about. But Heather's a grown woman. She can make up her own mind about where she shows up. If she'd rather not come to a big gathering here, she won't hurt my feelings."

Matt couldn't say the same. He'd been thinking of asking Heather to ride again. There was something about her that stuck with him. It wasn't only her thoughtful and curious light brown eyes and all that long wavy hair that drew him to her. It turned out she was easy to hang out with. Impressive, how she'd handled Pebbles like they were old pals. Come to think of it, she was that way with Nick and Lucy.

"Hey, Matt, it's getting late," Mom said. "You better head out if you're going to get to the school on time."

"Right, right." He grabbed his jacket off the hook. "I'll bring dinner home. I'm not sure how long this excursion with the tykes is going to take."

With that, he left the house and hurried to his mom's car, a more comfortable ride with twins than his truck. He felt like he'd pulled off a great escape. He and his mother rarely argued about anything, but she'd likely seen through his no-big-deal facade about Heather.

Before the twins had become his forever, Matt hadn't thought much about settling down and having a family. At least, not yet. He'd been having a good time running Finer Rides and meeting many women. He'd always found women to spend time with, but he'd never let things get too serious. With the twins in his life now, casual dating was one luxury he couldn't afford.

When he pulled into the pickup line at the school, he saw the two reasons he'd stayed a loner. Lucy and Nick were standing with their classmates waiting to get on the bus. He got out of the car and called their names as he approached. Two little faces lit up in surprise. They raced toward him and launched themselves at him just like they did at home when they got off the bus. How much longer would this uninhibited affection last? Realistically, not as long as he'd like. He'd give it a year, two tops, before they'd declare themselves too old for public hugs.

"We're doing something special today, little cubs." He waved at the teacher in charge of loading the buses to let her know he was taking charge of his two.

"Where are we going, Uncle Matt?" Lucy asked.

"I'll tell you when we're underway. But first you tell me what you learned today that you didn't know this morning."

"Me first, me first," Nick said, climbing into his booster seat in the back. "I learned that Byron Beatty is a mean kid."

Uneasy about what was coming, Matt waded in. "Tell me more, Nick."

"It's nothing," Nick said in a tone of resignation.

"If it was nothing, you wouldn't have said anything, buddy." With the two secured in the back, Matt got into the driver's seat and pulled away from the curb.

Lucy spoke up. "It's because I'm taller than Nick. So Byron likes to say 'Lucy's bigger than you, ha, ha, ha'. He won't stop."

Nick jabbed Lucy in the arm. "Why did you have to tell him?"

"Nick, I'd rather hear about these incidents, so I can keep track of what's going on." Matt glanced at Nick in the rearview mirror. "We don't want little things to fester. You know what that means, right?"

"Gram says if you ignore something bad, sometimes it gets a lot worse." Nick said the right words, but he sounded bored with the whole thing.

"Exactly. Now, as for Byron, he probably doesn't know any better." Matt purposely raised his voice but maintained his matter-of-fact tone. No sense making the trouble bigger than it was. "It seems Byron isn't aware that when you're little, kids grow at different speeds. That's why Lucy is a little taller today. Next year, who knows?" The Burtons tended to end up taller than average, so Matt could easily see Nick as a lanky, fast-growing teenager. Lucy, too.

"This is the way to Landrum," Nick said.

"Right you are. We've got a little shopping to do."

Lucy clapped her hands. "Really? Am I getting new shoes?"

"Yes, you are. You, too, Nick. And other things, as well. It's a surprise." Nick didn't show much of a reaction, but Matt assumed that was because he was still thinking about being teased. "As for Byron, the best thing you both can do is ignore him. He'll get tired of trying to get a rise out of you. Agreed?"

"O-*kay*," Nick said.

Nothing from Lucy. "That means you, too, Lucy."

"I get it. Can we go to the shoe store first? I need new sneakers. I don't run that fast in my old ones."

Lucy's excitement wasn't contagious. Glancing in the rearview mirror, Matt saw Nick's eyes close. "A little nap might be good for you, too, Lucy. Go on and put your head back and see what happens."

Lucy shook her head and squirmed in her seat.

Matt kept driving, reassuring himself that with school out soon, he'd have more time to keep an eye on Nick. He'd be outside more and get some sun back in his cheeks. Along with increasing his energy.

Last fall, Nick's teacher had made a point of saying the boy couldn't sit still for five minutes. Matt wouldn't mind hearing that complaint again.

CHAPTER FIVE

"TELL ME THE TRUTH, Heather, do you really like it?"

"You're stunning. I'm nearly in tears." Heather pretended to dab the corners of her eyes only because she'd managed to hold back the real tears at the sight of her friend in her beautiful dress. It wasn't surprising her heart would turn to mush in the wedding shop. As little girls they'd put on magical weddings for their dolls and played wedding dress-up with their moms' cast-off clothes. Bethany usually rode away with her prince Cinderella-style in a pink-and-silver coach. But not Heather. She rode off into the proverbial sunset with her guy, on their horses, semifluffy dress and veil and all.

Bethany had never looked so beautiful. But it was her happiness that added the finishing touch. Thrilled for her best friend, it was still a bittersweet occasion for Heather. In the last few years, she'd changed everything in her life except for the tight bond with Bethany. Four years had flown by, and now things were changing again.

The dress fitting was their last stop after shopping and lunch at Cyndy's Corner, Landrum's new café. Now Bethany stood on a platform in front of a mirror in the private fitting area of the bridal shop. Her dress needed only a tuck here and there and a tiny adjustment to the spaghetti straps. The seamstress had finished her part and was off helping another customer. Heather took out her phone. "Turn around one more time, Bethany. I want to get shots at different angles."

Bethany dutifully made a slow circle in the swingy robin's-egg-blue dress that hit just at her knee. "That blue is an exact match for your eyes."

"That was the plan." Bethany stepped into her heels. Now her legs went on forever. Bethany looked down and held one foot out in front of her. "I got the dress because I figured I could wear it again somewhere, someday. Hmm…but these shoes are another story."

Heather laughed. The two of them had

grown up in jeans and sneakers with the occasional switch to sandals or the ever popular and completely impractical fashion boots with pencil-thin heels. The allure of glamorous shoes had lasted only until they were old enough to actually wear them. Bethany's white five-inchers looked terrific and put her at over six feet tall, but their virtues ended there. "My feet hurt just looking at them. You'll have to practice walking around the bunkhouse in those."

"You, too, my friend," Bethany said. "We'll be in wedding march training together."

"Looks that way." Heather held up the heels that matched her blush-pink dress. Sleeveless with a cowl neck, it had a simple A-line skirt. Once the hem was shortened a couple of inches, Heather would be good to go.

"To answer your dress question, I adore it," Heather said, taking one last picture on her phone. "Jillian will give her ten-year-old's stamp of approval. It's exactly right for a wedding that suits you and Charlie. It will be intimate, and you're the only bride I've ever heard of who isn't breaking out in hives or something over the stress of it all. Avoiding an over-the-top approach is already paying off."

With Charlie's long absences and Bethany's demanding job in an orthopedic unit, an elaborate affair wasn't practical. More to the point, Bethany and Charlie put more energy and thought into planning their future life together than in planning their wedding. That was why they were now the owners of a gem of a cottage in town.

Careful not to stick herself with the straight pins, Bethany stepped out of the dress and Heather took charge of returning it to the matching blue-satin hanger and leaving it on the seamstress's rack. Like the room itself, the hanger carried the faint aroma of lavender. "I think they have your mom's lavender sachets tucked in all the corners in here."

Bethany didn't respond but pulled on her jeans and sweater and then sat on the edge of the riser and rested her weight on her palms behind her.

"Is something wrong?" Heather asked.

"No, I'm just feeling a little nostalgic. Having you around does that to me."

"For me, too." *May this conversation end with that...please.* Going down this road always ended with Bethany questioning Heather's move. "But that's all, I assume. You're still sure marrying Charlie is the right thing." It was a declaration, not a question.

"Oooh, no doubt there. Not that I'm in love with his job. He's gone for months at a time," Bethany said in a pouty voice. "But he tells me what he's doing is important, so it's easier to understand."

The way it stood now, Charlie was due back on the second of July, cutting it kind of close for a Fourth of July wedding. Bethany took it in stride, or at least that was the attitude she showed to the world.

"Did you get a job offer yet?" Bethany asked.

Heather shook her head. "You'd be the first to know. Seriously, I've only got a few weak feelers out for now. I'm not eager to rush back to work yet. Olivia's keeping an eye on house listings for me, but the job comes first."

"I get it." The corners of Bethany's mouth turned down.

Heather sat next to Bethany on the riser. "No, I don't think you do, but you need to." The room was warmer now, almost stuffy. "It's simple. You and the man of your dreams have a house and are planning to start a family one day. Those same things are what *I* want." She patted Bethany's knee. "It's taken me this long to decide to build myself a real life, full of good things. *Roots*. And a house and a horse. I can't count on it, but finding my own right guy, like Charlie is for you, would be the coconut icing on my chocolate cake." She nudged Bethany with her shoulder. "Got it?"

Bethany nudged her back. "Okay. When all the beans are counted, as my dad says, we want the same things, right down to our favorite cake." She got to her feet. "I'm such a hypocrite. If Charlie's job took us to a new place, I'd be okay packing up and having an adventure in some faraway place. When it comes down to it, I think you love this home-place of ours more than I do."

Heather kept her response to a quick shrug. They'd been over this ground before, and if she kept talking, the bitterness she still carted around might slip out despite her good intentions. "So what's next on our agenda?"

"I'm thinking we start with a glass of wine at Legends. Then, when we're ready for a feast, the Jury Room awaits. It's got a great menu and is only half a block away."

Heather picked up her handbag. "All right. Let's go."

After goodbyes to the shop owner, they started down the street, but Bethany tugged at her sleeve to stop her. "I owe you an apology. I keep telling you how much I wish you'd stay. It's like I can't help myself, even though you're clear the subject of where you live is closed."

Heather looked into Bethany's kind blue eyes. "Exactly. But I also want to celebrate this happy time in my best friend's life." Her voice caught in her throat when she added, "Today isn't about me. It's all about you and a blue dress and torture shoes."

MATT HELD THE door for the kids as they filed out of the shoe store carrying their shopping bags. "Okay, tykes, mission accomplished. You have new shoes to outgrow—with lightning speed."

"Don't call us tykes, Uncle Matt," Nick said, swinging the two small bags, one for his shoes and the other for a new cowboy hat from Western Wear.

"We told you we're too old for that," Lucy added. "We were tykes up until we were five."

Matt bounced the heel of his hand against his temple. "I keep forgetting that. I guess I'll have to stick with cubs and kiddos. The truth is you'll always be tykes to me."

Lucy gave him a solemn nod. "It's okay. We'll give you another chance."

"Lucky for me."

Suddenly, Nick pointed down the street and shouted, "Look, look. There's that lady who rode Pebbles. It's Heather."

Matt looked where Nick was pointing. Sure enough, Heather and Bethany were walking toward them, but with their heads together talking and laughing, they hadn't noticed him or the kids.

"Can we go say hello?" Lucy asked.

He could think of no reason to hold them back. "Sure, go ahead."

The two scampered down the street. Bethany spotted them first. Matt was a few feet away when he saw Heather's face light up when she recognized the kids.

She looked up and smiled. A big, warm

smile. There went his heart again, going from an easy trot to a full gallop.

"Nice bumping into you two." He nodded to the shopping bags. "Like the three of us, it looks like you've been shopping."

"I got a cowboy hat," Nick said, "and new sneakers."

"I got new shoes, too, and a skirt that has *fringe* on the bottom. I can wear it when the grownups come to the big bash at the ranch." Lucy stretched her arms out to the side to show them how big.

"That big, huh?" Bethany teased.

"That's what Gram calls it," Lucy explained. "Do you have your costumes yet?"

"I can't come to the bash because I have to work at the hospital here in Landrum." She turned her mouth down. "Poor me, I'm going to miss all the fun."

"Bethany is a nurse. Like me," Heather said. "She'll be busy that night taking care of people who need her."

"But she'll be free on the Fourth of July," Matt said, looking down at the twins. "Remember I told you we were going to a wedding. Well, Miss Bethany is the bride."

The twins delivered the wide-eyed reaction he'd expected. Lucy was full of questions about flowers and the wedding dress, which Bethany patiently answered.

"We came to town for a fitting for our dresses," Heather said as she took a few steps to the side and separated herself from Bethany and the twins. "So far, so good. My best pal is going to be a gorgeous bride." She snickered. "You won't believe how much taller the two of us are in our heels. Barely able to take five steps, but we'll *look* glamorous."

"I have no doubt of that," he said, grinning from happiness at running into Heather. "The two of you have all the glamour a guy can handle." He lowered his gaze to her shoes. "Right down to your fancy red boots. Your dancing shoes, huh?"

It had been a long time since he'd made a woman blush. That was why Heather's cheeks pinking up emboldened him. He had an idea.

"I heard that, Mr. Charming," Bethany teased as she approached. "You can throw compliments like that our way anytime. Right, Heather?"

Heather didn't answer but gave her friend

a good-natured eye roll and changed the subject. "So much is new in Landrum. I barely recognize Buffalo Street. We had a glass of wine at Legends and—"

"Well then, maybe you're ready for dinner. Want to join me and the kids at the Jury Room? We were just about to head that way." Not exactly, but he liked this change of plans. Sitting at a table beat going to a drivethrough every time.

Bethany's face lit up, so he knew she was in. Heather seemed preoccupied with Nick's humorous jibber-jabber.

"What do you say, Heather?" Bethany asked. "We were headed to the Jury Room, anyway."

Heather shot her friend a pointed look, for reasons not clear to Matt.

"Sounds good to me," Heather said, her attention focused on the twins. "Bethany tells me they serve more than humungous burger platters. So it's something new and different." She squeezed Nick's shoulder. "What about you?"

"I'm getting a burger with fries." Nick raised his arms over his head like he'd won a prize.

"Okay, it's settled," Bethany said. "Hey, you two, let's race Matt and Heather to the front door."

"The great twenty-five-yard dash is on," Heather said, laughing.

Matt was in no hurry to win a race. He was fine strolling along with Heather. "Charlie and I talked a couple of days ago. Even if everything goes just right, he'll have less than forty-eight hours to spare before the ceremony."

"That's what Bethany told me. No margin for error," Heather said, "but she takes it all in stride. Once he gets here, he'll have to leave in six days. Then it's goodbye for several months."

Matt smiled. "We came over here for new shoes, and even though Steak Fry Saturday is for adults, I got them a couple of things so they can feel special on the big night—until bedtime, that is. What about you? Have you come up with a costume yet? For the sake of history, isn't it your duty to dress up like the original Adelaide?"

"Not much pressure there." She pointed with her chin at Bethany, who was declaring herself and the twins the clear winners of the race. "Oh, I still have lots of time. Maybe I'll drop into Western Wear to see what they have." She gave him a sidelong glance. "And before you ask, I plan to visit the gallery before Memorial Day."

Maybe she really was a mind reader. He'd been about to ask if she'd ventured in there yet.

They reached the door and followed Bethany and the kids to the hostess station. It shouldn't be a long wait. Given the way the twins were bouncing around between Bethany and Heather, he hoped not. Even Nick had some extra energy.

"Okay, it's time for your restaurant manners," he said, putting one firm hand on Lucy's shoulder and the other on Nick's. "Am I clear?"

"Okay, Uncle Matt," Lucy stage whispered. "We'll use our inside voices."

He glanced at Heather, who gave him a look that clearly conveyed *nicely done*.

While they waited for the hostess, Bethany held out a menu and the twins went right to her and listened carefully as she read the list of special dinners for kids.

The distraction gave Matt a minute to talk

to Heather and act on an idea he'd had a couple of days ago. "I'm planning to move some of the herd from the basin to fresh pasture on the other side of the ridge. Probably after Memorial Day. It occurred to me you might like to come along and lend an experienced hand." He paused and added, "Any interest?"

For a second or two, she seemed startled. He'd caught her off guard.

"You mean work with you and Kenny?"

"Yep, that's what I mean. Between you and me and the dogs, though, I'm confident we can handle the job. It's not too far, and we've put in some fencing. I've been keeping Kenny busy seeding the pasture where it's sparse. We need more variety anyway."

Heather frowned as if deep in thought, but finally she spoke up. "I'm sort of…well, floored. It's been years since I've herded sheep. But I'll grab this chance. Count me in."

Nick came alongside Heather and whispered, "Can I sit next to you? Lucy said she wants to sit next to the bride."

Heather smiled down at Nick. "I think we can arrange that."

"And here comes the hostess now," Matt

said. "Since my tykes, uh, I mean cubs, have very particular ideas about where we sit, would you two oversee that?" He held up his phone. "I need to let my mom know her dinner will be coming a little later."

"Go ahead. We can handle these two," Heather said.

He stepped outside to send his text and return a couple of messages from Kenny. Mostly, though, he got a kick out of what had turned out to be his lucky day.

When he got to the table, the waitress was ready to take their orders, with the kids settling on child-sized burgers. Like Bethany and Heather, he took advantage of the varied menu and ended up with a pasta plate for himself and one to take home for Mom.

"So Charlie tells me all I have to do as best man is make sure I have a suit and tie," Matt said. "I told him not to worry. I can manage that."

Heather's eyes sparkled as she turned to Lucy. "Oh, wait till you see our dresses at the wedding." She raised her eyebrows and gave Lucy an intimate smile. "They are sooo pretty. I can't *wait* to wear mine."

Lucy giggled the way she did when Matt

used his whole face to exaggerate a point. Seeing Lucy happily talking to Heather played havoc with his feelings. He could almost feel his heart growing and taking up more space in his chest.

Dinner talk went from the wedding plans to Bethany and Charlie's house, and on to answers to Heather's questions about the trails they used for his pack trip company.

After they said good-night on the sidewalk, Matt settled the two sleepy kids in the car and enjoyed the silence. The only glitch in the evening had come in the middle of dinner when Heather's phone buzzed and her face brightened happily when she checked the screen and quickly responded. Maybe her smile had faded a little when she'd typed her response, but it could be she had business to attend to.

Wishful thinking. It was likely a text from her boyfriend. Matt tried to convince himself he had no reason to care one way or the other. She was here in Wyoming, and a boyfriend back home didn't mean Matt couldn't casually enjoy her company. Still, he envied the guy who could make her face light up like sunshine.

EVEN WITHOUT MUCH daylight left, Heather followed Bethany's directions and made the turn onto O'Malley Street. Given the size and layout of Adelaide Creek, she could have found the street blindfolded. Standing across the street from the white-framed house, it appeared even smaller than it had in the photos Bethany had texted. With its window boxes and shutters, it was the classic movie symbol of cute and cuddly romance. All it lacked was a white picket fence. The previous owners would be in the house a couple of weeks more, but Bethany and Charlie were now the proud owners of this cottage in Adelaide Creek.

"Aw, Bethie, it's so romantic." Heather was the only person allowed to revert to Bethie. *Rarely.* She took care not to push her luck, but this was definitely a Bethie moment. Heather took a couple of quick shots of the cottage and made it a point to include the small dogwood in the front yard just starting to bloom. "I admit I've had a hard time understanding why you wanted such a small house, but now that I see it, it's pretty irresistible."

"The house is dark, and I don't see cars in

the driveway, so let's get a little closer." Bethany hurried across the street to the patchy lawn, Heather right behind her. "It appears small," Bethany said, "but that's deceptive. The house has room for a baby when the time comes." She turned to Heather and gave her a sly smile. "Maybe even two babies."

"I can see that," Heather said, but a skeptical tone slipped in anyway. In her mind's eye, she saw herself in a big, sprawling house. It would have a couple of floors and big windows and a wraparound porch. Red Wing had lots of houses that fit that description. Some were fixer-uppers. She could handle that kind of physical work.

"All my life I've watched my parents toil away on our big barn of a home. Like your family's place," Bethany said. "My dad calls it repair and restore, and only when all else fails, replace." Bethany lifted one shoulder in a quick shrug. "But that was their choice. I like my work and thinking about grad school programs more than I like picking out paint colors and wallpaper." She extended her arms toward the house. "And our little newlywed hideaway is updated and freshly painted inside and out."

Bethany's clarity about her choices was something to behold, Heather mused, right down to the knee-length, blue cocktail dress. And who ever heard of a wedding shower where no gifts were allowed? Bethany owned that choice and didn't care what others thought.

They walked around to the backyard, where a couple of young blue spruces marked the corners of the property line. A field extended for a couple of acres beyond where the property ended.

"You can't see it in the dark, but prairie clover is coming in and spreading some purple around," Bethany said, "and I saw several iris and blanket flower on the edges. Wildflowers will be with us all summer long." An owl hooted in a stand of trees marking the next yard. "Listen to that. The birds agree."

Snippets of memories of her house on the ranch, with its built-in breakfront and cubbyholes and shelves in all the rooms, flitted through Heather's mind. Repair had been the watchword for her family. Restore or replace had barely made it into the vocabulary. She hadn't been inside the old house yet, but she imagined Matt and Stacey had decided it

was less expensive—and a lot less bother—
to skip the repair phase and go directly to
restore. Maybe that was why the challenge
of a fixer-upper in Red Wing had a certain
appeal. She couldn't bring back the original Stanhope home, but she might be able
to bring back another house suffering from
neglect.

"You're quiet all of a sudden," Bethany
said when they went back to the SUV.

"I was thinking about how smart you are."
Not really a fib, since she'd been thinking
about Bethany's choices a lot lately. "You
never fussed with material things. Keeping
it simple has always been your motto." She
paused, but not for long. "You're clever, too,
because you get your way—at least, most of
the time."

"You're pretty straightforward yourself,
my friend. When you get yourself a house
and a horse, and some coconut icing, you'll
be good to go," Bethany said. "Oh, by the
way, I noticed you got a text during dinner.
You looked happy, so I assume it wasn't bad
news from Minnesota or anything like that."

"Hmm…not really. It was Jillian. She'd
texted me earlier about an online chat. But

I'd told her I'd be gone all day and promised we'd schedule some face time in the next couple of days." She'd had no intention to bring it up at dinner, but something in the tone of Jillian's text had left her uneasy.

Heather settled in the driver's seat and started the engine, but she didn't pull into the street. "I always get a little thrill when I get a text from Jillian. Seeing her be a kid without the heavy burden of her illness is new for me."

"It's rewarding when we see our patients become whole again," Bethany said. "I see that with my patients whose new knees or hips give them a new life."

"It is rewarding, but Jillian wasn't really like herself, not this time. She claimed I'd promised we'd reschedule for tonight, but I did no such thing. It shook me up a little. We had a call yesterday morning."

"You covered it well. I didn't notice anything wrong. As for Jillian, she probably misses you more than you know," Bethany said. "Seeing her through some tough chemotherapy created a pretty special bond."

Heather had talked to Bethany often during some of the most heartbreaking days car-ing for Jillian. She'd counted on Bethany's listening ear as much as Olivia and Jillian had counted on Heather's presence.

"It was awful, and yes, she counts on me. But she's well now," Heather said. "I've already tried to clarify that things are different than they once were. It's hard for her to grasp it, I guess."

"She needs more time to adjust. That's probably all it is. She's not used to you being away," Bethany said. "It's good that you're planning to move into your own house when you go back."

Heather slapped the steering wheel with conviction. "When you're right, you're right. I'm making it complicated. I need to give it more time and be consistent."

As she pulled into the street, the small size of Adelaide Creek hit home. "Your new house is…what, a forty-five-minute walk to your parents' place?"

"A hair under three miles round trip. If our little village had sidewalks, it would shave off some time." As if she were afraid of someone listening in, Bethany spoke in a low voice. "Charlie and I figured we're close enough, but not too close to my folks. If you know what I mean."

Heather nodded and swallowed back a reminder that at least Bethany had parents. Saying that wouldn't be fair to her friend.

They were quiet on the rest of the way home, but as soon as they were in the house Bethany came to Heather's open bedroom door.

"What's up?"

"I'm sorry," Bethany said. "That remark about my parents was completely out of place. You know how I feel about my folks. I'm aware of how lucky I am to have them."

"No apologies allowed. I understand why you and Charlie want a little distance." Heather kept her tone light. "You're in the same town, but you don't need to be on the same block."

"Thanks. I was feeling bad about it." Bethany turned to leave. "Meet you on the porch. Ten minutes."

As she changed her clothes and slipped into her warm robe, Heather's mind was filled with images of houses including Bethany's cottage. But those things shared space with thoughts of Lucy and Nick and Matt. She had to remind herself she'd met them only a couple of weeks ago. As her thoughts jumbled in her mind, concerns broke through. Worries about Jillian.

CHAPTER SIX

Matt led the last of the four horses out of the trailer. He gave the mare a quick pat on her back before she trotted through the gate of the main corral and joined the three other newcomers. With the fence secured, he listened to the four horses neighing to each other before they broke into a trot and moved as a group to explore their surroundings.

"Saying hello, stretching their legs and sizing up the joint," Matt remarked to Nancy, Kenny's wife. "They don't take to being confined. Good thing I can give them plenty of space and new friends."

"With the four of them arriving together, it shouldn't take them long to adjust," Nancy said, wiping her forehead with the back of her hand on the scorching day. "It's when one horse gets removed that a little loneliness and even fear can set in."

"I didn't plan to take on more horses here

at the ranch, but it's worked out that way."
He tilted his head toward Nancy and smiled.
"Good thing I've got you and Kenny. Have
I ever told you that hiring you two was the
best decision I ever made?"

"Oh, maybe once or twice," Nancy teased.

Dirk, the driver who'd delivered the horses,
came up alongside Matt. "We're done here.
Good luck with them. I know Buddy hated
to let them go, but he feels better knowing
they're with you and not sold off cheap to
some fly-by-night."

Once a private trail guide, Dirk now picked
up occasional work with an older man who
everyone called Buddy.

Matt nodded. "Like I told Buddy, these
horses won't leave my ranch until I find a
home for them at least as good."

Dirk didn't linger and soon the empty
trailer bumped and rattled down the drive.
"I'm kind of excited about having new horses
to look after," Nancy said.

"I guessed that."

Matt was aware of Nancy's affection for
the horses, which was why he'd specifically
asked for her to be around when these four
arrived. That meant he could leave her to ob-

serve their mood and gauge how they were faring with the others. Not that he was too worried. These four were trained and already had a work history of sorts. They'd been Buddy's trail horses for a couple of summers, which meant they were good-tempered and capable of showing patience to tentative, even fearful, riders but still tolerate the confident cocky types who might not realize they had a lot to learn.

Buddy's company was closing its doors even before the season started. Couldn't meet expenses, he'd said. Matt had swooped in when he'd seen the horses offered at a fire-sale low price. Maybe it had been a little impulsive, he told himself.

Meanwhile, he'd enjoy these visitors. Maybe Heather would like to ride one of the newcomers, who were ambling closer to Pebbles and Bo. They were neighing and nickering and punctuating everything with an occasional snort.

"That Morgan's name is Miller. The other one is Branch," Nancy said, looking at the sales sheet.

Matt nodded, but now that the horses were in his corral, he was rationalizing his decision for his accountant, Zoe. She likely wouldn't approve of what sure looked like an impulsive purchase of four horses. But then, it didn't take much to displease Zoe these days, starting with the jittery markets of the last couple of years. She'd warned him that the wool and lamb prices had barely kept pace with expenses.

Matt sighed. He followed trends, too, and he saw at least even odds that the price for his high-quality, pasture-raised lamb would be up by the fall when it came time to sell. He squared his shoulders and took in a deep breath. *I know what I'm doing...this venture is working.*

Giving himself pep talks now and then gave him a shot of the confidence that had led him to buy this enterprise in the first place. He'd done pretty well in life by believing in himself. This was no different, no matter what.

Matt asked after Lisa, a curious two-year-old now. Kenny and Nancy were over the moon when they'd had that little girl. Nick and Lucy found the toddler endlessly entertaining. The couple occasionally babysat for the twins, and his mom watched Lisa once in a while, too.

"All looks well in the Burton corral, but I missed meeting the twins at the bus. I'll go see what's doing up at the house," Matt said.

Nancy pointed behind him. "Looks like they're saving you a trip."

Matt pivoted to see the kids racing through the front yard and taking a shortcut in front of the barn, directly toward him. His mother followed. "Right you are." He took a few long strides and opened his arms for a hug. "I was just coming to find you two. Come see our new friends."

When they ran to the fence and stood on the lower beam and rested their elbows on the railing, he stopped guessing what market conditions would be months down the road and put his mind on his twins.

"I want to know *all* their names," Nick said, bumping his hip against Lucy's.

When he did it again, she scooted over a few inches. "Stop it. I don't like it when you push me."

Nick grimaced and poked her arm. "Ha, ha."

"You keep poking me and I'll poke you back."

Lucy stuck her tongue out at him, which led Nick to whine, "Uncle Matt said you're not supposed to do that."

"And you're not allowed to pick at Lucy," Matt said, glancing at his mom, who had her eye on the twins and not Nancy or the horses. He had a feeling she was thinking the same thing he was. The twins were bickering more. Undeniably, Nick usually instigated the annoying—almost mean at times—pushes and pokes. So far, Lucy's retaliations were mild, but Nick complained anyway.

"Enough," he said, stepping between the two. "Nancy can't make the introductions if you're fighting."

Nancy distracted the twins from each other by introducing Miller and Branch and pointing out their markings. "Such pretty faces with their white stripes for Branch and a couple of circles for Miller. And we have two quarter horses, Harris and Night Magic. She's the shiny black horse with markings on her face."

"She gets a *two-word name*." The note of awe in Nick's voice amused Matt. It reassured him a bit, too, because that was something the charming Nick might say.

"Will you let Heather ride one of the new horses?" Lucy asked. "She might like Night Magic."

"She can ride her if she wants to," Matt said, noting again how often Lucy brought up Heather now.

"She's going to help Uncle Matt and the dogs herd some sheep," Lucy explained to Nancy.

"Really, Matt?" Mom asked before Nancy could respond. "You asked Heather to come here—again?"

"Yeah, I did." He turned away, hoping she'd get the hint and his lead. "So, kiddos, I don't know how long the horses will stay, but we'll treat them right, won't we?"

"We treat *all* our animals right, Uncle Matt," Lucy declared.

"They get all the food they want," Nick added as if that settled the matter.

A truce. He could leave them with Nancy for a minute and catch up with Mom, who was hurrying toward the house, Scrambler on her heels. "I'll be right back," he said as he broke into a jog.

When he caught up with her, she raised her hands in surrender. "No need to explain,

Mathis. Who you invite to the ranch is none of my business."

"You don't approve. Is that because you took an instant dislike to Heather? Or is this about who she is?"

Stacey waved him off. "Oh, please, of course it's about who she is. How could I dislike her? She's a nurse who works with kids. What's not to like?"

Matt noted his mom's softening gaze. She had a tender spot for nurses, whose jobs, like her teaching, were all about service.

"Someone is going to get hurt, Matt." Stacey stared at the ground and let out a frustrated sigh before she met his eye. "She's a lovely young woman. Under other circumstances, I'd say the two of you have a lot in common." She raised her head and sent a knowing arched eyebrow his way. "You don't fool me. I see how you look at her."

He waved her off. "None of that matters. She probably has a boyfriend, anyway."

In an instant, relief took over his mom's expression. "Oh, really? What makes you think so? Are you sure?"

"Don't go hiding your feelings, Mom," he said sarcastically. "Uh, no, I'm not sure, but it's a fair assumption based on a clue or two. I do know she's established in that town in Minnesota. She talked about getting herself a horse after she buys a house. That sounds settled down to me." He chuckled. "She's got a thing for horses, but I can tell she also understands sheep. That's why I invited her here to help me herd."

"You talk a good game, but there's something—a spark—between the two of you." Stacey cocked her head. "Sometimes I think you're doing the impossible. Raising the twins plus working this new ranch at a time when they're folding all over the state. I only bring that up because I want the world for you, Mathis, happiness and all good things. Not more heartache."

He had no answer for that. Mom wasn't a twin herself, but she understood the extra dose of pain lingering from a broken twin bond. Until they were eighteen years old and living in dorms in two different colleges, he and Susannah had rarely spent more than a day apart.

"You need to trust me on this." He kept his voice low but forced a smile. "Heather, appealing as the lady is, falls into that category known as unavailable. Herding sheep is definitely not a date."

His mom's wry smile showed her doubt. "So you say. Given her history with this place, the prospect of a little sheep handling might be much more exciting than dinner and movie."

Matt snickered. "Okay, I'll concede that point, but nothing else."

She gestured toward the corral. "Go on to your horses and send the kids in for their snack. Maybe Nick has settled down a little by now. He was kind of crabby when he got off the bus."

"We can hope he's brightened up."

"He's testing the limits. It's what kids do." She started walking to the house, but Scrambler headed over to chase Nick, who was scampering around in front of the barn.

Now that was the boy Matt knew. His mom was right. Little kids tested limits. End of story. Matt had to stop worrying about him.

"I'M NOT SURE why Jillian expected me to call last night, but her return texts were full of impatience, near anger that I wasn't available," Heather said. "I was in a restaurant and ended up shutting my phone off."

Olivia sighed. "I'll admit it, remission or not, it's been so hard for Jillian not to have you around. It's not your fault."

"It's not anyone's fault, Olivia, but I have to reach her somehow, get her to understand that I'm not always available. That's why we make appointments to talk." Heather chuckled. "Like playdates."

"Things should ease gradually on their own. I've got a high school girl lined up to take her to the pool and to a special art camp this summer. But the teenager isn't you, Heather. I've explained about Bethany and the wedding and why you need to be there," Olivia said, "but she forgets all that when she gets tired and cranky."

"We talked about this, Olivia. A little anxiety, a little depression, it's all part of the recovery. Or readjustment. That's a better word for what she's going through."

"I never expected this kind of overreaction when you're not available," Olivia said. "I told her you can't drop everything you're doing any more than I can at work."

"And I can't let her pin me down to a date

when I'll be back," Heather said. "Even if I decide to leave right after the wedding, that's still several weeks away."

"Oh, I thought that was the plan," Olivia said. "To come back after the wedding?"

"Well, more or less." Heather rubbed a spot in her chest as if that would release the pressure building there. "But I'm seriously thinking about staying through July, so I can help Jen with her herbs and vegetables. I don't want to walk away during her busiest time. Besides, I'm not ready to get serious about a job search yet." She paused. "And being here isn't as hard as I thought it might be."

"You know there'll always be a job around here for someone with your skills." Olivia paused. "Is there something else keeping you there?"

Was there? Not really. Matt? Bethany? Jen and Dan? The storybook Icelanders? They all beckoned to her, but none of that meant anything long-term.

"Not at all. And I don't want Jillian to feel like out of sight is out of mind. But I can't leave Jen's vegetable fields to take a call or walk out of a restaurant because Jillian wants to see me and chat." Heather exhaled before she realized she'd been holding her breath.

"Do we need some new boundaries?" Olivia asked.

"That's a good idea, Olivia. I'll make those boundaries with Jillian, but I wanted you to be aware of the situation."

"Okay, I'll keep a hands-off attitude unless you tell me you need me to get involved," Olivia said. "Oh, wait, I ran into Rudy the other day—he asked after you. He mentioned he's looking forward to another date when you get back."

"Oh, please...that was *not* a date. It was afternoon coffee." Heather hadn't even thought to tell Bethany about the hour she'd spent drinking hazelnut coffee and talking with the perfectly nice head of the physical therapy department."

"I don't know. Rudy said he had an awfully good time. He wants to see you again. Maybe for a real date this time," Olivia teased. "Like dinner in a fancy restaurant."

"I'm hanging up before you go on and on." Rudy had texted her while she was in the middle of South Dakota somewhere. He'd wished her a good trip, and she'd thanked him. One more text had come in last week and she'd replied politely. "I'll contact him when I get back. He's a nice guy, so unless he's found someone else by the time I return to Red Wing, dinner with Rudy is a go."

"You could go a little higher on the enthusiasm meter, but at least you're game," Olivia said. "We don't like the idea of some handsome rancher luring you to stay."

"*Pfft*, as my friend Bethany says when she thinks I'm being ridiculous." Heather laughed. A little too loud, a little too long. It was all she could do not to blurt, "Rudy? Rudy who?"

CHAPTER SEVEN

HEATHER STOOD ON the corner of Buffalo and Main, where sunbeams bounced off the Landrum County Gallery's storefront windows on the cold, windy day. Some things were about the same as she'd left them, but other parts of Landrum were nearly unrecognizable. The gallery was one of them. Dan Hoover liked to say that, to be successful, big towns like Landrum and even small towns like Adelaide Creek had to adopt twenty-first-century means and methods, while also convincing tourists very little had changed.

Based on her trip here with Bethany, and now wandering around today, Landrum was living up to Dan's prescription for success. On one side of Main Street, Legends, the upscale bar catering to a younger crowd, sat next to a tack shop, which itself was across from the Arts & Craft Co-op and an arcade of shops, including Western Wear. Heather planned to comb that place for whatever hodgepodge items she could put together for a costume.

The dome on the Adams County Courthouse was made from copper mined in Wyoming back in the days when mining was an important industry. The Jury Room was its neighbor on Buffalo, and across the street, the two-story gallery dominated the block. An unfamiliar push-pull had taken over since Heather had parked. She wanted to see her mom's painting installed in the gallery, but apprehension about seeing the Stanhopes' past in the ranching display pulled her back. To her, that history didn't seem like the past at all.

When she finally opened the door, the first thing she saw was a glass case of Wyoming jade, and the first scent she inhaled reminded her of the inviting smell of a library.

Bright and modern, the gallery had a welcome counter, but no attendant was in sight. Heather wandered into the main room, which included a gift shop where touristy trinkets like key chains, mugs and carved long-horned steers were mixed with old maps, landscape photos and puzzles.

A wooden arch ahead of her matched the typical entry markers for the ranches. They struck Heather as both a welcome and a warning, just like those authentic ranch arches themselves. In either case, crossing that threshold meant entering a different world.

She intended to visit the temporary ranching display, but it was the art on the walls that drew her like a magnet.

The first painting Heather saw was of a train barreling toward the viewer. A Douglas Hamilton original any gallery in the country would covet. Famous and controversial, the 1930s artist's work warned about change, with green pastures turning brown and storm clouds gathering above the trains that appeared in almost every painting.

Heather scanned the walls until she spotted one of her mother's landscapes of a setting sun behind mountaintops. The colors ranged from pinks to lavenders and finally deep purples. She'd never tired of creating more of those pieces. Those colors, always mentioned in write-ups about her, were the signature feature of Noreen Stanhope's work.

Walking closer to the painting, Heather

smiled at the memory of peering over her mom's shoulder in the corner of the dining room where the light was the best and she had a view of the mountains. She'd want to see how Mom's latest canvas was progressing and tease her about using Velvet and Corkie as the horses in half her paintings and a mountain color palette in the other half. "I play favorites," her mom had said. "I know we have other beautiful horses, but you and Jeff love Velvet and Corkie, so they're my stars."

It was that simple.

Heather looked at other work in the cluster that ranged from calm and meditative pastorals to sheep huddled in shelters in the harsh winter snows.

Mom's second painting was installed with the portraits of identifiable people. And there they were, Heather and Jeff, two teenagers sitting on the fence behind the stables. This painting was more detailed and lifelike than her usual work. From a distance, it could have been a photograph, and Heather knew for sure it had been painted from one. Heather appeared self-conscious, an awkward fourteen-year-old, but Jeff's prominent cheekbones and square chin made him manly at only seventeen.

Heather recognized a few of the names and faces in other paintings on the wall. Adams County had no shortage of talented artists.

Coming out of the gallery, Heather meandered into the ranching display, where oil portraits caught her eye.

Only a few of the county's early ranchers were so grand as to have real portraits painted, and the Stanhopes were not among them. Most of the images of Landrum County's cattle and sheep ranchers, at least those whose images were preserved, were seen in photographs. The oldest of those in this display showed unsmiling people in formal attire and posed with the patriarch sitting in his thronelike chair, the missus standing with her hand on his shoulder. Even as a child, Heather had hoped these families were happier than they looked in the austere late-nineteenth century photos. Other treasures like letters, diaries and ledgers were protected in the glass cases. The photos graduated to more modern ones, too, with people of all ages smiling or hamming it up for the camera.

Heather recognized many names. And although lots of ranchers had left their mark in this region, for reasons traced to weather and markets and family issues and disputes, they had scattered. Heather had gone to school with the kids of several long-time ranchers, but their current families were seldom still in the business. One of her classmates was the granddaughter of the family that opened Adelaide Creek's still-surviving Merchant Street Diner.

Heather was certain she would come across photos of her dad as a child with his parents and grandparents. Generations of Stanhopes had produced enough sons to keep the name along with the ranch, but not so many that disputes hindered the family's earlier prosperity. In her dad's generation, he was the one interested in the ranch, while his older brother left early to become a doctor and came around to visit but never to stay.

Ready now to move on and confront the Adelaide Creek and Stanhope sections, Heather pivoted and came face-to-face with a familiar but greatly enlarged image of Adelaide herself. Stunned, she closed her eyes and opened them again to make sure it wasn't an illusion. It was real. The photo was at the top of a long panel, one of four on a glass pillar descending from the ceiling to a foot or two above the floor.

Maybe it wasn't *exactly* like looking into a mirror, but it was close enough, starting with the dark hair pulled back in a bun, although not so severely that it stopped the natural wave from framing Adelaide's face.

Like the subjects of the other photos in the collection, Adelaide wasn't smiling for the camera. Instead, her expressive dark eyes under arched brows hinted at a defiant streak. And why not? Adelaide had defied the odds. When William Stanhope had died and left her with three teenagers, two boys and a girl, she'd refused to give up the ranch in the town that already bore her name—thanks to William. That was the common version of the tale, confirmed by a couple of letters Heather had read when she and her mom had dug through the crates in the attic.

Adelaide's defiant streak showed itself when she'd convinced the local bank to loan her the money to buy out a neighbor and add to her grazing acres. She'd turned the simple space into a full-on ranch, where her two sons built houses and raised their families.

Heather circled the four-paneled pillar and saw the photo of the ridge on the edge of the basin where she'd stood with Matt the other day. The panels were filled with pictures mostly taken in front of the growing and improving house. A few were from the county fair and, as expected, weddings.

Heather came across one she hadn't remembered seeing before. Maybe it had been forgotten at the bottom of an old box of papers. Adelaide and her grown children were on the porch, dressed as if they were on their way to church. Adelaide, likely around age fifty, wore the same jacket as the one in the portrait shot and the same white blouse with a lacy ruffle at the neck. But in this photo, the bolero cut of the jacket was visible, along with a round-brimmed leather hat with braided trim. Great-great-grandma Adelaide had style. Her boys and her daughter towered above her, but she stood out as a powerhouse.

Staring at the photo of Adelaide and her children, Heather was a little ashamed of herself. Adelaide had become an adult when she'd married William Stanhope at age sixteen. According to the stories, they'd taken the horse and wagon to the church in Grisham, where a traveling preacher stopped once a month. Married on Sunday, they greeted Monday in the two-room house on a few acres that were the start of their spread. After that, risk followed risk. Buying sheep, borrowing money to buy more acres...more sheep, more pasture. Adelaide and William endured everything together, from droughts to blizzards, until a lightning strike during a violent thunderstorm killed William.

As if she'd never seen the other photos before, Heather took in the color snapshots of the next generations and of her parents as kids—especially one of her mom, a member of the Warner family. Not much more than a toddler, she was pictured eating cotton candy at Spring Fling decades ago.

Heather battled to hold back tears when she stood in front of the fourth panel labeled *Adelaide Creek Now.* It covered her parents and followed the thread of the Stanhope story through to a simple statement about the sale of the ranch. The next line summed up a sad state of affairs.

The Stanhopes' two children, Jeffrey Warner and Heather Adelaide, currently reside out of state.

Plain talk, Heather thought. It seemed fitting since neither of these adult children had a real home.

Heather's sadness eased when she saw the open pages of ledgers from other ranchers showing precise records of lambing and shearing. They filled in the story of ranching in the region.

Heather had avoided thinking about Steak Fry Saturday, especially the need for a costume. But Jen had pestered her about it until she'd finally joked that she'd follow Nick's lead and get herself a new cowboy hat. She'd embellish it with some sequins to give it a feminine flair. Good enough? Maybe not.

As if discovering her all over again, Heather got a sense of Adelaide beyond the legend of the town and the creek. Who knew? Maybe Adelaide liked to dress up a little. With any luck, Heather could find a long skirt, maybe even a leather hat. She'd brought a white peasant blouse with her, and she had her red ankle boots. Her dancing boots, Matt had called them. She was halfway there already.

Staring into those dark eyes in the photo, Heather asked herself if Adelaide had taken on her defiant expression because so many people told her she couldn't make it as a rancher on her own. She'd showed them, hadn't she? What would Adelaide have done if she couldn't have worked the ranch after William died?

Heather was still speculating about Adelaide's resolve when the sound of her name grabbed her attention, along with the quick tap on the back of her shoulder.

"It's really you, Heather. Come to visit us from the big city." The woman smiled and said, "It's about time."

"Big city? Get real." She gave Willow Lancaster, her old high school friend, a disbelieving look. "Red Wing, Minnesota— population 16,000, give or take."

"Oh, well, bigger than Adelaide Creek and Landrum combined." Willow looked her up and down. "You haven't changed a bit. Are you here for good?"

"No, no, I'm only visiting for a few weeks. I'm Bethany Hoover's maid of honor." Not wanting to answer more questions about Red Wing or her visit, she turned the tables. "I haven't been in every nook and cranny here, but I can see it's a beautiful gallery. Do you work here?"

"A little over two years now." With a proud smile, Willow pointed to the panels and the case. "I'm in charge of the rotating displays, like this one. We combed the library archives and came across your family's records. Others gave us information they'd uncovered, and we came up with what we needed to show this one important story in a region with many stories."

Heather glanced at Willow's nametag again, which showed her title, Assistant Director. "I'm glad our records helped. It was important to my mother that researchers could get a picture of what it was like in the early days of sheep ranching."

Willow's eyes softened. "That's the goal. Naturally, we're digitizing everything, but we're also preserving handwritten ledgers and diaries. I like the feel of them in my hands."

Willow's voice exuded both excitement and a little awe. Heather smiled. "I can tell this job suits you." A native of Adelaide Creek, Willow's grandparents had been cattle ranchers, but her dad had chosen real estate instead.

"Turns out I have a passion for things new and old." Willow gestured around the room. "Especially in my own backyard."

Heather pointed at the picture of Adelaide inside the case. "Speaking of backyards, I'll be in town for Steak Fry Saturday and I heard I'm supposed to dress up. Do you happen to know where I might find a bolero jacket and a long skirt like the one Adelaide is wearing in the photo? Everyone says I resemble her, so I'd get a kick out of, you know, sashaying around in a getup like hers for a night."

Willow stepped back and eyed her up and down. "Yep, the resemblance is huge, even without a costume. Not hard to picture you sashaying like a fashionista of old." She offered another smile and curled her index finger a couple of times at Heather. "Come with me. We'll take a trip. I *might* be able to help you out."

Amused by her old friend's attempt to add a little drama to the costume quest, Heather followed Willow through a doorway in the back and down the stairs.

Willow opened a door to a room about the size of a large walk-in closet. "Ever since the display began, people have been donating old clothes they found in their parents' and grandparents' attics. We've kept a lot of items so staff and volunteers can do research or preserve the items, or fix them up for inclusion in the gallery. But they could be used for costumes, too."

Heather scanned the room and stopped when her gaze fell on a wide-brimmed leather hat almost exactly like the one Adelaide wore in the picture. It sat on a shelf filled mostly with cowboy hats of every size and description. "That's it. It's like the hat in the photo. Light brown leather, and that circle of braiding gives it a jaunty look. And it's as close to identical as I'll ever find."

"Go head, try it on." Willow lowered her voice when she added, "I'm probably not supposed to do this, but since I met you in *kindergarten*, I'm sure you won't skip town with the vintage clothes."

Heather chuckled. "You have my word I won't abscond with the treasures."

Willow started riffling through the racks like a saleswoman in a store. "I know exactly what I'm looking for. It will be perfect, and best of all, I predict it will fit you like a seamstress made it for you."

Her friend's enthusiasm was contagious. "Such optimism. You must know this collection pretty well."

"I do, and I know that only a few people can wear what I'm scavenging for." She pulled out a white blouse with a high collar trimmed in lace and pleats running down the front. Handing it to Heather, she said, "I wasn't looking for this, but hold on to it. You'll need it."

The blouse was sheer enough to have an almost silky texture. The descriptive tag said it was from the early 1900s. The era fit.

"And it matches perfectly with this." She held up the suit for Heather to see.

Heather took in a breath at the sight of the outfit. "You're right. It's as if it were made for me." The bolero jacket had a thin line of looping brown stitching on the edges of the cuffs and around the neck.

"I'm not sure what to call the fabric, but

it's a twill weave, I'm guessing. And I'd say the color's sort of natural."

"Reminds me of butter," Heather said, "or shortbread."

"Shortbread it is." Willow glanced up and grinned. "Go ahead, try it on. I better get back upstairs, but if the suit fits, wear it. And the hat and the blouse." She made a quick exit and hurried up the creaky stairs.

Heather slipped on each piece and stood in front of an antique full-length mirror. Piece by piece, she—or rather, Willow—had created the look she'd been going for. The jacket camouflaged the less-than-perfect fit of the blouse. She stuck her sneakered foot out in front of her, imagining her red dancing boots peeking from under the skirt.

Dressed in the suit, Heather saw Adelaide as the woman in the photo who'd already lost a husband and raised a daughter and two sons. She saw this relative doing her work and managing her ranch day after day, making decisions and taking risks but never knowing how any of it would turn out. Guarantees are scarce, her dad used to say.

Heather turned away from the mirror and shrugged out of the jacket. What had triggered these random and rapid thoughts jumbling in her head. She took off the hat long enough to twist her hair into a loose bun at the nape of her neck and moved her head this way and that. Yes, this was how she'd wear to the steak fry.

She changed back into her jeans and sweater and folded the suit and blouse, trembling inside over the strange effect of holding these clothes in her hands. Heather had been transported as if inside a dream.

She closed the closet door behind her. Once upstairs, seeing Willow at the front desk broke the hazy spell. With her feet firmly planted in her own time, Heather browsed in the gift shop while Willow completed a sale at the counter.

An adult coloring book caught Heather's eye. Filled with images of the Wyoming wilderness around Jackson and Yellowstone, it was perfect for Olivia. She'd tried grown-up coloring to help her tamp down stress and anxiety during the months of Jillian's treatment. Now it was a hobby.

With one gift chosen, Heather saw a series of three books about a twelve-year-old girl raising horses and solving mysteries while living with her dad in a town near Yellowstone. She picked up all three. She had a hunch they'd be a happy surprise for Jillian.

When the customer left, Willow glanced at the hat on top of the pile of clothes. "What did I tell you?" she said with a cocky grin. "I bet you look stunning."

Heather put the clothes and the gifts on the counter. "And you're gloating over it, too, aren't you?" she teased.

"You bet I am. It's one of the best outfits we have. And like I said, not that many people can wear it." Willow picked up the coloring book. "For you?"

"Gifts for some people in Red Wing. It was the longest I stayed in one town these last years."

"Are you going back there after the wedding?"

Heather nodded. "There'll be a position for me somewhere, likely at either the hospital or the county health department."

"So it's like home, huh?"

An innocent question, yet so unexpected. And absurd. Her first instinct was to deny any such notion. But she caught herself in time and mumbled something about putting down roots.

"I'm glad to see you. But you have to promise you'll stay in touch." She gave Heather a chastising look.

"Agreed, and I'll see you at the steak fry ."

Willow leaned across the counter and whispered, "I've got an amazing getup, too."

"I bet you raided the costume closet, huh?"

Willow snorted. "No, ma'am. I raided Mom's attic and found a costume for a high-wire dancer, as they were called back then." Showing off a little talent for drama, Willow struck a pose with her nose in the air and arms extended to the sides. "I'll pretend to have run off with the circus to dazzle audiences with my daring feats of skill and courage."

"Hey, like you said, if the costume fits…" Heather said with a laugh in her voice.

Suddenly, Willow raised her eyebrows. "I didn't think of it while we were talking, but the steak fry…it's at your old ranch."

"It's okay." Heather spoke fast to cut off the conversation. "I've already been out there."

"Really?" Willow pursed her lips but then spoke in a low tone as if sharing a secret.

"Word spread pretty fast about you and Matt Burton dancing at Spring Fling."

"What?" Heather's low groan came from deep in her chest. "You have got to be kidding."

"C'mon, you remember how nosy, I mean, curious people are. We should rename the county Gossip Basin." Willow paused and stared into the room before she finished her thought. "It was good talk, Heather, not the malicious kind. And as for the Burtons? Well, once we all got used to the idea of a new family in town, we took them into the fold, such as it is."

"That's good." Heather kept a neutral expression, but she was eager to leave and be alone for a while. She needed to process what she'd seen—her mom's work, the photos, the clothes. She even needed a moment alone to make peace with being the object of local buzz. "I better run," she said, "but the next time I see you, I expect to see stage makeup and a high-wire dancer's tutu."

"I'll do my best," Willow said. "But maybe I'll run into you at the Memorial Day ceremony first."

"Ah, yes, Memorial Day. Of course."

Heather picked up her bags, waved goodbye and went to her car, her thoughts drifting to the Burtons. The twins had lost their mom before they were old enough to have clear memories of her. And Adelaide Creek had accepted the new family completely. At one time, that would have bothered her. She'd have acted like someone had snatched away something of value that belonged only to her.

Anger would be the easy route. But that would mean staying in denial. Her feelings about being back here were much more complicated now. All Heather's life, Adelaide had been the legendary woman who would scale tall buildings, given the need and a chance. When Heather had driven away from town four years ago, it was with an image of herself as part of the family that had lost that legacy.

Today, though, Heather saw a woman in a stylish suit and a cool hat who'd lived her whole life never knowing if any of her plans or hard work would pay off. And if they hadn't, the legendary Adelaide would have forged ahead and found another way to build a life. She likely wouldn't have had time for guilt or apologies or self-pity.

By the time she picked up an extra-cheese, extra-mushroom pizza to share with Bethany, Heather couldn't help thinking she'd been looking at her losses through a murky lens.

CHAPTER EIGHT

MATT HELD LUCY'S hand as they joined the small group gathered at the war memorial adjacent to Adelaide Creek's cemetery. His mom followed with Nick and came to Matt's side. "Seems odd to think this cemetery was part of the original ranch," she said. "It wasn't even a real town yet."

The war memorial had been added later, to honor a man who'd been killed in France in World War I at the age of nineteen. Since then more names had been added, including a Walter Stanhope, killed in World War II. The most recent addition was a local woman who'd lost her life in Iraq.

Matt focused on taking deep breaths so he could hold it together while two young vets guided an older man to the row of chairs up-front to join other residents who'd served. If Susannah were alive, Matt was sure she'd have stepped up to lend a hand to other former military men and women. She might even have spoken at the ceremony.

Susannah was buried in Fortune, their hometown in Saylor County. The twins knew their mom had died in a war, but he believed they were still too young to see either Susannah's grave or even a veterans' monument with her name listed.

Matt wouldn't call this a huge crowd, but he was impressed that in a town with a population that hadn't hit five hundred yet, almost one hundred somber people had gathered. There was little chatter, other than moms and dads trying to get the little kids to speak in library voices. Some folks planned to drive over to Landrum, which held a more formal Memorial Day commemoration every year. Matt preferred the quieter atmosphere here in Adelaide Creek, followed by his solo trip to Fortune.

Jen and Dan Hoover slipped into the crowd on the opposite end of the semicircle. Bethany came behind them with their family friend, Cookie. Heather slipped in next to Dan. Matt kept his eyes on her as she scanned the crowd and spotted him. A surprised smile animated her expression. And then, as if she remembered the occasion, her smile disappeared, replaced with a subtle nod.

"Uncle Matt, Uncle Matt," Lucy said, pulling on his arm. "Do we have to stand here? Why can't we go to the park?"

"Gram will take you later, honey. But we need to be here for a little longer." Matt looked on as two of the volunteer firefighters took their places on each side of the memorial, one with an American flag, the other with the state flag. "They're going to start talking, so it won't be too long."

Matt watched Nick, who, unlike fidgety Lucy, was standing in the grassy space nearly motionless and watching everything going on in front of the simple stone memorial. The names were etched on a bronze plaque about five feet tall. After a moment of silence, a woman asked the veterans in the crowd to come forward and give the gathering their names and when and where they'd served. There were a dozen or so altogether, including four women, two of whom had served in Iraq and Afghanistan. Susannah's colleagues, Matt thought, living their lives and now mothers to the kids they had at their sides.

Matt gave his attention to Lucy, who was more observant now.

Joe Ellison, the emcee, asked for military families to identify themselves, too. Matt looked at his mom as they raised their hands, along with close to half of the crowd. Without hesitation, Matt told the twins they were old enough to raise their hands, too.

"Of course, you'd all be here today," Joe said. "For so many people, this is a day off or a time to grill in the yard..."

"Not for us," one of the young vets yelled. "I'm missing my buddies who didn't come back and worrying about all the guys trying to start over here at home."

Those words brought murmured agreement. Matt's thoughts always went one step further, though. *At least they got a chance to start over.*

Out of the corner of his eye, he saw Dan Hoover slip his arm around Jen's shoulders as she lowered her head. She'd lost her much older brother in Vietnam, as Matt recalled. And from the looks of it, she still ached. He got it.

Matt knew what was coming. Susannah was buried where she'd been born, but when it came to reading the names of the fallen, she'd be included, simply because her survivors—especially her children—lived here.

The vets read the names from World War I on. His mom slipped her hand into his and held on tight as the names progressed until the last one: Susannah Burton. Matt was conscious of many pairs of eyes on them, including the twins. Lucy looked up at him, her eyes big and full of questions. But Nick said, loud enough to be heard in the hushed atmosphere, "That's our mom." He leaned against his gram's leg and she pulled him close.

Lucy watched Nick, her face pinched. Matt lifted her and settled her against his hip. He looked down at Nick and then at Lucy and whispered, "Yes, that's your mom."

Joe closed the event with a moment of silence, and then one of the vets played "Taps." When it ended, people dispersed. Dan still had his arm around Jen while they stood and talked to Cookie and others they knew. Stacey left to join them, but Matt stayed put with the twins to say hello to Bethany and Heather who were approaching. A distraction, Matt hoped, not only for him but for the twins, too.

"Look who's here," Matt said. "You remember Heather. And here's Bethany."

"We're coming to your wedding," Nick said, "'cuz Uncle Matt has a job there."

"Exactly, Nicky," Bethany said. "He's got a very important job. It's called being the best man."

Nick's mouth turned down. "Uh… I'm *Nick*, not Nicky."

Bethany's hands flew to her cheeks. "Oops, I'm so sorry. I made a mistake."

Nick smiled shyly. "It's okay."

"Whew…all is forgiven," Heather said.

"Did you hear the man say our mom's name, Heather?" Lucy asked. "Her name was Susannah. She died. In a war."

Heather crouched and glanced at Nick to include him in her answer. "I did hear her name. I was sad when your uncle Matt told me about your mom. You can always be very proud of her."

"I don't remember my mom," Nick said, "but we have pictures."

"It's okay if you come to the ranch and ride Pebbles again," Lucy blurted.

"Thanks so much, Lucy." Heather glanced up at Matt. "I may do that."

"Maybe even this coming week," Matt said. They had yet to firm up the day, but it would be soon.

"I'll look forward to that," Heather's exaggerated, big-eyed expression made both kids grin. Then she looked away. "I need to go say hello to someone. But it sure was nice seeing all of you."

Bethany began talking about Charlie and the new house and the wedding, but Matt had a hard time listening to her. The kids apparently felt that way, too, because they watched Heather walk over to a woman who looked familiar to Matt, though he couldn't place her.

"For someone who's been away for so long, Heather knows a lot of people," Matt remarked to Bethany.

"Oh, that's Willow Lancaster. She works at the gallery in Landrum," Bethany said. "We went to school with Willow."

"That's where I've seen her," Matt said, keeping up the conversation.

"Heather finally went over to Landrum to visit the place," Bethany said. "She wanted to see her mom's paintings hanging there. She ran into Willow at the same time."

"Good. I was hoping she'd go and check it out."

Bethany frowned, as if puzzled. "Well then, you'll be happy to know she was really impressed. And full of surprises."

Like what? He wanted to ask, but Heather came back to Bethany's side, and so did his mom, who said she was ready to take the twins to the playground down the block. Bethany left the circle and joined her mom and a couple of other women.

"Are you going to leave for Fortune from here?" Stacey asked.

"I thought I would," he said.

"Well, we'll be off to the park then. And maybe we'll eat lunch at the diner."

Nick and Lucy waved to Matt and hurried ahead.

"Any chance you're up for a ride over to Fortune?" he asked Heather. "I like to put a flag on Susannah's grave. We haven't taken the kids over there, yet. Mom and I go separately. She prefers to pick more random days, rather than a holiday."

Heather's clear eyes were thoughtful, serious. "Are you sure I wouldn't be intruding? I would imagine that's a private."

"Very sure."

"Well then, yes. I'd like to go." She frowned for just a second. "I do need to make a call, though. I'll need to reschedule an on-line meet-up. But I can handle that later, if you don't mind a quick interruption?"

The mystery person, he assumed. When Matt hung out with Heather, he forgot all about the likelihood that she had a boyfriend. And why shouldn't she? Fun and smart, a great dancer, and easy to be with—and to look at. Heather probably attracted a lot of men.

The competing voices in his head continued to debate until he and Heather were underway in his truck.

Two hours later, after a quick stop for lunch, they reached Fortune. Matt had taken advantage of the ride from Adelaide Creek to his hometown to fill in some details about Susannah's deep ties to Wyoming, her trips home on every leave, and how she'd been looking forward to settling when she came back.

Heather asked Matt if Susannah had decided what would be next for her after the army.

"The two of us had considered the idea of

working together and expanding my company. She also thought of hiring out as a private trail guide." Matt glanced at Heather in the passenger seat. "That seems so long ago now. I can't believe how much our lives have changed."

"And Stacey's as well, I suppose."

"Oh, for sure," Matt said. "At the time of Susannah's death, I didn't think about how much my mom was giving up to help me. Not just her home, but the teaching job she expected to have until she retired."

"And it's not like she's an older grandma," Heather said. "Stacey reminds me of Jen. Lots of energy, not to mention really pretty with her auburn hair like Lucy's."

"My mom would smile hearing those words. I imagine you've heard yourself described many times in much the same way, apart from the auburn hair."

She scoffed and flicked her hand at him. Then she pointed to the sign. "Saved by the Welcome sign. We're here."

"The cemetery is at the end of this road." He flipped on his turn signal and let out a sigh. "This is always the worst part of the trip for me. Maybe it's because the cemetery is up at the top of a hill with a view of all the graves."

She nodded but didn't comment. He was silent, too, preparing himself to walk through the cemetery to the cluster of graves connected to him and his family. "My dad and grandparents also are buried here."

"Hmm…that's hard," Heather said. "Before I go back to Minnesota, I'll visit Mom and Dad. They're buried in the town cemetery, so it's not like it's a big undertaking. I just haven't felt the need." In a voice barely above a whisper, she added, "Maybe I'll stop on my way out of town."

"A lot of mixed feelings, I suppose."

She didn't respond right away, but when she did, her tone was light. "My dad used to refer to our section of the cemetery as the 'family reunion.' His attempt at a little joke. Mom would act like she disapproved and give him one of her looks, but that was for show."

"My father used to joke like that but when my mom sent one of her schoolteacher looks his way, he shaped up fast." He chuckled. "Susannah and I saw through all that."

Heather laughed. "Right. Like your mom is so fierce."

If she only knew. His mother's recent warnings about spending time with Heather came back to him, along with her slightly grudging admission that Heather was quite a woman. He slowed at the entrance to the cemetery and inched along the paved drive until he parked on the shoulder behind another truck.

"I always see so many other vets' families here on Memorial Day," Matt said, stepping out of the truck.

"Speaking of that, do you want to be alone with Susannah?" Heather asked. "I can hang back while you take whatever time you need."

"No. I've been here by myself the last few times, so I'd just as soon tell you a little more about Susy." Matt took a small flag out of the glove box and they fell into an easy pace along the narrow path to reach the top of the hill. "Ever since that first day you rode Pebbles, I've had a feeling you understand that twin connection. Better than most people."

"Working in pediatrics, I see it on display. Your twins have it, yet they are distinct individuals, too. Beyond looking so different."

That was also his observation.

"You called her Susy." Heather tilted her head and offered a sad smile.

"I did, didn't I? I call her Susy when I talk to her in my head. She was Susy as a kid, and I sometimes forget."

Matt led the way off the path and up to the grassy rise. The headstones were simple for both his dad and Susannah. His mom had wanted it that way. Susannah's had the words "Mother. Daughter. Sister." engraved above the years of her birth and death. Without mention of unit or rank, "US Army, Afghanistan" was inscribed in smaller letters.

"Mom added that because she wanted people to remember that women also died there." Matt moved closer and ran his hand over the top of the stone before he planted the flag in front of it. "The words seem so ordinary— mother, daughter, sister. If it had been up to me, I'd have left off those role labels and said something like, 'She loved her family, horses, dogs, and the moon and stars.'"

Heather sighed. "Aw, yes, that paints a clearer picture."

"That's why I enjoy seeing you on her horse. You don't look like Susy, but maybe you understand horses and kids how she did."

"I grew up with a lot of four-legged friends." She opened her mouth as if to speak, but then closed it again.

"You were saying…" he encouraged her.

"Ah, you caught me," she said, looking down as if self-conscious. "It's just that sometimes, girls with horse pals prefer them to boyfriends."

It did him good to laugh from deep in his chest. "There you go, sounding like Susy. I'm laughing because I remember complaining to Mom that I couldn't catch a break with Susy's friends. Not a date to be had."

Heather pursed her lips and cocked her head. "Oh, poor you."

"So mean. No sympathy for my tender teenage feelings."

Her gaze kept returning to the headstone. He didn't talk about Susannah and men very often, and never with his mother. Now, with Heather, he wondered if she might offer clues. "She was super choosy about the guys she dated in high school and college. When it came to the twins' dad, she declared him a big mistake, end of story. Now he's gone, too. We don't know who he was." He hesitated but decided to add, "It's a puzzle. Somehow, it didn't seem like her."

"It was a blessing the kids were already settled in with you." Her tone had shifted from casual to professional. "They didn't have to be yanked out of one environment and whisked off to another. Kids are resilient, but stability is best." Heather offered a small smile. "Sorry, I didn't mean to deliver a lecture."

Matt dismissed that apology in a hurry. "Nah, not a bit. You're correct. We also were relieved. Mom called it a blessing amid the pain."

"They like their hugs, those two. I've seen them catapult into your arms. And they adore their grandmother."

"Oh, yeah. They learned all about hugs and kisses and reading books from their mom long before we had them." He smiled at the memory of seeing the toddlers curled up with Susy and reading a story.

Heather shifted her gaze away from him, and when he turned to see what had grabbed her attention, he stayed silent, too. A group of a dozen people traipsed up the hill. Two teenagers each cupped an older woman's elbows as she took slow steps toward a small headstone several rows up the hill. He didn't know their names, but recognized them as people from Fortune and waved to acknowledge the connection.

Heather glanced back at Susannah's stone. "I can only imagine your shock."

Matt inhaled deep into his lungs. "I had this odd feeling that she couldn't be dead because I was still alive. I went through the motions, but it took me a long time to face reality."

She looked directly into his eyes. "Something went missing, but you didn't know how to find it."

"Exactly." He sidestepped to his dad's stone. "I think Susannah got her fascination with the moon and the stars from our dad. He was the dreamer. Mom's more down-to-earth. Dad taught us about the night sky."

Matt stepped back. "Mission accomplished, Heather. I needed to come here today and I'm ready now to move on."

They started down the hill.

"My mom was like your dad," Heather said. "She was the artist and the sky-gazer.

Dad was more of the no-nonsense type, but oh, how that man could dance."

"Oh, yeah? So that's where you get your flair for the two-step and waltzing across the floor so smoothly." His heart filled just thinking about her warm fingers resting in his palm.

"Seems you like my favorite boots?"

That sly, flirty smile got him every time. "Yes, ma'am, I do."

"I may just wear them to the steak fry," Heather said. "Seems to me Jen said something about live music and a little dancing on the grass."

"And I hope you'll save me a dance."

She cocked her head. "Oh, you bet."

On the way home, they stopped at Basin Diner, sat at an outside table, and Matt went to the window to order the ice cream flavor of the day: peach-vanilla swirl. When he returned, Heather was on her phone, but she was frowning, which signaled a troubled state of mind. A couple of seconds later, though, the muscles in her face relaxed and a smile had returned. She nodded a few times and then ended her call.

He sat opposite her at the table for two. Now or never time.

"So what's the guy's name?" he asked, pretending casual interest.

She frowned and glanced around. "Uh, what guy?"

"The one who makes your face light up like a sunny day. Though maybe some clouds are rolling in this time. Seems someone special is waiting for you back in Minnesota."

She lowered her head. "Busted!" A smug grin came and went in a second or two. "I'll have to reveal the mystery person."

He should have kept his mouth shut. He had a feeling he was about to look ridiculous. "Should I prepare to be red in the face?"

She let out a hoot. "*Very* red." She scrolled through her phone and then held it close to her chest. "Last chance...wanna see?"

He swallowed and nodded. "Okay, break the news."

"Yes, this is the one." Her face broke into a big smile when she passed him her phone. "That's Jillian, my patient, my ten-year-old sweetheart."

Matt groaned. He felt silly looking at the photo of a smiling girl in a Minnesota Twins

T-shirt, pointing to the short brush of red hair coming in on her head. "Well, well, don't I feel a fool?"

"Oh, don't fret over it. I'm only having a little fun with you." The broad smile appeared again but didn't vanish in an instant this time.

"Mystery solved. Now I can see who brings out your radiant glow." Matt cleared his throat. "I suppose that's why I assumed it was a guy."

Ignoring his comments about a guy, Heather filled in the details about her young patient's leukemia treatment. "Jillian is proud of her pretty red hair. It all fell out with chemo, but she's in remission now. So she's excited to see her hair grow back the same color."

Matt plunked his elbow on the table, rested his chin in his palm, and listened to Heather describe her last year. The more she talked about Jillian and Olivia, the more her eyes softened with affection.

"When I was in the gallery the other day, I bought Jillian mysteries about a Wyoming girl and her horse. I'm hoping Olivia will get over her fear for Jillian and let her ride in the next couple of years." She filled in details about Olivia, too.

Only someone with the hardest of hearts wouldn't be affected by this child's story. He didn't even know her, but she'd touched a tender spot in him.

"Olivia and Jillian don't really need me anymore, so when I go home, I'll look for a house of my own in Red Wing." The corners of her mouth drooped. "Have to find a job first, though."

"So Minnesota is home," he said. "It's been decided?"

She glanced away but nodded. "It's time I put down some roots and get myself a real life."

"You have deeper roots than anyone I know," Matt blurted.

She stared at him, a puzzled look in her eyes, and put the phone back in her handbag. "Anyway, I didn't see it coming, but Jillian's having a tough time breaking away from me. She tried to talk me into making this a quick trip, just fly in for the wedding and come back right away."

Heather swallowed a huge spoonful of her melting ice cream before continuing. "I've sent her the pictures I took of Velvet, and a few of Jen's sheep."

"I bet she enjoyed that."

"The night we had dinner in Landrum, she had wanted to have a FaceTime. But we hadn't scheduled it, and when I told her I was out with friends, she got upset about it."

"Were you supposed to talk to her today?"

"We had a tentative date, but I shouldn't have planned a call today in the first place. I rescheduled it for this evening.

"Jillian needs to gain her independence now. Part of that means understanding that I have a life apart from hers. I love them both, but I needed a break before my next job. That's why I showed up almost two months before the wedding." She paused, as if considering her words. "That, but also wanting—needing—to spend time with Bethany before everything changes again."

Getting a glimpse into Heather's work, her commitment to both her patient and her best friend, shone a light on what kind of person he was spending time with. She grew even more attractive, more compelling every time he saw her.

"I have to get better at setting boundaries."

She sat a little straighter, as if to reinforce her resolve. "We didn't talk about necessary adjustments when Jillian got well." She raised her head and met his gaze.

"Maybe she's a little afraid you won't come back period."

Heather bit her lower lip. "That's possible. Her dad disappeared the week she was born. Just walked away."

"When you say you need to find a real life, what's your definition of that?"

"Nothing radical," she said with a shrug. "I want what most everyone wants. Satisfying work, a family, a place to call home."

The backflips in his gut were waging a battle with his urge to ask her to stay. Give them a chance to find out if this electric current between them was real or just a flirtation. Instead, all he managed to say was a weak, "You obviously love your work."

For a few seconds she stared into space, seemingly lost in her thoughts. Finally she said, "Turns out I like a lot of things. And little Jillian is one of them."

Since Matt now lived where she had once

been planted, he couldn't argue that her roots were still in Adelaide Creek.

So much for the boyfriend question. It turned out it didn't matter.

CHAPTER NINE

A MORNING LIKE this was familiar in the way old shoes were easy to slip on. In good times and bad, Heather had known she could count on birdsong and the sunrise over the pastures, even when nothing else remained the same. When she and Matt trotted to the crest of a hill, he stopped to point out familiar ravines, rocks and slabs where sage and primrose had pushed their way through the cracks and crevices.

"There are a couple of narrow creeks crisscrossing the land up ahead," Matt said, bringing Bo alongside Heather and her horse. She took their stop as a chance to talk to Archie, the quarter horse Matt had readied for her to ride. Unlike Bo, Pebbles hadn't trained for herding work.

"Everything is green," Heather observed, smiling. "Except for all the places where it's not and never will be." To her right, the fresh grazing land eventually became patchy and rocky until it turned into desolate country, where what grew at all was wild. The ancient cottonwood trees, often whipped around in storms, were turning into skeletons. "Not everything is like a postcard, is it?"

"Would the younger ranch-hand in you have said that? Maybe some tidier views have jaded you for all this." Matt's eyes looked especially blue on this unseasonably warm but hazy day. They were teasing eyes now.

"Not a chance," Heather said. "But there's something to be said for the ocean and sandy beaches and spotting herons standing like statues in the Carolina marshes." Heather thought about the dairy cows on the rolling fields in Minnesota. "I felt like I'd stepped into a postcard many times."

"I know you didn't want to leave your original home, but seeing other parts of the country must have had its upside."

She nodded, but it was hard to sort all that out when she was on a new horse traveling old ground that didn't feel like the routine ride it once had been. She was tentative now, as if she'd lost a step in terms of her skills and instincts.

On the other hand, there was Matt and Kenny, who confidently separated groups of sheep moms and fast-growing lambs. Kenny worked with Spice, an Australian shepherd, deliberately moving quicker toward the new pasture. Meanwhile, Matt had the other dog, Casey, a classic black-and-white border collie.

Kenny's wife, Nancy, had raised both dogs from puppies, Heather had learned. That was when, Matt had told her, that Nancy and Kenny had once managed a sheep ranch for an owner who rarely took an interest in the operation. "They said the best thing to come out of that was hard-won experience," Matt said. After a couple of years, the gentleman farmer must have learned that raising sheep was challenging work, even with good hired hands.

Casey expertly circled the group of sheep and held them together while Matt stopped to check the terrain before taking this group down the hill. From where they were at the crest, a few old oil rigs, shut down now, were visible in the distance. They'd left behind the fields Kenny and Matt had planted to provide hay over the winter when they'd depleted the summer pastures. They'd get there by navigating areas where nature's upheavals had produced hazardous broken rocks and ravines.

"When I hired Kenny and Nancy, I got their dogs as a bonus," Matt explained, "which is why they live with them. Meanwhile, we're lucky to have Scrambler at our house. His only job is to entertain."

Without fanfare, Matt rode ahead of her down the hill and called out, "Way to me," as Casey started circling the sheep counterclockwise to guide them across a scrubby part of the landscape. Heather watched the border collie expertly run alongside the group, slipping to the other side to move some wayward ewes and lambs back into the herd. Then Casey stopped on a dime when Matt called, "Down."

Heather followed his lead and stopped when he signaled for the dog to do the same, so he could briefly assess what was ahead. Memories of this stretch came back to her, particularly one year toward the end of their run when Jeff had stepped in and taken over the job. Heather had been on Velvet and turned her around to head to the stables with

their exhausted dad. Everything should have
ended then, if her parents had been clear-
eyed. They'd have admitted Dad's com-
plaints were about more than being under the
weather, his usual understatement. In truth,
his heart was wearing out.

As only an observer along for the ride, she'd
expected to enjoy herself, maybe even feel
like she had as a teenager training for what
would surely be her future life. But it wasn't
like that. Instead, she was intimately connected in some ways, yet simultaneously—
a disconnected stranger taking it all in.

Matt and Casey made good progress across
the next stretch of ground. Heather continued to hang back so she could take in the big
picture of the work in progress. Eventually,
she picked up speed and was about to lope
ahead and catch up, but faint bleating and the
louder baas of a ewe stopped her. Aware of
how deceptive sounds could be on the open
range, she closed her eyes and listened. She
determined the sheep talk rose from a stretch
of the plain across from her. She turned Archie to her right. "C'mon, let's see what's up."

Archie knew the terrain better than she
did now and sprinted across the open space,

dodging dips and rises until they'd reached the edge of a small crater. The lamb had either fallen into danger or walked headlong into it, as Heather had witnessed lambs do more than once. The unhappy ewe had already picked her way out as far as she could, but slanted slabs and boulders blocked her.

Heather had never taken the sound of bleating casually. She was a lot like her dad in that regard. He could move thousands of sheep and worry over the bleating of the single lamb that got away and the sound of a frantic ewe. Heather brought Archie as close as she could and dismounted. She hurried around the perimeter until she saw an opening. When she found a path as free of stumbling blocks as she was likely to get, she scrambled down the slabs and around the boulders until she reached the lamb.

"You got yourself in big trouble, didn't you?" She hoped her voice would help calm the animal.

The sounds from the mama were coming close to bellows. Bent on rescuing her baby, the ewe had gone into the ravine from the wrong angle and was struggling to stay where she was, unable to move either down to her lamb or up to safety.

Heather breathed deeply to quiet her nerves, but fearful noises coming from a sheep in trouble had triggered action. She might as well have been twelve again, with adrenaline surging and fueling the energy that wouldn't let her quit. When she reached the lamb, she put her arm around its legs and lifted it up to a flatter spot. She hadn't choreographed the next move before she heard the beat of hooves hitting the ground.

"Man, you're quick on your feet," Matt said, dismounting and picking his way to Heather's side. "Why don't I get behind her and push her up? She'll move her feet if she's forced to. Then I'll pick her up and get her back to her mama."

Heather studied the slope and the rocks between her and the edge. "Why don't I push and you lift? I'll know soon enough if I'm still strong enough to force the lamb up and over. It's too rocky to carry her all that distance."

"Okay then, let's give it a try." He positioned himself higher up the slope where he could brace his boot securely. "Kenny and the dogs are with the herd, but they're spreading out across the pasture. There's water in that smaller creek. That'll keep them for now." He smiled. "Except for this rescue operation, our work is more of less done today."

Getting behind the lamb, Heather pushed the animal's hindquarters, while making sure her own feet between slabs were stable.

Matt waited between the ewe and the lamb until Heather coaxed the lamb close enough for him to reach down and lift it into his arms. Then he twisted around to put it on flat ground. They did a similar dance to back the ewe off the slab and onto a rocky patch. With a little encouragement and a couple of pushes, she reached the edge and Matt brought her to the higher ground and Heather pushed her the rest of the way. Heather quickly retraced her steps, while Matt blocked the lamb to keep it from running off. The ewe didn't waste much time fussing over the lamb. A quick sniff and a light nuzzle, and some extended baaing for good measure, brought the lost lamb incident to its good end.

"So what do you think?" Heather asked the white-faced ewe. "Everything okay now that you've had your sniff?" She put her hands on her hips and took a couple of deep breaths. Getting lambs out of trouble wasn't easy. "Your baby is safe and sound. A little rambunctious, maybe, but all is well."

Matt chuckled. "You've been spending far too much time with the Shetlands and Icelanders. Are you expecting the sheep to give you an answer, add a little commentary about the weather?"

"It's tough," Heather admitted with a tsk. "So far, the Icelanders haven't picked up much English." She struggled to keep a straight face.

"Oh, too bad. That must make reading stories to them at night a little tricky."

Heather let out a hoot. "I deserve that. I've gone completely soft. I'm like a city kid looking around for Bo Peep. The other day when we came back from Fortune, I grabbed a beer and wandered through Jen's upper pasture and had myself a good time telling them about my day."

Matt's only response was a teasing chuckle. "You have turned them into pets, haven't you?"

Heather gave that some thought. "It changes things when you know the sheep has one job, to produce wool. Lamb markets are irrelevant for that bunch. That's why I can allow myself to get more attached." She shrugged. "I'll always have a soft spot for all kinds of sheep."

"I get it," Matt said, his eyes fixed on her. "But you're a pro out here when anything can happen." He nodded to the ewe and the lamb. "We're a good team. Let's get these two back to the herd."

With the ewe and lamb between them, they got to the pasture, and Heather and Matt stopped to watch them rejoin the fold.

Heather rode around the edges, examining the familiar land with its shelters and troughs in place. The modern version of the sheep wagon, a small trailer home sat away from the pasture. Kenny and Nancy would stay there with their baby for a couple of months while the sheep reigned over the food supply. Unlike the old days of sheep wagons and lone shepherds tending the flock for many months, a dirt road gave Kenny and Nancy access in and out and enabled them to bring in their own supplies. Heather could see how much smaller herds changed this way of life. Maybe something was lost, but life was a lot easier on the families.

Seeing that Matt was busy talking with Kenny, Heather pointed Archie down an old trail. If she kept riding until the end, it would run parallel to the plain and take her to a wooded area on the far side of the ranch. The last time she'd been out here, she'd been on Velvet and Jeff had been on Corkie. It wasn't a planned part of the ride, but Matt would understand, and Archie wouldn't mind.

Heather hadn't slept much last night or the night before that. Thoughts of Matt had kept her restless and wakeful. Alone with him for the better part of Memorial Day, she'd seen another side of him. He wasn't Matt the loving surrogate dad, or Matt the determined sheepman, or Matt the business guy. He'd been Matt the surviving twin, and he'd also showed her a little of Matt the son.

Not a man to sleepwalk through his life, as her mom would have said. He managed to shoulder a full load of responsibilities and keep his sense of humor sharp in the process. Today, though, was a flesh-and-blood kind of day, with jobs to do and certain ways to do them, but Matt and Kenny had been prepared to expect the unexpected. Horses, dogs, sheep, humans—everyone had an assignment.

Heather understood that. She'd lived it. But no matter how bound to the earth she was sitting on this horse under the sun, the whole day had passed like one long dream. She had to shake herself awake. This wasn't her life.

"WHERE DID HEATHER GO?" Kenny asked, looking behind Matt.

"She took off in that direction," Matt said, pointing to the line of trees that marked the end of the pasture. They were next to the trailer that sat an acre or two back from one set of shelters and troughs. Stumps of dead cottonwoods were serving as chairs at the moment. The trees had probably been cracked open by lightning during violent storms or felled by winter winds bringing snow across the plain.

"If she keeps going, she'll reach the end of the old Stanhope ranch—those four hundred or so acres sold off years ago are just beyond the trees," Kenny said. "So did she like being out here again?"

"Oh, yeah," Matt said, grinning. "She hung back a little but had no problem helping a lamb out of a tricky situation. When I got there, she was figuring out a way to reunite that lamb with its mama by herself." Teaming up had made it an easier job, though, and without the need for a lot of words. Matt liked that.

"Seems odd no Stanhopes live anywhere near here anymore," Kenny said. "But you know the history, probably better than most people."

"I made it a point to learn."

They turned to the sound of Nancy arriving in the truck. When she joined them, she had a bag of turkey sandwiches along with lemonade and cups.

"Here she comes now." Matt had come to expect the familiar lift in his chest at the sight of Heather. She smiled at all of them when she dismounted Archie and gave him a friendly pat before walking toward them.

"I don't believe we've met," Nancy said, "but I know you're Heather."

"And you're Nancy, but I don't see your little girl." Heather smiled.

"Grandma has Lisa for the day." She held out a sandwich and a cup of lemonade. "How did you like being out with the sheep?"

"Ah, great. Hard to find the words." Heather wiped the sweat and grime off her face with the bandanna Matt had given her before they'd started out. Then she drained the cup of lemonade.

She'd put her hair in a long braid but it wasn't inclined to stay in place, Matt noticed. It might bother her, but he enjoyed every glimpse of that hair.

Heather asked about Lisa, and Nancy was off and running. When Nancy changed the subject to horses, the two women were like kindred spirits. Heather got a faraway look in her eyes as Nancy told her about the four newcomers and Heather hung on every word.

"Uh, Matt?"

Kenny's voice seemed distant but it flipped his attention switch on fast. "Sorry."

Kenny frowned. "You were a million miles away."

Matt chuckled. Not really. He was content sitting with these people and the animals and taking in the dreamy look in Heather's eyes.

CHAPTER TEN

"DID YOU EVER think you'd be a guest on your own ranch, Adelaide? It never once crossed *my* mind." Ever since her visit to the gallery, Heather felt a new kinship with the first Adelaide. Like magic, putting on the shortbread-colored suit and leather hat brought Adelaide to her side like an invisible companion.

When she joined the party already in full swing in front of the house, she could easily picture her ancestor milling about and greeting guests. Yes, it had to be the clothes, even the red dancing boots now peeking out under the ankle-length skirt.

She remembered very well her first reaction to hearing about Steak Fry Saturday. Fire and fury, both about the event and Stacey's audacity to think she would come.

The proud and pretty house in front of her stood in stark contrast to the lonely, run-down place she'd left behind. Fresh white paint brightened the frame home, and a new wraparound porch had replaced the old shabby one. Long tables set up in the yard were covered with red-and-white-checked tablecloths. Heather guessed close to one hundred people were already there.

She fell into step with the McCormicks, a couple who'd followed her up the long drive. Ursula and Finn had been old friends of her parents', fixtures in her childhood, especially because Finn had been a science teacher at the high school in Landrum. This was the first time she'd seen either of them since she'd been back.

"Aren't you something in that getup?" Finn grinned, doffing his beat-up stove-pipe hat.

"I should call you Adelaide," Ursula said. "I bet she had a suit exactly like that."

Heather glanced down and smoothed her hand across her skirt. "That was the idea."

"You could be the town's schoolmarm back in the day," Finn observed.

"I suppose so—but nobody teaches biology like you do, Finn," Heather teased. "I think Bethany and I got our inspiration to become nurses from you." She looked him up and down. "President Lincoln, I presume."

"At your service, ma'am," Finn said as he gave her an exaggerated bow.

Heather turned to Ursula. "And here's Mrs. Lincoln in her blue taffeta dress. You've done wonders to match her look."

Ursula nudged her husband with her elbow. "See, I told you folks would know who were."

"It's good to see you, Heather," Finn said. "So many of my students had to leave the area to find jobs, but some are like you and finding their way back."

Heather let that ride. She nodded toward a young couple dressed up as 1980s rock stars with matching wigs that gave them wild blue hair. The woman wore shiny black platform boots and the man struggled to walk in leather pants. "I wonder if they plan to dance in those getups," Heather mused. "I hope they'll be okay."

Finn and Ursula turned to look at the couple and smiled. "Two more of Finn's students," Ursula said.

"They look awesome. Nothing timid about those costumes." Finn waved to the couple. "He's a former student of mine and has just become the new math teacher at the high school."

"Nice," Heather said to acknowledge Finn's proud smile.

Finn gestured toward the house. "Don't know if you heard that the guy who bought the ranch, Mathis Burton, and his mom are raising his sister's twins. She was killed in Afghanistan."

"Actually, I've already been out here. I've been lucky enough to meet Lucy and Nick."

Ursula didn't hide her surprise, but seeing Matt heading their way, Heather was saved from more questions or comments. A good thing, too, since she was busy being impressed. Speaking of impressed, she spotted Matt. He stood tall and handsome in a black suit with wide lapels trimmed in leather. His string tie and black hat completed his look.

"Well, aren't you the respectable type in that suit, Mathis?" Finn glanced back at Heather. "I guess you two have met."

"We have." Matt squared his shoulders and offered his arm to Heather. "I'm hoping the fine lady will dance with me later."

Maybe because Ursula and Finn were watching and could see the amused sparkle in Matt's eyes, Heather's face warmed.

"Well, lucky you." Finn grinned. "And I

see you've made my former student blush."
He and Ursula gave them a quick wave and
walked toward a trio of loitering zombies
Heather recognized as the firefighter crew.

Heather slid her arm through Matt's
crooked elbow. "What can I do to help?"

"Not much at the moment. Mom and her
friends are keeping an eye on the buffet table,
but the caterers are doing most of the work.
Kenny and a couple of other guys are grill-
ing the steaks. We've got volunteers collect-
ing the dinner fee."

"Oops, let me go and take care of that. I
like knowing it's for a good cause."

"No need. I covered it."

That didn't sit well. It sounded way too
much like a date. She withdrew her arm.
"Why would you do that? I mean I can pay
for my own dinner."

"Whoa, I didn't intend it as an insult." He
pointed to the house. "It just didn't seem right
that you should have to pay to be here." He
held her gaze for a few long, awkward seconds. "Besides, we're friends, aren't we?"

She exhaled and her irrational irritation
drained away with her breath. "Seems so.

To be perfectly honest, I didn't expect you'd turn into a friend, but here we are."

"Let's start again. Miss Heather, may I accompany you to Steak Fry Saturday?" Matt added a bow for effect.

"Why, yes, Mr. Mathis," she said, chuckling, "I'd be happy to have you escort me to the dance."

"See? It's a date," Matt said.

Still looking into his eyes, she said, "You made your point. Thanks for dinner, Matt."

Matt nodded but then stepped back to have a better look at her. "Then, from one friend to another, I think you look real nice. You could be a formidable businesswoman in that getup."

"Or a schoolmarm or a preacher's wife," Heather said.

Grinning, he pointed to her feet. "Only if you lose the flashy boots."

Heather glanced down and lifted her skirt above her ankles. "Right. They're a little daring for an upstanding woman of her time." Heather pretended to be serious. "I might not have fared well back then, after all."

"I think you would have done just fine." When he stepped to the end of the buffet line, Matt said, "Now, this is the kind of celebration I like. I don't have to do a thing except stand around and look important in my black suit."

Heather pointed to the block-long drive to the road. "When I was teenager taking my turn to plow the drive, I'd complain about the house being set back so far from the road. But it's what makes this place just right for a town gathering like this."

"If it happened to rain, unlikely as that was, we were going to move everything to the barn and stables," Matt said. "A tight fit, but we'd have made it work."

In the distance, the musicians started to test their sound and lighting. "Is this party just an excuse to have music and dancing?"

"You're on to me." Matt's voice trailed off, but that's because he was focused on something over Heather's shoulder. "Man, will you look at Willow?"

Heather turned around and laughed at the circus performer in a red leotard and tutu-like skirt, matching tights and black ballet slippers—and an abundance of black eyeliner and the brightest red lips Heather had ever seen.

Willow approached and raised her arms over her head in a ballet pose. "Here I am, the Great Willowina." She tapped her blue glasses. "Intrepid high-wire gal or not, I need to see where I'm going." Smirking, she gave Heather a head-to-toe glance. "Whoever wore that suit before was your body double."

Heather put her index finger over her lips. "Don't tell anyone, Matt, but Willow let me borrow these clothes from the historical society's stash."

Matt patted his heart. "You two are dazzling beauties. A guy can barely breathe around here."

Willow rolled her eyes at Heather. "All for a good cause. Right, Heather? New equipment for the firefighters and books for the library."

"Absolutely." Heather studied Willow. She'd pulled off a showy look, glasses and all. It had never occurred to Heather to be a little daring with her costume. Yet the Adelaide she'd recreated with her suit was a gutsy risk-taker. For the first time, it dawned on her that her other relatives had also taken big chances when they'd walked away from the ranch—must have been at least one that had run off with the circus. It was as risky to leave as it was to stay.

"I have to go. I'm theoretically helping Alice manage things." As Willow hurried off, Heather snapped back into the moment and shook off her confusing mix of feelings. She'd bristled at the suggestion that this was a date, but now she was pleased to call it that.

Matt handed her a plate and they moved toward the grills where a team was serving steak and chicken. Adelaide Creek's mayor, Alice Buckley, greeted people going through the line. She was dressed as an astronaut and even had the round helmet tucked under her arm.

When Matt introduced Heather to Alice, the mayor's face lit up. "Well, well, your reputation precedes you." She grinned. "I work part-time in admissions at the hospital, so I run into Bethany now and then and she'd mentioned how much she misses you."

"I've missed my best pal so much, too," Heather said. "I don't have family around here anymore, but I'll always have Bethany and her folks."

Alice's whole being was animated when

she explained the reason behind Steak Fry Saturday, an event that made fundraising fun.

"We're growing and most of our newcomers are young families. It's exciting," Alice said, "but it means the needs of the town are changing."

Suddenly, Matt broke in. "Something's going on, Heather. I'll be right back." He broke into a jog and headed to the pyramid of crates Matt called the Twins Topper.

"Must be some mishap with his kids," Alice said. "What a guy. If I didn't already have Cody..."

She didn't have to finish the sentence and Heather didn't need to respond. That left her free to focus on Matt and Stacey hovering over Nick. They'd moved him back from the Twins Topper, and he was trying to pull away from Matt. "I wonder if Nick is hurt or maybe just tired," Heather mused.

"It's probably typical kids' stuff."

Maybe. Heather wasn't so sure. She'd already wondered what was up with Nick. He didn't seem able to keep up with his twin sister at times.

"Speaking of kids' stuff," Alice said, "Bethany mentioned you're a pediatric nurse.

Then you'll be pleased to hear that next week the county is having our second annual Child Wellness Clinic. Parents like it because it's free and fast. We do quick screenings—hearing, vision, that sort of thing—before we send the kids off for the summer."

"Another positive development around here," Heather said, trying to keep her attention on Alice and not on Matt and Nick. "And who would have predicted Adelaide Creek would evolve into sort of a suburb of Landrum?" She put air quotes around *suburb*.

"Certainly not our grandparents," Alice responded.

Someone called Alice's name and she took off at the same time Matt returned. "Nothing serious. A stubborn little guy balking at bedtime." Matt injected a light tone into his voice, but his eyes showed worry.

"A lot of excitement in his yard, so I can imagine he wouldn't want to get ready for bed no matter how sleepy he is." When Heather held out her plate, the guy at the grill filled it with a steak cooked exactly the way she liked it.

After they served themselves from a buffet of side dishes, Matt steered them to the empty end of a long picnic table. When the waiter, dressed as a court jester, came by with a tray of glasses of red wine and mugs of local beer, Heather helped herself and so did Matt.

"A toast to friends and family, and the power of giving," Matt said, raising his mug, "and to rock stars and presidents, zombies, circus performers and ladies wearing suits the color of butter."

"I'll happily toast to that. But Willow and I decided it's the color of shortbread."

Matt tapped her wineglass. "Even better."

The sweep of sky behind Matt showed the last brushstrokes of pinks and golds and a touch of violet lingering as the sun went down. Cooler evening air had already descended. For a couple of seconds, Heather was light-headed, as if nothing around her was quite real. Then, as fast as the feeling had come over her, it vanished.

She took another sip of wine and glanced at the house she knew like the back of her hand yet barely recognized in its spruced-up state. That was surprising, but not in a bad way, much like being with Matt at this event seemed as natural as breathing. Studying Matt's face, so often full of fun and good humor, her heart beat a little harder. This feeling went way beyond pleasant and fun—it was thrilling.

"Heather? Are you still with me?"

She started at his words. "Oh, yes. I'm enjoying all this so much."

"I can hear the band warming up." Matt frowned and scanned the other tables and the buffet line.

"Is something wrong?" Heather asked.

"No, not really. I'm looking for Grey and my mom. I don't want Mom feeling like she has to spend her whole evening monitoring Nick and Lucy. The kids were really worn out after a big day. We had a little struggle with Nick earlier. He was overtired, I think." His eyes narrowed in thought. "I'll go check on them now before the dancing starts."

"Sure. Do you want me to come with you?"

"No, that's fine. I'll deal with it." He craned his neck to look past some people in clusters. Then his expression brightened. "Mom just gave me a double thumbs-up sign. Everything must be okay. I'll check on the kids in a little while. If Nick wakes up, he's likely to come out here looking for me or his gram."

"I imagine so." Heather hesitated, but finally decided to say what was on her mind. "Your life is so complicated right now. And I don't mean because of the kids." She gestured to the barn and stables. "Managing this operation isn't easy."

He gave her a tepid nod and looked away. Then he tilted his head toward the band. "Can you hear it? The warm-up is turning into melodies."

He'd barely finished the sentence when the lead singer shouted to the crowd, "Let's get this party started!"

Matt got to his feet and held out his hand. "May I have this dance, Miss Heather Adelaide?"

"My answer is yes, you may." Heather followed Matt to the grassy area in front of the band as the fiddles and bass kicked up a fast beat, more rock than country.

"We're the first ones out here." Matt took both her hands and turned her under his arm so they were side-by-side syncing small lively steps, stepping apart and moving closer and laughing from the fun of it.

Heather could have revved up her energy another notch if they hadn't been alone on the dance floor. Suddenly self-conscious, she slowed.

"Something wrong?" Matt asked.

"We're out here by ourselves, Matt."

He looked around and snorted. "Guess they didn't have the benefit of years of lessons like we did. They didn't win dance contests in every state west of the Mississippi River, like us." He twirled her twice and the music stopped. "You have to admit we're pretty good at this."

"For a couple of near strangers."

He pulled her closer. "We don't dance like strangers."

Fast comeback. She had to hand it to him.

The singer kept up light banter leading into the next song and after that the ice broke when people of all ages were coaxed onto the grass for the Electric Slide.

Then, when the drummer performed a classic drum roll, Alice came to the front, grabbed the mic, and gave a quick welcome speech that brought whistles and cheers.

"This event is Alice's baby," Matt said, "including its name. She's rooting for it to become another Spring Fling, a signature event." The music started again and Matt gave her an expectant look. "Want to show everyone the Texas two-step done right?"

"You know how to apply the pressure."

"I think you can handle it."

And she did. At the expense of her hair. She'd already taken off her hat and tendrils started falling out of the bun she'd fashioned at the nape of her neck. She didn't care. She took out the pins and freed her hair. A bun wasn't her style anyway.

She danced with Dan, who looked like an authentic Dracula, during the next set and then waltzed with Finn. Almost all the one hundred or so people spread across the grass for an only slightly awkward Cowboy Boogie. When that music ended, Matt excused himself and jogged to the house, but came back a few minutes later.

As the sky darkened, the light from the torches and lanterns hid the stars in the clear sky, but not the half moon. The band slowed way down to a languid waltz. Heather relaxed in Matt's arms as if they'd danced together all their lives. Maybe the wine had gone to her head a bit, enough to slough off concerns about the many pairs of eyes settled on them as they moved.

When the music ended, Matt held on to her hand. Breathless, she didn't pull away or protest when he led them from the dancing.

"What's your pleasure?" Matt asked. "A glass of wine? Another dance?"

Neither. Her pleasure was to be away from the crowd in her light-headed state. "Since you asked," she whispered, "I'd like to say hello to Pebbles."

"I think that can be arranged. Come with me." They walked past tables where guests taking a break from dancing were mingling. Heather kept her focus straight ahead and hoped Jen or Cookie hadn't spotted them. Or Stacey. That was ridiculous, really. They were only going to visit a horse. Hand in hand after nonstop dancing with the best partner of her life. But who's noticing?

The horses weren't in their stalls but inside the corral with its lean-to shelter. They stood closer together than they did when they were in the larger pasture during the day. "They like each other's company," Matt said. "I've noticed that about horses. They don't need to be shut away in their stalls all the time. Not on cool, dry nights like this one."

"Bo and Pebbles are nose to nose," Heather

observed, "almost like they're carrying on a conversation." Her own words embarrassed her a little. "I know. I sound like I'm turning them into people. I don't think they're chatting about the weather."

"What? You're spoiling my fun," Matt teased. "I imagine horse conversations all the time. We always keep carrots around for the kids to feed them. It gives them a way to connect with the new horses. I'll get a few, and we'll see what they have to say about that."

Heather moved along the fence closest to the horses. She tilted her head back and inhaled the fragrant smell of new grass and pines, and especially the heady scent coming from the clusters of mock orange across from the barn.

No matter where she'd been these last four years, nothing measured up to the fragrance of the air here among the pines and cottonwoods in June.

Matt sidled in next to her and called the horses' names. He waved the handful of carrots. "Got their attention now, haven't I?"

The two horses meandered over and bobbed their heads. When Heather held out a carrot, Pebbles wasn't shy about helping herself. Something about this horse touched Heather in a way that she barely understood let alone was able to find words to express. A small and gentle Appaloosa, with a great big heart. "It won't be long before Lucy can ride you, pretty Pebbles." She turned to Matt. "I bet Lucy will make a great friend in this horse."

"Pebbles sure takes to you. I saw that on our first ride."

Heather patted the horse's face and held out another, smaller, carrot. Matt was doing the same with Bo. Both horses nickered softly, liking the attention and the treat. Heather's arm brushed Matt's, but she stayed put and so did he.

In the background, the music and mixed sounds of conversation and laughter seemed so far away. She glanced up at him. "It's almost strange how removed it feels here, like all that music and dancing is a world of its own."

"That's so," Matt said softly, "and it's filled with beautiful things." His fingertips touched her cheek and lightly traveled down to rest on the curve of her jaw.

She could have stepped back, but instead

she closed her eyes, put her hand on his arm, and welcomed what was coming. His lips brushed hers. She tightened her grip on his arm and he kissed her again, a firm, hungry kiss. She wanted another and another. Finally, she moved back and reluctantly lowered her arms.

"Aren't you glad my horses like a late-night treat?" Matt whispered in her ear. When he wrapped his arms around her, she rested her head on his chest. But he lifted her chin and kissed her again and ran his fingers through her hair.

Confused, breathless and tongue-tied when they broke the kiss, Heather pivoted to Pebbles and fed her the last carrot. "I didn't forget about your treat, you sweet thing." No, but she had forgotten most everything else.

Matt sighed. "I could stay right here and kiss your sweet lips until the sun comes up, but I need to get to the house again and check on things. Nick has been so unpredictable lately."

Heather patted Pebbles's neck and whispered goodbye as she turned her back to the fence. "Of course. I'd never want to be in the way. I'll go back to the table."

Matt took her hand and they started toward the house. They were almost at the barn when a loud wail put them both on alert.

"That's Nick." Matt made a fast turn around the corner and nearly slammed into his mom, who was holding Nick in her arms.

Nick wailed again and squirmed to free himself.

"Here you are, Matt. I've been looking all over for you." Stacey gave Heather a quick glance. "Apparently, Nick decided not to listen to me tonight."

"I'll take him." Matt lifted Nick and held him against his hip. Or tried to. Nick still struggled. Finally, Matt put him on the ground and crouched. "Hey, buddy, what's all this about?"

"I want to be at the party. I heard the music, but Gram's making me go back inside."

"It's already way past your bedtime, Nick. And you can't disobey your gram."

"Yes, I can." Nick tried to show some bravado, but his tentative, meek tone got the better of him. Defying Gram was not allowed. He hid his face.

Stacey reached out to Matt with both hands. "Listen, Matt. People are starting to call it a night. One of us needs to be there to help Alice and thank people for coming." She sounded frustrated. "I can't be host and settle Nick down."

"Nope. No settling down." Nick peeked out from behind his hands. "I want to settle up."

Heather swallowed back the quick laugh that wanted to come out of her mouth. She glanced at Matt, who appeared to be having the same reaction. Not his mother, though. Heather knew an exhausted adult when she saw one, and that was Stacey this very minute. She'd had it.

When Stacey glared at her, Heather took another step back and tucked her hair behind her ears. She wanted to concentrate on Nick and not on Stacey's obvious disapproval. Shaking her head, it occurred to her that a couple of lovely minutes had complicated Matt's life even more.

"Is there anything I can do?" Heather asked.

"Uh, thanks, Heather, but I think we've got this," Matt said softly.

"I'll get out of your way then. Good night, Nick." She nodded to Stacey and avoided Matt's gaze as she took a shortcut through the grass to her car, hoping to avoid curious eyes.

A few minutes later, she was home and had plunked herself into one of the rockers. Intentional or not, she'd made a mistake with Matt. Now, even knowing Bethany wouldn't like it, or understand, there would be no lingering after the wedding. No more thoughts of staying an extra month. Bethany had counted on her company for at least a few weeks after Charlie left again. But staying was out of the question—why postpone the inevitable? It was already going to be hard to leave her home behind. Again.

Heather hadn't fallen in love in a long time, but her memory wasn't blurry. What had happened went way beyond a few dances at Spring Fling that had added fodder to the local rumor mill. That was bad enough. But then to spend the whole evening eating and dancing with him at the steak fry, too... The gossip would follow Matt around long after she was gone. She hadn't been thinking straight, acting like no one noticed the two of them sneaking off to the stables like a couple of teenagers. Holding hands, no less.

She struggled to keep her mind on making her plans, but her face was hot, her heart beating fast and hard. Matt's cool lips and memorable kisses were to blame. Yet even the memory of first-kiss sweetness wasn't enough to keep the other nagging, troublesome thought from gaining strength and demanding her attention.

Something was way off with Nick.

"You and I don't disagree that often, Mom, but when we do, watch out." Matt's attempt to keep his tone light, even a little jokey, landed with a thud. "But right now, let's keep this about Nick, okay?"

They stood in the kitchen, his mom in the doorway to the dining room. She'd said she was heading to bed but had obviously changed her mind. She was back in front of him with plenty more to say.

"It was more than a couple of dances this time, Matt." The exasperated sigh that followed wasn't typical of her at all. "You're letting this thing with Heather interfere with our lives now."

He wasn't buying it. "If it hadn't been for Nick acting up, you wouldn't have noticed I left the dancing and went to the corral. You wouldn't have paid any attention. Neither would anyone else."

Mom frowned. "Not true. *Everyone noticed*." The scoff that followed carried a grudging tone. "Like Grey said, it didn't help that you two were the best dancers out there."

In spite of how the evening had ended, a pleased smile tugged at Matt's mouth. "If I two-stepped any other woman around our front yard, you'd think that was a good thing. It's not a crime to enjoy Heather's company."

"This is different. And you know it. How are you going to feel when Heather packs up her car and heads back to Minnesota after the wedding? Have you asked yourself that?"

"Look, it's not like that." That was no small lie. More like a whopper. The magic they'd created on the dance floor...well, that counted, but it only was a little of the magic. Heather's lips were irresistible, and she'd responded to him with kisses of her own. It had been a long time, if ever, since a woman had left him feeling so alive. When had he hung on every word a woman said? Or felt his heart expand every time he looked at her.

"It's *exactly* like that," Mom said. "You're

not good at self-deception, and I'm not blind. I just don't want to see you hurt."

"Things change," he offered. "Plans change. It's not like this is a one-sided teenage crush. She likes me, too."

"I don't doubt it. She looks at you with the same dreamy expression you have when you look at her. It's like the two of you are in sync. Who would ever guess you'd only met her a few weeks ago? No one."

"Well then, why are you hounding me about her?"

"Because it can't work, Matt. It's not only that she's a *Stanhope*. We live in her family home. Do I really need to spell it out?"

"Oh, so what?" He knew why it mattered, but he no longer cared.

"Have you forgotten what it was like in this tiny town the first year or two? All we heard was Stanhope this and Stanhope that. Even the town has a Stanhope name. No one told us *that* until we got here."

He wished he could contradict her. "I know, Mom. We didn't own the Burton ranch, we lived on the Stanhope ranch, like we were squatters and didn't have a right to be here." Matt put that on the table before Mom had a chance to.

"At least we agree on that."

"But it's behind us now," Matt insisted. "We just hosted the town's newest festival on *our* ranch...the Burton ranch."

"But, Matt, she grew up in this very house." She twisted her upper body around and pointed to the staircase. "I'll bet she remembers which step creaks."

Matt knew what came next, because this wasn't the first time they'd discussed Heather. "We're not going to lose the ranch, Mom."

"That's what you say now, but you've hit a bad patch," his mom said. "You may want to sell the place, Matt. It could be a good thing down the road. But..." She raised both hands in a helpless gesture.

Matt leaned against the counter and crossed one ankle over the other. He couldn't deny that any more than he'd try to deny his growing feelings for Heather. But it wasn't the bad patch that worried him the most.

They fell silent, with the only close sound the hum of the fridge. It seemed they had nothing more to say, but Matt's unspoken thoughts grew louder in his head. Finally, he cleared his throat. "I'm officially changing the subject. No more talk about the ranch or Heather." He took in a breath. "I don't care what Nick's doctor said before. He's not okay. This is no 'stage.'"

His mom shifted her weight and uncrossed her arms. "Let's get another opinion."

"We'll take the twins to the clinic this week," Matt said. "Even if Dr. Nielson is the guy doing the screening, I'll demand he take a second look."

Matt sighed. *We'll figure this out, Susy.*

CHAPTER ELEVEN

BEING ASTRIDE A horse and herding sheep heightened all her senses and left her exhilarated and fulfilled. Same with dancing. Heather took a quick inventory of the supplies lined up in the freestanding cubicle and smiled in satisfaction. Nursing exhilarated her, too, and sharpened her focus, and nothing fulfilled her more.

"You're Heather, I take it," a voice behind her said. "I'm Tom Azar. Glad to see you. Everyone calls me Dr. Tom."

Yanked out of her musings, she exchanged a quick handshake with the doctor before he went on to explain how the clinic worked.

The young, energetic Dr. Tom brought to mind an oncologist on Jillian's team who sported pink sneakers embellished with cartoon animals that always coaxed a giggle out of her patients—and usually their worried parents. Dr. Tom's sneakers were white, but his jeans and the blue T-shirt under his white coat likely put kids at ease, while simultaneously telegraphing to adults that they were dealing with a new type of doctor.

"It's wonderful to be here," Heather said, lifting her shoulders in a happy shrug. "Alice's call came as a complete surprise, but my schedule is wide open." In the days since the steak fry, Heather had thrown herself into helping Jen, mostly tending the vegetable gardens, while trying to pretend nothing had changed between her and Matt.

The community room in the town hall had been transformed into a makeshift but functional clinic with two separate examination areas—one for the screener nurse, the other for the doctor. The minilab allowed them to draw blood, and she had a tablet for charting that fit into the pocket of her white lab coat.

Alice joined her and Dr. Tom and elaborated on the county's plans to expand health screening for seniors as well as for kids. It had been a couple of years since she'd done routine wellness screening, so Heather took a minute to study the protocols. Even before she'd taken care of Jillian, all her young patients had been hospitalized, some with serious conditions. Concussions were common, and she'd tended to many kids with complex bone fractures. Sadly, Jillian hadn't been her first leukemia patient.

"I can't thank you enough." Alice put her palms together and raised her head as if sending up a prayer of gratitude. "If I hadn't run into you at the Burtons' the other night, it wouldn't have dawned on me to call you as a substitute in this pinch."

The surprising call from Alice earlier that morning had interrupted Heather's first cup of hot coffee on the porch. It was a chilly morning, so she'd wrapped herself in a throw a customer of Jen's had made from Shetland wool. Heather had been deep in thought about Matt, but she'd at least tried to pivot to thoughts about a job search and house hunting. She'd decided to give it a couple of days before she opened a conversation with Matt about Nick, but she refused to bottle up her concerns about him.

The scheduled nurse had had to cancel because of a family emergency, and Heather had jumped at the chance to fill in. The mayor herself had volunteered to be the greeter and handle the check-ins of parents and kids showing up for the pop-up clinic.

When Alice left the cubicle, Heather quickly surveyed the setup before the first patients arrived. A carpeted play area took up space in the waiting area, where Alice had positioned a check-in table. She'd put books and blocks as well as crayons and coloring books on a child-sized table. Back in her cubicle, it didn't take long for Heather to arrange her supplies of gloves, swabs, tongue depressors, penlight, blood pressure cuff and the tablet for charting.

She used her own stethoscope, one she carried with her in the emergency first-aid kit she kept in her car. The kit had come in handy now and again, including an episode of cardiac arrest in a restaurant in Charleston, and six or seven years ago, a multicar accident on a highway outside Adelaide Creek. She still remembered the relief that came from knowing she could grab her kit and swing into action. Seeing the lineup of her nurse's tools fueled her confidence about stepping in to help Alice with the clinic.

Heather watched as Alice checked in the early arrivals. Most were pleasantly surprised to see their mayor as the greeter. From the looks of it, they'd have a steady flow of patients.

Until Alice's call, and now seeing children come in with their parents, Heather hadn't realized how much she missed the everyday clinical work of pediatrics.

Alice waved a mom over. Holding her fully awake and cooing baby in her arms, the mom followed a sulky, slouchy, teenage boy into Heather's curtained exam room.

After Heather introduced herself and took a brief history, she weighed and measured the infant and checked her muscle tone and reflexes—and her crooked social smile. The baby's big blue eyes matched the mom's and the boy's. The teenager, Mason, had yet to speak so much as one word. But he had all the right numbers in all categories, height and weight, blood pressure and heart sounds. A little on the skinny side, but still in the normal range.

"Any issues or questions? I see your regular doctor cleared you to play sports, Mason. Any questions about that?"

"What about this? What can you do about

it?" Mason pointed to the acne on his forehead, then looked away.

"I can do three things for you." She kept her tone crisp and professional. She rolled the stool to the portable desk with its rack of pamphlets on various health topics. She chose one on adolescent acne and handed it to Mason. "That's the first thing. Read this, cover to cover. Lots of good information here. And two, as soon as the doctor is ready, I'll send you in so you can talk with him. I can recommend products you can buy but talk to him first."

She turned away to type notes into the tablet and waited.

Mason cleared his throat. "Uh, what's the third thing?"

Pretending she'd forgotten all about it, she tapped her temple. "Right, right. The third thing is what *you* can do. It's called patience."

Mason's face fell. It was slight, but she didn't miss it. She told him the truth, that teenager acne clears up in the vast majority of cases. But then she added, "It's part of your journey from changing from a boy to a man."

She'd used that phrase before with teenagers, and sometimes it shifted something inside them. She saw it in the subtle changes in their eyes. Eyebrows lifted, eyes opened a little wider. Like now with Mason. He didn't need jokes about hormones and bad skin, sometimes delivered by well-meaning adults in a teasing tone. Like other teenagers, Mason needed to see himself as part of something bigger. The sulky expression was replaced with one of curiosity.

Mission accomplished. "I'll let the doctor know you're here. You can have a seat. You'll be first up."

Over the next hour or so, Heather developed a rhythm and the exams went quickly, and other than one notation about the need for an extended vision exam, the kids of Adelaide Creek were a healthy lot. She gave out pamphlets on diet, exercise and sleep to everyone whether they asked for them or not. Dr. Tom went along at a fast clip as well, with a minimum of babies' protests or toddlers trying to escape their captors.

"I expect most of these kids will soon become Tom's patients," Alice confided during a lull, "if they aren't already. He's great with kids."

"I couldn't agree more, Alice." Heather

caught Mason's eye. He stood holding the baby against his shoulder and swayed side to side while his mom talked to Dr. Tom. Heather waved and he nodded back.

Heather had planned to hold out for a job in the pediatric department in a hospital in Red Wing or one of the other pretty towns on the Mississippi River. Now, seeing these kids, a few a little scared, some chatty and all curious, had an appeal. Maybe it was time to help healthy kids stay that way.

One of her patients, Dakota, strengthened Heather's resolve. A cute fifteen-year-old, Dakota was taking medication for anxiety and to keep her calm. The meds appeared to be working, although she was unnaturally quiet and listless, her mother said. It made Heather wonder. "I see you're actually Dr. Nielson's patient," she said, puzzled. "You had a checkup with him a couple of weeks ago."

"Yeah, well, Dakota wants to see a counselor," her mother replied. "I want that, too. I figured if we showed up again, maybe he'd give us a referral this time. Now I see that he isn't even here today."

Heather asked enough questions to find out

the girl had sought therapy, but Dr. Nielson had maintained the drug would be enough. The girl herself perked up to call the doctor's attitude dumb.

"We'll make sure you can talk with Dr. Tom. Who knows? New doctor, new ideas." She kept her tone light, but she was on Dakota's side all the way. Most kids rebelled about counseling, and here was one who'd asked for it and was refused. Ridiculous.

"Really?" Dakota asked. "You mean I can talk to the new guy? Today?"

Dakota's mom smiled, obviously happy to see her daughter pleased.

"Yep, that's what I mean. Follow me." Heather finished her notes and directed Dakota and her mother to the empty chairs. "He'll be free soon."

After a big thank-you from Dakota and her mom, and a quick break for lunch, Heather again fell into a rhythm with the steady parade of kids. She discovered all over again that she was good at helping kids relax and trust her. She bantered easily with the older ones and teased the younger ones.

She'd known she needed this break but

going back to work would give her a chance to flex new muscles.

As the afternoon went on, the atmosphere was upbeat, even boisterous and fun. One teen balked at seeing a pediatrician. He wasn't a *child*, after all. But then he saw Dr. Tom walk by at the intake table. Maybe it was the doc's younger age, or the jeans and cool white sneakers, but suddenly the idea of talking to the doctor wasn't so off-putting anymore.

When she went out to greet her next patient, she heard a voice she recognized shout, "There's Heather, Uncle Matt." Heather turned her head in time to see Matt's face light up and Stacey's eyebrows knit. Nick was still pointing at her, and Lucy was waving.

"Good to see you," Heather said as she approached. "I hadn't realized you were coming in for the clinic today."

"Heather is our friend," Lucy explained to Alice. "She's been to our ranch, and she rode *my* horse."

"Then I guess I don't need to introduce her, do I?" Alice remarked with a wry smile.

"You won't have to wait long." Heather was deliberate about addressing Stacey as well as Matt. She wasn't prepared for the wave of relief traveling through her body. A chance to take a closer look at Nick had fallen into her lap.

She gestured to the next mom and three school-age kids. "Come on back."

Heather settled herself with a deep breath and tried to forget Stacey's frown and Matt's smile when they'd seen her. After what had happened between them in those few passionate minutes, she was self-conscious, unsure what it all meant. Or what it didn't mean. Whatever it was had nothing to do with her intuition about Nick.

Putting on her mental blinders, Heather focused on the kids in front of her. Theirs was strictly a fact-finding trip. One of the boys wore glasses, and he complained that they'd fallen off when he was playing baseball. He was convinced he not only didn't need them but that they were holding him back. "But the glasses give you perfect vision," Heather said. "All the better to see a fastball coming across the plate." He conceded the point with a smile showing permanent front teeth his face hadn't quite grown into yet.

"You can get the kind that are so light you

barely know you're wearing them," Heather said. "Or ones with bendable arms. They're great if you're playing sports. You can find frames in your favorite colors—or clear, no color at all."

"I want the clear kind," the boy said.

She smiled and patted his shoulder and sent the boy and his mom on to see Dr. Tom.

Heather hurried to welcome the twins and Matt and Stacey into her space.

"I'm fine," Lucy said. "I don't need any needles today."

Matt squeezed her shoulders. "We'll let Heather and the doctor have their say about that, sweetie."

"I had fun at our party," Lucy said. "Our whole yard was filled with people, maybe thousands of them."

"Really? Thousands?" Heather teased, trying to ignore the flutters in her stomach at the mention of the party. She forced herself not to glance up at Matt or his mother.

"Nick got sick," Lucy said. "Right, Nick?"

Nick nodded, which gave her the opening she needed.

"Why don't you tell me about it, Nick?" She picked up the tablet and showed it to him and Lucy. "I'm going to write down what you tell me so the doctor can read it when you see him." There was no question in her mind that Dr. Tom would need to order some tests. With Nick sitting this close to her in the well-lit room, it was even clearer something was off. Pale skin and dull eyes made him appear worn out. She reached over and affectionately squeezed Lucy's hand and then Nick's. Lucy's skin was warm, but Nick's was cool, closer to cold. She noted that on the tablet.

"Sometimes I get tired at the wrong times."

Stacey leaned forward in her chair. "We had a hard time settling you down the other night, Nick," she said. "You didn't seem like yourself. Not at all."

"We'll tell Dr. Tom you're tired at the wrong times," Heather said.

"Sometimes I get mad about things. I don't like the rules."

"Oh, I see. Is it like a bad mood that won't go away?"

"Only *some*…times," Nick insisted.

"Right. I'm typing that word in this tablet. I think Dr. Tom will be interested in hearing more about that." And putting together the clues of cold hands and pale skin. No child should have dull eyes.

Heather caught Matt's look, hoping to convey the right level of concern, but not panic. She had a hunch about Nick, and if she was right, the treatment wasn't difficult and could start right away.

Starting with Lucy, she had the twins stand on the scale, noting that Nick was smaller and at the low end of normal weight.

She documented the rest of Lucy's and Nick's stats. "So the twins were declared A-OK not too long ago, huh?"

Matt and Stacey nodded simultaneously. "But we still have questions," Matt said. "Telling us it's just a stage doesn't cut it."

"Got it." Heather turned her attention to the twins. "Here's what's going to happen next. I'm going to talk to your gram and your uncle while you wait for your visit with Dr. Tom."

Stacey held out her hands. "Come on, you two. I'll walk you back to the chairs in the front."

"I didn't expect to see you here," Matt said when they were alone. He spoke softly, his mouth slightly turned up.

Heather had trouble not smiling, too, as she explained how she happened to be there. "I'm pleased I could fill in, last minute or not. To tell you the truth, this could be your lucky day." She was quick to add, "I'm not saying Dr. Nielson isn't a good doc. He's been around for decades. This new guy is different. He's kind of a child magnet, and the parents look relaxed when they leave. Need I say more?"

"You figured out that something's wrong with Nick, didn't you?" Matt asked.

She nodded. "Yes. Most likely it's not serious, though. But my guess is anemia. Dr. Tom will look over what I wrote in the chart and likely order the tests. Nick shows all the typical signs, including being argumentative and short-tempered. Nick has swings in his energy, and in a little kid that mimics mood swings we see in older kids."

"Anemia?" Stacey whispered as she came back inside the cubicle. "That doesn't sound so bad."

Heather started to answer but Matt spoke first. "Dr. Nielson insisted his low weight was only a lull in his growth. A stage. Like growing pains or something."

"To be fair, these signs are often missed. I mean, a child acting up isn't a novelty." Heather spoke directly to Stacey, more at ease with her now that health was the focus. "But Nick appears listless. He's pale and his hands are cold." She explained the symptoms she noted. "He livens up when someone is talking to him, and then he loses energy when they stop."

"Wow. That showed itself the other night," Stacey said.

"That kind of agitation and defiance is a sign of anemia, or it's related to the kind of fatigue that comes with it. There was so much going on at the ranch. It was too much for him." Heather shrugged. "Some six-year-olds are unhappy a lot, but Nick doesn't strike me as that kind of child."

"He isn't." Stacey sighed and rubbed the back of her neck. "I've been so tense."

"We both have," Matt said.

Heather held up her tablet. "In any case, all the findings and my observations are on the record." She hesitated but was obligated to offer another option. "It's your choice, but you can bypass Dr. Tom and make an appointment with Dr. Nielson."

Matt shook his head. "No way. I went against my own instincts once. I'm not doing it again. I wanted another opinion. Now I have yours. That's good enough for me."

Heather tightened her jaw. She'd never met Nielson, although he'd been around when she was a kid, but parents shouldn't leave a doctor's office filled with self-doubt. Even Matt, not a guy who lacked confidence, questioned his own instincts.

"Uh, Heather, you don't think it's anything more serious?" Stacey asked.

"Not if it's straightforward childhood anemia, but there are different types, and some are tricky to handle. That's why it's best to run the tests."

"Is anemia genetic?" Matt asked, lowering his voice. "I think I mentioned we don't have much information about paternity."

"Matt... Heather doesn't need all the details."

"It's okay, Mom. I've filled her in about what we do know."

Stacey winced as if Matt's words had hurt her. "I don't want anyone delving into what's your sister's business and talking to who knows who about—"

"Mom," Matt interrupted, his face and tone putting his obvious shock on display.

Heather extended both hands to break into the conversation. "Wait, wait, wait. Stacey, I would *never* repeat anything Matt told me about Susannah. Not to anyone." She lifted the tablet in the air again. "As a nurse, I'm pledged to maintain privacy. Everything I noted is to help Dr. Tom. All I want is what's best for Nick."

She got it. Stacey didn't like her. But no one had the right to question her professionalism. "Besides, you won't need to worry about me spreading gossip." She kept her clipped tone when she added, "I'll be gone for good no later than the end of July."

Stacey cupped her cheeks in her hands and closed her eyes. She looked contrite, and as if she might say something. Heather stood, pulled the curtain back and left the cubicle with Matt and Stacey.

One more patient to go, she thought, when she returned.

Heather focused on Mags, a fourteen-year-old with braces and a severe case of freckles. Her braided strawberry-blond hair fell over one shoulder, and her bright-eyed gaze followed Heather's every move.

"You have an interest in medicine, Mags."

"Critter medicine," she said, flashing her braces. "I'm going to be a vet. Horses will be my specialty."

Heather patted Mags's knee. "A girl who loves horses, like me." This girl with curious brown eyes was rapidly finding a comfy place to settle in Heather's heart.

She pulled out pamphlets and handed them to Mags. "These cover all the good stuff—you know, diet, exercise, skin, sleep, vision. If you'd like to talk to Dr. Tom, he'll be available soon."

"Nah, I'm good." Mags tugged on her braid. "I'll read these. Can I call you sometime if I have questions?"

Much as she wouldn't mind talking with this horse-loving girl, she had to nix the idea. "I'd like to say yes, but I don't live here anymore. I'm in a town for a visit and next month I'll be going…home. To Minnesota." Those words were hard to get out. Today, working at this clinic, Minnesota was a faraway place.

Mags's mom's face took on a look of sudden recognition. "Wait, I thought you looked

familiar. You were at Steak Fry Saturday."
She introduced herself as Lexie. "You had
on a very smart suit and hat from the old
days." Her gaze went to the name tag Alice
had made for Heather. "Of course. Stanhope. Didn't your family once own the Burton ranch?"

"A *long* time ago now."

"Yes, Matt and I chatted before while
we waited to see you. Nice guy." Lexie
grinned. "Terrific dancer, but you know that.
I thought…" A puzzled frown appeared, and
Lexie quickly said, "Never mind. Doesn't
matter what I thought."

Suddenly, Heather imagined Lexie as one
of those who'd had eyes on her and Matt
slinking away from the crowd.

Heather left the cubicle, got Dr. Tom's attention and introduced him to Mags and her
mother. After a couple of questions, he signed
off. "Anything else on your mind, Mags?"

She flipped her braid from front to back.
"Nope. I'm cool."

"Yes, you are, Miss Mags," Dr. Tom said.
"But you can always call me if anything
comes up." He gestured to the Burtons and
all four headed toward him.

Heather walked Mags and Lexie to the front. "I'm glad I met you. It's always good to meet a girl who lives for her horse."

Mags nodded. "I wish you weren't leaving. You seem like the kind of person who belongs here." She narrowed her eyes and cocked her head. "What's so great about Minnesota, anyway?"

"The Mississippi River and Lake Superior," Heather shot back, amused by this uninhibited girl. She leaned toward Mags and whispered, "I'll let you in on a secret. They even have horses in Minnesota."

Mags's wide grin bloomed. "Okay, I get it. I just wish I could see you. You probably know as much as any doctor."

"Oh, Mags," Lexie said with a laugh in her voice. "Once she grabs hold of an idea, Heather, look out."

"I can see that," Heather said watching them walk out into the hall.

"We're done," Alice said. "I'll bet you're happy with that news."

Heather didn't say anything one way or the other. The truth was, she'd had fun with the babies and teens and all the others between. Ages ago in her training days, she'd discovered she had a way with kids, not so different from her ease with horses. She understood them. They understood her.

"It was an enjoyable day for me, Alice. One of the best since I've been back."

She went to the cubicle to box up the supplies and enter the stats for the day. She was almost done when the twins rushed to her.

"Dr. Tom filled a whole tube with Nick's blood," Lucy announced.

Nick held up his arm with the taped gauze. "But Dr. Tom said I have plenty left."

Lucy chimed in again. "He said Nick was very brave about the needle."

"I was, Heather. It didn't hurt much, anyway." As soon as the words came out of Nick's mouth, he sighed and his little shoulders drooped. He'd run out of steam.

As the adults walked to the door, Matt put his hand next to his ear and mouthed the words *I'll call you*.

Heather nodded before turning to the kids. "You better skedaddle. Looks like it's time to go home."

"Skedaddle," Lucy repeated. "That's what Gram says when she wants us to get moving."

She skipped ahead of Nick, who lagged behind but turned around and waved goodbye.

Mason, Dakota, Mags, Lucy, Nick. They sealed the deal. A change was in order for Heather's next job. A walk-in clinic would suit her. Or maybe she'd find Red Wing's equivalent of cool Dr. Tom. She'd like that.

CHAPTER TWELVE

LONG AFTER THEY'D had their fill of moo shu pork and cashew chicken, Heather and Bethany filled their wineglasses and strolled out to a wooden bench that sat on the edge of the ridge. The spot offered an unimpeded view of the starry sky on the clear, cool night. The panorama was like a tapestry embroidered with constellations. Bethany and her dad could not only connect the dots, they were also familiar with the dozens of myths and legends behind them.

"Are you going to miss this vista when you move into town?" Heather asked.

"Oh, a little," Bethany answered. "Charlie likes it out here, too. Good thing we're on excellent terms with the nice couple who own this spot," she joked. "I don't think Mom and Dad will mind if we picnic out here. The more important question is if you'll miss all this after you head east again."

"Of course I'll miss it," Heather said. "But I know the owners, too, and I'll be back." She paused to take a sip of her wine and to gather her thoughts. "Today started out with a phone call about being a fill-in nurse. But it morphed into something bigger."

"Tell me more," Bethany said.

"It nudged me to follow my heart about the type of nursing I want to do. No more hospitals for me right now. I'm going after wellness, not illness. That means finding a job in a pediatric practice—or maybe a school or the health department."

"You have the qualifications. Are there job openings?"

Heather shook her head. "I'll look online soon and let Olivia in on my new plan." She could always work fill-in shifts at the hospital until something opened up. "I got a kick out of the kids who filed in and out." She told Bethany a couple of stories from her day. "I shouldn't play favorites. But that last patient, Mags-the-equine-vet-to-be, was the most fun of all."

She closed her eyes and concentrated on the cool night breeze brushing her face. As the days passed, memories of Matt's fingertips caressing her cheeks and his warmth enveloping her when he'd taken her into his arms were intruding more and more.

Before Bethany noticed she was off in a different world, she coaxed herself to keep her eyes on the stars and sip her wine. They were tangible, real things, not wispy Matt moments that would fly away on the breeze. Besides, were her reactions to Matt truly about him, or did they only illuminate what was missing in her life?

"I don't have any specific strategy yet for my next steps, but if this trip accomplished nothing else, it added oomph to my resolve to get a horse. I don't need a partner for that or to buy a house. But if I'm lucky like you, I'll meet the right guy." Being around the twins had also fueled her desire for a family.

"Hurry up, then, girlfriend. Wouldn't it be great if we had our kids around the same time? The other night, Charlie and I were saying we're so ready for a baby."

"Aw, you'll be a beautiful mom, just like your mom."

"I'm getting really excited about the wedding. It used to feel so far off, but now all I can think of is the two of us with our arms around each other." Bethany held out her hand and it trembled.

"Are you nervous?" Heather asked.

"Nope. I want to say something, but I'm a little scared."

"Scared of what?"

"What do you think?" Bethany said, impatiently. "I'm scared of *you*."

"Me? Get out." Heather sighed. "Besides, I know what you're going to say."

"Right, right. The psychic is back."

"You're too predictable. You want to know why I don't look for my house and horse here." Heather pointed behind her. "But this is about the past. Other than having an admittedly showy place in the gallery, the Stanhopes are more or less forgotten."

"So what?" Bethany blurted.

"*Huh?* So what?"

"My point exactly." Bethany grunted, leaving no doubt about her frustration. "For years now, you've acted like the Stanhopes are the only people who count around here. But people have always come and gone from these parts." She swept her arm across her body. "You've had relatives who didn't want any part of this struggle. Other families burned out or were bought out, until there wasn't a cow or a sheep in sight."

"Maybe so, but not the Stanhopes. We lost ours." Heather thought about the photo of Adelaide in her hat and suit, with her two sons on either side of her. "There's no shame in wanting a different life, Bethany, setting a different course. I get it. But a bank we did business with decade after decade ended up owning our ranch. Remember?"

"You bet I remember. You won't let anyone forget. You wear that loss like a logo. You take it everywhere you go. All along you've acted like what happened was your personal failure." Bethany sighed. "I'm... I don't know. I shouldn't have said—"

Heather waved away the attempt at an apology. Anger simmered. But something else, another reaction, competed for her attention. "Everything you said describes the best reason to build what I want in a new place. Losing the legacy *wasn't* my personal failure. I finally know that. But it adds up to the same thing—moving on."

"Your dad was worn out and ill long before he went to the doctor and was diagnosed with heart issues. He'd already spent most of his life digging out of the problems *his* parents left him. The handwriting was on the wall, Heather."

"That doesn't change the problems Jeff and I were left to handle." The minute the words were out, she wanted to breathe them back in. She diverted her attention by topping off Bethany's glass and then her own.

"I get it now," Bethany said. "You plan to keep punishing yourself for mistakes and bad luck that had nothing to do with you. You still blame yourself because you were powerless to fix everything that went wrong."

Heather opened her mouth, ready to deny Bethany's words, but she took a sip of wine instead. What Bethany said had shaken her. Mostly because it was true.

"You've been back to the ranch a few times now," Bethany pointed out. "You survived." She scoffed. "Quite well, as a matter of fact."

"What's that supposed to mean?"

"I told you about Mathis Burton's sweet smile and his cute twins," Bethany said, lowering the volume of the conversation. "I didn't have the inside info about what a cool dancer he is."

Heather started to protest but, really, what was the point?

"Don't bother denying it. People see things. Dad told me he spotted you and Matt slipping away and heading toward the stables. Were you feeling sorry for yourself then?"

"You're on a roll, aren't you?" She still nursed anger over Bethany's remarks like she nursed her white wine. Sort of. Staying mad at her friend was a tough job. "He actually told you that Matt and I left?" Heather didn't wait for the answer. "I adore your dad, but c'mon, Dan, like everyone else around here, likes a little gossip."

"If you want to know the truth, Dad thought it was nice." Bethany smiled and tilted her head back. "My dad is a romantic guy. He notices things. Like the way Matt looks at you and pays attention when the two of you are conversing…that's what Dad calls it."

"Well, the romantic conversation was all about Pebbles—the horse." She made light of it by telling Bethany about Matt getting the carrots for Pebbles and Bo. "We had fun. You know I like to dance. I like horses. Why wouldn't I enjoy myself?"

"From the minute you met him," Bethany said, "you liked him, despite who he was."

Heather laughed. "The first time I saw the man, he was holding a happy little girl against his hip and waltzing her around the dance floor. He gave all his attention to that adorable child." She directed a pointed look at her best friend. "Let's get real—a scene like that makes a guy hard to despise."

"I don't mean to be hard on you," Bethany said. "You're my Best Friend Forever. I *want* to see you happy."

Hmm...that was exactly why Heather was tempted to tell her about Matt's kisses. A nervous laugh escaped, and Heather put her fingertips over her mouth like a self-conscious little kid.

"Something did happen," Bethany said. "I see it written all over you."

Heather tried to flick away such a notion, but a giggle escaped. "I'm not good at hiding things. So yes, I have a secret. We had a sweet, lovely kiss." She laughed lightly. "Okay, we had a few kisses. I got caught up in the moment."

"Caught up in the moment, huh?" Bethany teased. "I got caught up in moments like that with Charlie, too. That was one of my early clues."

"Clues?"

"That I was *falling in love* with him."

Heather tried to find words to deny that was what was building within her. But she gave up and just shook her head. Finally, she said, "I can give you another reason this thing with me and Matt wouldn't work, not at all."

Bethany gestured toward Heather. "Don't hold back. Spit it out."

"Stacey doesn't like me."

"What? I doubt that's true."

"Oh, yes, it is. She was seething when she had to come looking for Matt to help with Nick." Heather still smarted from the glare directed at her. Earlier, at the clinic, Stacey had all but accused her of gossiping about Susannah. Her leftover anger at Heather barely concealed. "She found us together, coming back from the barn. And Nick's acting up disrupted her date with Grey Murtagh."

Heather winced. Another mistake. "Oh, no, I never thought of that. No wonder she glowered at me."

"She's a mom, too. She likely senses you're

halfway out of town already. Could be she fears for Matt's heart."

They fell silent long enough to listen to the hoot of an owl Jen had spotted in one of her cottonwoods near the shed. The breeze picked up and filled the air with the low swoosh of the grasses on the path.

Matt's heart, her heart. Two hearts at risk.

"Okay, I'll shut up now." Bethany smirked. "*Almost*. I told you what Dad-the-romantic thinks. Do you want to hear what Mom added?"

Heather swallowed a mouthful of wine. "Go ahead. Lay it on me. I love your parents no matter what they say."

"Mom said Matt was happier hanging out with you at the steak fry than she'd ever seen him."

Heather tried to be nonchalant as she suppressed a smile. Who didn't like a little flattery?

"That's not all." Bethany spoke slowly and barely above a whisper. "Mom said the same thing about you."

Heather stared at the stars in hopes one would inspire a snappy reply to Bethany.

No such luck.

"WHY CAN'T THE new horses stay, Uncle Matt? We like them," Lucy insisted. "We want them with us."

"Gram and I like them, too, honey, but the woman who's taking them today needs them for her guests to ride. That's why we're letting her borrow them for the summer and fall."

Not long after Matt and Ruben had determined it was unlikely they'd need the horses for Finer Rides this season, he'd made a fast deal with Erin Perez. She needed to rent them for her start-up, an adventure company targeting the as yet weakly tapped women's market. She had spent a decade as a wrangler and a private tour guide, so she had what it took to make a go of this specialized business.

Matt and Erin knew each other by reputation—important in any dealing where horses were involved. The four relative newcomers were healthy and good-tempered. Matt had believed they'd earn their keep and then some. He'd been right, and that made Ruben and his accountant happy. They'd agreed that leasing them out was even better for the bottom line than selling them.

"Here she comes now," Mom said, pointing to the trailer turning onto their drive.

The twins rushed to the fence where they'd have a good view of the horses as they were loaded.

"I'm like the kids. I don't like to see them go," Stacey said. "I've enjoyed watching them pal around with the others out in the pasture these last couple of weeks."

"Me, too, but Erin came along at the right time." He and his mom followed the kids down to the fence where Erin had pulled in and stepped out of the truck. Another woman appeared from the passenger side.

"Mornin'," Erin called as Matt and his mother approached. "This is Roz, who can do all the jobs—cook, guide and wrangler."

Matt gestured to the trailer large enough to transport the four horses and the tack. "You're going to have my twins as an audience while you're loading these beauties."

"They aren't happy campers about seeing these four leave," Mom added.

"If they're anything like I was at their age," Erin said, "then the more the merrier. Of everything. Dogs, horses, hot dogs, cupcakes…"

"And wilderness adventures for women," Stacey added. "We can use more of those."

"Seems I'm one of those people not cut out for a nine-to-five job," Erin said with a happy lilt in her voice.

"Me, neither," Roz said, grinning.

"It's a pretty big club, I'm finding," Matt said.

Night Magic balked some. Harris raised his head and flattened his ears in protest at being led into the unfamiliar—and small—space. But after having the last word, he settled down when Matt patted his flank. He stopped neighing once Miller and Branch joined him. Erin's voice was soft and reassuring when she spoke to all four horses.

The kids ran back and forth between the truck and the corral and the stables while Matt finished up the paperwork. When Erin and Roz took off, Stacey went inside with the twins to get ready for a birthday party that afternoon. Matt kept his eye on Nick, hoping he'd be okay for the party.

When he turned his attention to the corral where Pebbles and Bo were hanging out, in his mind's eye, he saw Heather riding next to him.

His mom's latest warning words about getting involved with Heather echoed through his head. He'd brushed them off. They were too late, anyway. The woman with a generous spirit for kids and horses, not to mention sheep, already had a piece of his heart. With an idea taking form in his head, Matt got out his phone and sent a text.

CHAPTER THIRTEEN

"He's coming here? Now?"

"That's what he said. He's riding Bo and leading Pebbbles. We're going to ride across your fields to the other end of his ranch." Heather pointed to the back of the bunkhouse, which looked out on the long ridge that connected the Burton acres to the Hoovers' pastures. "He's riding down over Pointy Rock, like we used to do. He cleared it with your mom."

From her expression, the news astonished Bethany. "Pointy Rock? I haven't thought of our made-up name for a decade. Maybe longer."

"I hadn't thought of it, either," Heather said with a laugh, "but it came right back to me like it was yesterday. We must have been about ten years old when we gave those hills and the trail that name."

"Lots of slabs and pointy rocks to dodge.

The name fit perfectly," Bethany added, curling one foot under the other in the rocker. "Matt didn't need to call Mom. He's welcome here anytime." Bethany gave her a goofy grin. "In fact, Mom probably sent a text to Dad at the hardware store to broadcast the Heather–Matt breaking news."

Heather rolled her eyes, trying to play it off as nonsense. But the excitement deep in her gut told a different tale. "Apparently he thought he needed to ask. He hasn't seen the Icelanders up close, you know." She waved her phone. "That's what he said."

"Right. Matt's walking a horse across the trail so he can look at some sheep. Such a novelty for him."

Heather laughed at Bethany's dry tone. From the time they were girls, her friend had always had a way of cutting through the layers to get to the heart of things. "C'mon, Bethany. You know these sheep are different."

With that, Heather went inside and put on her riding boots then changed into a tank top for what was already building to a sweltering day. She grabbed a denim shirt and a bag of trail mix and went back out to the porch.

"I'm glad you're having a good time here,

Heather." With a touch of hesitation in her voice, Bethany added, "And putting aside everything else I said the other night, what's not to like about Matt?"

Heather lifted her hand in a halt sign. "The ride today is about distracting himself while he waits for Nick's test results. They should be coming in later. He'll send them to me, so I can help explain what they mean." That was one way to deflect personal talk about Matt.

Heather had told Bethany about the kisses but not about her sharp awareness of him in every cell of her body when he was near, or how his eyes could be blue one day and green the next. Ironically, as dangerous as it was to let his feelings for her into her heart, she'd never felt as sure around any man.

"I suppose Stacey is with the twins?" Bethany asked.

Heather nodded. "Matt said something about a birthday party." A subtle flutter in her stomach interrupted her train of thought as memories of Steak Fry Saturday passed through her mind. "I wonder if a party will be too stimulating for Nick. It hurt to see his lovely brown eyes fill with confusion. When he gets agitated, he doesn't know why he's upset."

"Hey, Nurse Heather, you're off duty now." Bethany gave her a knowing look. "The birthday party isn't your problem."

That didn't stop Heather from wanting to protect Nick. "I don't like kids being judged as bad when they act up, especially when a physical problem is the cause."

Bethany's smile was soft, affectionate. "I think you need a passel of little ones of your own." Suddenly, she stifled a yawn.

"Looks like you need to crawl into bed for a few hours," Heather said, spreading sunscreen across her shoulder and down her arm. Bethany hadn't been ready for sleep when she'd first come home after her nightshift, but she was now. To wind down, Bethany had joined Heather on the porch and they'd spent the bulk of the morning chatting about Charlie and the wedding.

Heather was in awe of Bethany's ability to cope with Charlie's absences. As if reading Heather's mind, Bethany said, "In another year or so, Charlie will be able to work from home or from a secure office in Landrum."

Knowing Charlie's work was a secret,

Heather put a lid on her curiosity. Even if Bethany knew where Charlie was and the exact nature of his work on this stint, she'd never betray the demand for silence. "I still think you're more patient than most of us would be."

As if it was the most natural thing in the world, Matt came around the corner from the side of the bunkhouse, loping astride Bo with Pebbles on a lead.

"That was fast." Heather grabbed her denim shirt and the trail mix and approached Pebbles, who raised her head and snorted her greeting.

"See? Nothing subtle about that. Your best horse friend misses you," Matt said before nodding to Bethany.

"That trail you took over here is the same one the Heather and I used to ride back and forth to each other's houses," Bethany said. "We claimed it as our own and named it Pointy Rock. It was a special spot for a couple of teenagers to share their secrets without any eavesdroppers except for the birds."

"Sounds like fun," Matt said. "I bet Lucy or Nick will do the same thing one day."

Heather stroked Pebbles's face and sweet-talked her a little before settling into the saddle. "You sleep well, Bethany," she said, leading the way to the trail.

They rode side-by-side behind the bunkhouse bordered with sage and a hodgepodge of scrub pines mixed in with flat slabs and rocks. They took a shortcut through the pasture, where Jen's sheep grazed on the far end of the sloping land.

Matt nodded at the Shetlands and Icelanders. "They look like they were delivered from central casting. What a great place to film a Western."

"They're hardly even curious about us," Heather remarked. "They gave me the once-over when I first got here, but I bring them water, so they're used to me now. They don't seem to mind this heat."

Matt's blue T-shirt was already dampening a little. "Maybe this wasn't such a good day for a pleasure ride."

"Every day is a good day to be out here, Matt." She'd spoken so quickly, she surprised herself. Even worse, he was unsettling her. She fought back the urge to babble something about looking for a job with the school system in Red Wing. That would clarify her intention. See? She already had one foot firmly planted on Red Wing soil.

Instead, she pointed to a destination beyond the pasture. "Let's go see how the spring is running."

They moved at a slow pace in the heat of the afternoon. The sun was high and hot in a clear, bright sky. They dismounted when they got to the spring that crossed the Hoover and Burton ranches. The water was low enough to expose the shallow network of willow roots on the bank. "Is it my imagination or is it getting dry earlier than usual?" she asked.

"Not your imagination." He paused. "People around here argue about this, but one of the biggest ranches on the other side of Landrum shut down. Suddenly, too. Like, last week. I'm told water figured into their decision. That's the best reason to stay on the smaller side."

"I guess tourism can't support the whole state," she said with a cynical laugh. "Don't ever quote me, but maybe I left at exactly the right time."

"No," Matt asserted as he came a little closer. "No. There's a lot you can do here. Think what you did for the kids at the clinic.

You have a skill you can use anywhere you choose." He fixed his gaze on her. "And I wish you'd choose to stay here."

She took in a breath and forced herself to keep silent. She could see he wasn't done.

"I want you to be here with me." In one motion, he gathered her in an embrace and she stood on tiptoes and circled her arms around his neck. She felt no hesitation in returning the kiss and inhaling his tempting masculine scent.

No way could she pull back from the next kiss or the one after that. But, finally, they broke the kiss and she caught her breath. "You know I like you, Matt."

"Like me? I don't think that was the question." The next words came out fast. "There's a whole lot more going on between you and me." He pointed to his chest. "You stole a big piece of this heart of mine. And I don't want it back."

With her heart racing, she stepped away from him and mumbled, "I know. I don't know…it's hard."

Matt paced and then stopped to catch her gaze. "Can you explain why that is?" he asked, his voice quieter now "All the reasons you could check off on your list are just head things…logic." He scoffed. "And if you ask me, they're weak, too."

"Yeah, right, like logic doesn't count."

His heavy sigh showed his exasperation.

She looked away. She couldn't escape Matt. Not that she wanted to. But she needed to flee from a conversation that made her jittery because she wasn't ready to have it.

His phone buzzed. He scanned the screen and held it up her. "Nick's results."

MATT FOLLOWED HEATHER up the slope to a cottonwood that shaded the phone screen from the bright sun. He tried to follow the summary of findings, but he was tense and unsure what they meant. He handed Heather his phone. "Can you explain these results? I'm not sure what to look for."

He kept his eyes on Heather's face as she read and scrolled. "Good news, overall, Matt." She clutched his arm. "From what I can tell, it's a straightforward case of childhood anemia. Nothing iffy or borderline about the diagnosis. It doesn't spell this out in the lab reports, but based on my experience, it will reverse with treatment." Her exhale was loud with relief. "And I can almost guarantee it won't take that long."

"Your hunch was on target," Matt said. "I feel like someone lifted the weight off my shoulders."

Heather studied the report again. Nodding, she said, "Yep, I'm sure about this. You have every reason to be relieved."

"But it's not easing my mind." He shook his head. "It never should have happened. It's my job to prevent things like this." Memories flickered one after another like frames in an action movie. He and Susannah at the kitchen table before she deployed. They went over lists of things he should know about the two-year-olds. Backup files and paper copies of vaccination records, last checkups, notes about naptimes and bedtime rituals. She'd even jotted reminders about their morning moods—Lucy less cheerful than Nick. *Oh, Suzy...*

"Susannah trusted me with her children. She believed I would keep them safe. They've been super healthy—a couple of colds and an ear infection for Nick." He drew in a breath and on the exhale he said, "That's why I'm upset."

"Aw, Matt, don't do this to yourself. I can see—everyone around you sees—that you love your twins with your whole heart. And you're a wonderful parent." She squeezed his arm. "Trust me on this. These things happen all the time. When you weren't satisfied with what the doctor said, you brought Nick to the clinic for a second opinion."

"You're right. It's just…"

"Look, I can't speak for Dr. Tom, but the treatment isn't difficult and it's safe. Nick will be checked regularly." She smiled. "I can pass on a tip or two to help manage it."

Matt closed his eyes and took a deep breath to apply the brakes to his overreaction. Heather was right. He had no cause for the knots of guilt in his gut. Or maybe it was something else. He was a levelheaded guy, so what was throwing him so wildly off his center?

"Parents want their kids to be well and happy all the time, but things come up no matter what you do." She gave him a look that said, *It's always something*.

Her words were just that. They were probably what she said to every parent…people who were strangers to her. "Don't say stuff like that. You don't know us. We've put a lot of effort into keeping these kids well and happy."

Heather stepped back. "Hey, I wasn't implying otherwise. Do you seriously think I'm not aware of all that you and Stacey do for those children every day?"

Matt compared himself to the spring in front of him. It had been high a few weeks ago, but now it was depleted. That's how he felt, dry and depleted, as if he'd lost something because of numbers on a test. Numbers that showed all wasn't right with Nick's blood. The results were supposed to put him back on an even keel. A puzzle had been solved. But now he felt worse.

Matt tapped his temple. "Up here, I know what you said about raising kids is true. Of course, I'll listen to Dr. Tom. We'll do whatever it takes."

"I don't have any authority here, and I can't guarantee anything," Heather said, again examining the image on her screen. "But I see nothing that indicates a more serious form of anemia."

"I get that in my rational mind. But not where it hurts."

She frowned. "Which is?"

He briefly squeezed his eyes shut. "You want to hear the real reason I'm acting like this?"

She folded her arms across her chest. "I'm waiting."

He looked at her square in the eye. "It's not just about feeling like I let Susannah or the twins down." He saw her react and held up his hand before she could interrupt him with what were likely reassuring words. "My poor ol' *pride* is wounded."

She jerked her head back in surprise. "Your *pride*?"

"I know, I know. It sounds silly."

"No, no, it's not silly. You've had reasons to be confident in lots of ways, but this time the bravado you show to the world took a hit. The adage you live by doesn't always pan out."

Matt frowned. "What adage?"

"The notion that if you do everything right, everything will come out fine—maybe even better than fine."

She had him dead to rights. He'd been like that in school and as a wilderness guide, with his company, with the twins, and now with the ranch. "In a nutshell…"

"Olivia went through that when Jillian was diagnosed. And she's a doctor herself. Even so, she couldn't shake off the feeling there had to be something she should have done to prevent it or at least spot it earlier."

Matt nodded. "Yep. I prided myself on the twins being—" he shrugged "—fine, happy. Full of life."

Suddenly, she snickered. "They are all that—charming, too. I get a big kick out of your lively twins. They never miss a chance to throw themselves into your hugging arms."

Her words were like a pleasant hum in his ears, going a little way to replacing the harsh screech of doubt and worry. "Coming from you, that means a lot."

"Thanks." She pointed down the stream to a flat section of grass that led to a stand of cottonwoods. "Let's walk our friends farther downstream where there's more shade. I need a hit of trail mix and a water break."

"Sounds good." As they led the horses away, he considered what he needed to say. It was too much to think he could recapture what had happened before his phone had interrupted. If he was honest with himself, his pride had been wounded before Nick's results had popped up on his screen. Walking next to her in the silence now, he didn't need to write a whole speech when a few words would clear the air. "I'm sorry I spoke harshly. There was no call for that."

She waved away his words. "Don't worry about it. I've got thick skin. In the pediatrics business, anxious parents tend to do a little lashing out at whoever is nearby. I don't take it personally."

Heather's easy take on what had happened only made him like her more.

He didn't think that was even possible.

CHAPTER FOURTEEN

MATT GLANCED AT Scrambler coming toward him. The dog, as if sensing something wasn't quite right with Matt, plunked himself down, not only at his feet, but with a paw resting on Matt's shoe.

"The financial news isn't that awful." Zoe studied the screen, but Matt knew she was giving him time to adjust to what she'd laid out. "These are cautionary signs, and I'm doing what any good accountant would do— warning you about what I see."

"Flashing red to get my attention." Matt thumped the desk. He and Zoe were sitting side-by-side in his small office in the barn. He'd always known he couldn't manipulate the markets, but he'd confidently moved forward with his vision because of his belief that his updated approach to sheep ranching would pay off. For all his trouble, he'd been dead wrong. And he'd said as much to Zoe.

"No, Matt. I wouldn't put it that way. Your original loan was structured to help you through tougher years, so you've got some time. Buying and leasing the horses was a good short-term move."

"Helped a little," Matt conceded.

Zoe pointed to the screen. "Between the dude ranches and the adventure business, the need for good horses is going to go up. That's a projection, too. A solid one. And you have an eye for that business."

That was true, and it wasn't bragging to say so, although Susannah deserved the credit. "I picked up what I know from my sister. When it came to horses, she was a great teacher." He leaned back in his chair and released a pent-up breath. "My eyes are open about the risk I'm taking and I can find my way through it. But I can't ask someone else to share it with me." He let out another heavy sigh.

Zoe looked at him over her glasses. "Are you talking about Heather? I've heard a little gossip around town."

He offered a quick smile. "I'll tell you another time. As for today, I'm having a hard time accepting that I won't break even on the lambs."

"Still, it's just a slump at this point. You're up to date on the loan." Zoe spoke as if that was all he'd need to quiet his fears. She ran her fingers through her spikey salt-and-pepper hair. He'd seen her do that before when she was searching for new schemes and plans. "What's the worst that can happen? You play that out, and you can sell this venture and move on to something new. Or you and Ruben can expand and diversify Finer Rides. With you actively working as a guide again, you could probably double the adventure side of the business. Look how successful you've been. Plus, you can always buy and sell—or lease—horses to bring in some money."

With that, Zoe closed her laptop and got to her feet. "No need for this gloom. You're in a wildly fluctuating business, but you've got other options. You knew that going in. This ranch would bring in a good price on its own."

"And we have the buildings and the house."

Zoe's scoff was blatantly cynical. "Last month, a friend of mine sold a spread much like yours. They're keeping the buildings but razing the house. They wanted something double or triple the size of an older farmhouse like yours."

Matt never saw himself as a stuck-in-the-past kind of guy, but the image of a wrecking ball having its way with the house where his twins were growing up made his gut churn. "Not a pretty picture."

"Maybe not, but this is a lot of property," Zoe mused. "You could certainly go smaller, fewer acres but plenty of room for horses. You have a good reputation. That's worth a lot, Matt." She paused. "Whatever happens, we don't want surprises. Better to make contingency plans now."

"Right you are," Matt said thoughtfully. "I can support the twins no matter what. That's what counts."

With Scrambler on his heels, Matt walked Zoe to her car. Heather was due in a couple of hours for a ride out to see Kenny and Nancy at the summer place where the fresh grazing land would keep the sheep fed.

Zoe's sobering visit had handed him a lot to think about. He needed time to sort it out and decide on his next move. But he wouldn't drag Heather into his troubles. He wrote a text.

Something came up...need to cancel today.

Not giving himself time to second-guess his decision, he hit Send.

BETHANY'S ANTICS HAD been entertaining Heather since the two could crawl across the floor and babble hellos. Nothing had changed. Bethany was in the middle of her new living room, performing a dramatic and exaggerated tango with a broom to music she made up as she went along.

"Too bad there won't be a band in your front yard at the wedding, or you and Charlie could really show off."

"*Charlie?* Not a chance." Bethany lowered her voice to sound like a tough ol' cowboy. "When I get a mind to tango, darlin', I tango alone."

Heather snorted. "Good one, Bethie." Through mental mind games, she'd managed to get her thoughts off everything except this wedding shower. The guests were due to start arriving any minute. "You've got plenty of room for dancing here if you can persuade Charlie."

"A perfect nest for Charlie and me…and whoever else shows up. Maybe a couple of whoevers, huh?" She scoped out the room, as if seeing it for the first time, and nodded to the two wide windows in the front. "I'll be thrilled with a couple of little people pulling themselves onto the window seats."

"Here's an idea—put in an order for twins and be done with it." Heather grinned. "Matt's two little tricksters are a good combination. Sharp as tacks and up for fun, but well behaved, too." She nodded with conviction. "Nick will be himself again soon."

"Thanks to you," Bethany said, propping the broom up against the wood-and-tile fireplace. "Have you made a decision about the job offer?"

Heather had considered little else. It had come suddenly, thanks to a friend of a friend of Olivia's. When she wasn't thinking about the potential new start, Matt's disappearance from her life competed for her attention. He'd cancelled a ride, but hadn't rescheduled, and then he'd begged off her invitation to the bunkhouse for dinner. When she'd texted to ask if everything was okay, he'd given a one-word answer. Yes. End of story.

Too good to be true. That was how Olivia had described the offer from the outpatient pediatric clinic at the hospital in Red Wing. The position was hers if she wanted it. The woman in the human resources department had understood when she'd used the wedding as an excuse and bought herself time to make a decision.

"Right now, I've got my mind on other things," Heather said. "Like maybe it was a mistake to have this not-a-real-wedding-shower here rather than at your mom's." While not exactly empty, her friend's new home wasn't quite prepared for prime time. A glitch in delivering the few pieces of furniture Charlie owned had left the living room with a couch, a coffee table and one lamp. They'd brought chairs from the bunkhouse, and Jen would supply a few more.

"We don't have much time before the food arrives." On Jen's recommendation, Heather had ordered appetizer combo platters from Adelaide Creek's one and only caterer. "Let's get the chairs we have in a semicircle. Then I can put out the candles and flowers."

The kitchen, dining area and living room flowed together and created a light, airy space. The early evening light slanted through the vertical blinds on the sliding doors from the kitchen to the patio. The previous owners had left behind a long pine table, which Heather could use to serve the food.

The scorching heat of the previous days had broken. And when they opened the bay windows and the patio doors, the fresh, dry breeze set the daisies Heather had put in vases to bobbing in the draft.

Bethany opened her arms to the sides and spun around. "This is exactly what I wanted, Heather. More like a get together for a special bunch of women. Good food, good wine."

"No gifts, no games. You're a cheap date," Heather joked.

"It was Charlie's idea to nix the gifts and suggest donations." Her eyes misted over. "He wanted this quick and quiet, even more than I did. We have so little time..."

When the caterer's van pulled up, Heather went outside to help the owner, Donna Kay, carry in platters of wings and barbecue ribs, shrimp salad and crackers, vegetables and dips, and loaves of bread and spreads they could warm up.

"Wow," Bethany said. "You got all my favorites. Even strawberries and dark chocolate. What more could a girl want?"

"Enjoy…and congratulations," Donna said cheerfully. Then she was gone.

Stacey and Jen arrived together, and then Bethany's work friends, Maria and Iris, followed. Heather recognized Maria from Steak Fry Saturday—she'd come as a daring dance-hall girl. Now fully recovered from her surgery, Cookie came up the walk minus the cane. Heather spent the next several minutes filling wineglasses and setting out plates and napkins.

Refusing offers of help with the setup, Heather listened to the banter, the familiar conversation between Jen and Stacey and the two younger nurses, one married with a new baby. Heather might have been a girl years ago in her own living room listening to Mom chatting with Jen and Cookie and their other friends. Whose wedding or anniversary party was coming up, or whose child was headed off to boot camp or college. Her mother would have been thrilled to see Jen beaming over Bethany and Bethany beaming like a happy bride.

While she tried to catch snippets of the conversation, Heather busied herself putting the bread in the oven and arranging plates. But the vivid presence of her mother was dizzying. She took deep breaths to help her stay in the present and not drift further into the past.

"You said you don't need help," Cookie said, "but I'm wondering how you're doing. Are you still planning to stay through July?"

Heather forced a casual tone when she said, "I'm not sure yet. We'll have to see."

"Jen mentioned you've got feelers out for jobs in Minnesota, so I imagine that will affect how long you stay."

"That's right. It's the reason my plans are open-ended at this point." Talking way too fast, Heather went on about how Bethany had made moving look so easy. And when she'd milked that dry, she described the new wine store in Landrum. Anything to avoid talking about the job offer. Or her mom.

Cookie came closer to Heather and whispered, "Are you okay?"

It would have been so easy to brush her off

with quick reassuring words, but she couldn't coax them out. Instead, she whispered, "I don't know. You and Jen being here with Bethany and me, it's like old home week. Things are catching up to me as the wedding gets closer." Surprised by her admission, she had no need to explain to Cookie that her mother was the missing woman at the party.

Stacey complicated everything, too. Sitting between Maria and Jen, she had said a polite hello and then steered clear of the kitchen, apparently avoiding Heather.

Cookie raised her nose in the air and sniffed. "I'm catching a whiff of that bread. Who can resist?"

"It's a party, Cookie," Heather teased. "You're not supposed to resist."

"Hmm…good point." She gave Heather a lopsided smile. "Stacey told me about you helping Nick at the clinic the other day."

Heather kept her focus on the bread. "Well, I did my job. He got tested and now he's being treated. Matt and Stacey brought him to the clinic because they were concerned."

Before Cookie could comment, Bethany came into the kitchen doing happy dance steps. She leaned on the counter next to Heather. "Okay, pal, when do we eat?"

"Right about now," Heather said, putting her arm around her friend's back.

The other women converged in the kitchen, and Jen stepped in to help arrange the bread in the basket while Heather took the covers off the trays of hot food, releasing aromas of barbecue and garlic and honey mustard dipping sauce.

The nurses led the food line, and Heather filled her plate last, smiling about the laughter and good-natured and familiar teasing about marriage and men. This was her world as sure as it was Bethany's and Jen's. It hadn't judged or turned its back on her. It caught her up short to face the truth of what Bethany had said. She'd rendered the judgment all by herself.

Maybe it had been impossible to stay four years ago, but now it felt impossible to leave.

CHARLIE'S CALL CAME in while Matt was in the stables. He picked it up immediately knowing calls from Charlie were hard to schedule. And, given his funky mood, bring on the interruptions. He went into the office in the barn, determined to sound upbeat.

Matt put his feet up on the corner of his desk and leaned back in his chair. "I know you can't say anything about what's happening wherever you are or even what time it is there, but I can tell you, your beautiful bride has everything under control on this end."

"Good to hear." Charlie's tone was beyond happy. "Every time we talk, she assures me she's doing great, and I tell her not to let her feet get cold while she waits for me to show up."

Matt laughed along with Charlie. "Heather, my partner in your non-fussy ceremony, seems to think this is a wedding made in heaven—and the same goes for the marriage."

"I hear the two of you are talking. Bethany was a little afraid at first because of the Stanhope history."

Matt thought of Heather's warm lips, which he'd never forget. "She's quite a woman, as it turns out, a nurse whose hunch was right about what was wrong with Nick." Matt chuckled. "Besides, with a wedding like yours, Heather and I don't have much to do in these exalted roles."

"Funny you should say that about Nick. I talked to Bethany earlier and she told me Heather has a job offer—a good one, or so she said."

Matt's heart dropped fast, and the positive energy he projected, phony in the first place, circled the drain. "Well, I knew she was looking for a job in Minnesota. I'm not surprised someone would snap her right up." And when it came to kids, her heart was open for business.

"Minnesota, huh?"

"All along she's talked about finding work in Red Wing, a town in Minnesota on the Mississippi River." A heavy stone settled in his gut. "So do you know if she accepted it?"

"No, man, I get news piecemeal," Charlie said. "Bethany mentioned it during our five-minute conversation this morning. You'll get the details before I do."

"Of course, of course. I'm just surprised, that's all. I haven't seen Heather in a couple of days or so."

"I hope I'm not speaking out of turn, but

Bethany said you two were becoming good... uh, friends. Is that the right word?"

Not sure how to answer, Matt settled for admitting, "Uh, close enough."

"I've known you a few years now, Matt, and it's been a while since you mentioned anyone special in your life," Charlie said. "Is there something I should know about my best man and the maid of honor?"

Matt fumbled around for words, staying silent for one beat too long.

It wasn't lost on Charlie. "Hey, man, that's great."

"No, no...don't jump to that conclusion. It sounds good until you dig deeper. Right now, I'm sitting in the office that her grandparents added when they built this barn." And ushered in the decades of debt. "I'm rambling around in what was *her* house. She's fun and whip smart. She rides Susannah's horse like she's owned her all her life." As if it were an afterthought, he slipped in, "And she's beautiful."

"I recall that. We met a couple of times when she was halfway out of town," Charlie said. "Not a good time for her. But that was four years ago. What's the deal now?"

He filled the groom in on a few details Charlie might not have heard. Like Jeff running off. "The worst of it was her seeing the foreclosure as a personal failure."

"That's a heavy burden," Charlie said.

"She likes me. I know she does. If I only lived on the other side of town…"

"But you don't. I wish we could chew on that, but I'm due in a meeting in about two minutes. Keep me posted."

When the call ended, Matt stayed put in the chair and stared at his phone. He could call Heather, probe for details. Or not. Maybe she'd text him. He got to his feet and hurried out of the barn and down the road. His thoughts about Heather's job offer could wait. Meanwhile, his spreadsheets weren't going anywhere.

Given Zoe's warnings, and Heather's job offer, this was probably turning out for the best. The twins were due home from their first morning of day camp. They were all that mattered before he'd met Heather Stanhope. They were still all that mattered now. He knew what he had to do.

CHAPTER FIFTEEN

IN THE WEEKS since she'd arrived at the bunk-house, Heather had made the trip up this driveway a surprising number of times. This would be her first visit inside the house.

The twins and Scrambler met her at the front door and showed her through the dining room to the kitchen. Stacey was sitting in a chair at the kitchen table holding a cold-pack wrapped up in a dish towel against her cheekbone. Her other hand gripped her opposite shoulder. Heather made her way through the kids, Matt and Scrambler to get closer.

"Gram fell," Nick said, "but we don't think she cracked anything."

"Uncle Matt said he's not taking any chances on her bones, so he called you," Lucy added, taking hold of Scrambler's collar. "C'mon, boy, give Heather room."

Matt's eyes showed how amused he was by the twins' talk. "Why don't we let the expert diagnose Gram?" Smiling at Heather, he said, "The dog's pretty excited to see you."

Stacey scoffed. "Wish I could say the same. I liked it better the other night at Bethany's. It's a lot more fun to be with a raucous bunch of friends gorging on ribs and fresh bread and chocolate and…" Stacey's wince interrupted her recap.

"Yep, we had ourselves a good time, didn't we?" If she put aside the way Stacey had dodged her. "It's probably best if you don't talk while I take a look at your cheekbone." She opened her emergency kit and took out her penlight.

Stacey lifted the pack off her cheek and Heather aimed her light on the red, rapidly swelling area to get a clearer look. Stacey instinctively pulled away from even the featherweight pressure of her fingertips on the swollen spot.

"Do you need a bigger flashlight?" Matt asked, leaning in.

"No, this is good. Looks like fairly superficial skin abrasions…scratches, really. A tiny bit of blood is drying. But your cheekbone still took a hard hit. It's swelling fast."

"That's what these cold-packs are for," Stacey said. "I wrapped it in a towel because it was too cold on my skin."

"It's fine for the ride to the ER in Landrum," Heather said. "Your cheekbone could be fractured. And I haven't looked at your shoulder yet." She walked her fingers up the side of Stacey's arm and hit the tender spot along the joint and around to her back. Stacey jolted but then lifted her shoulder and was able to give it a weak roll. A good sign. "How did you fall?"

"Stupidly," she said with a scoff. "I was carrying an armload of towels and forgot I'd left a pile of area rugs on the floor—a concrete floor."

"You probably went down hard. I have a hunch your shoulder is just badly bruised. It broke your fall and then you rolled over," Heather said, illustrating with her own upper body how both Stacey's cheekbone and her shoulder were injured. "But you need to go to the ER to make sure. They'll probably want to X-ray both injuries, especially your cheek."

"Will Gram turn black and blue?" Lucy asked.

"I'm afraid so. Probably by tomorrow." She

reached into her bag and took out the blood pressure cuff. "I'll do a quick check."

"Is that really necessary?" Stacey asked. "I don't have a history of high blood pressure."

Heather smiled. "Necessary? What's the cliché? An abundance of caution? I'll feel better if we get a reading. That's why I carry my bag of tools." Stacey extended her good arm and all eyes stayed on the wrist cuff. No one made a sound, not even Scrambler. When the numbers came up, Heather said, "Completely normal. We can all exhale now."

Heather gently touched the area from Stacey's cheekbone to the side of her eye. "I can feel the swelling extending up closer to your eye. Yep, Stacey, this needs attention." Heather asked Matt to bring her two dish towels. When she had them in hand, she secured a cold pack on Stacey's shoulder.

"Is Gram going to be okay?" Nick asked, taking a few steps closer to Stacey.

Heather was struck by the worry in the boy's and Lucy's eyes. Stacey and Matt were everything to them. "She's going to be just fine," Heather said. "You two don't need to be concerned about your gram." She glanced at Matt. "You should leave for the ER. I can stay here with these two…cubs." She turned to the twins. "Is it okay if I call you that?"

"Better than tykes," Nick said. "We're done with tykes."

Heather waved her finger side to side at the two. "Okay, then. I won't make that mistake."

Nick took her seriously, but Lucy giggled, as she usually did when Heather exaggerated her words and widened her eyes.

"They shouldn't be any trouble. It's just about bedtime," Matt said.

"And they're already in their pajamas, I see." Heather smiled at the twins, who hadn't budged from Stacey's side.

"I hate to impose on you, but Grey is away on business. Are you sure you don't mind staying?" Stacey asked.

"Not a bit," Heather said. "Maybe I can talk your grandkids into telling me a story or two."

"Uncle Matt and Gram usually read us a story," Lucy said, "or two. Sometimes *three*."

Behind Heather, Matt guffawed.

"I see. Well, lucky for us, I know how to read, too. We're all set." Heather lifted her hands in the air. "And I have nowhere else I need to be." She sent a pointed look to Matt and Stacey. "You need to go."

Stacey got to her feet. "With any luck, I'm just banged up."

Heather squeezed Stacey's hand. "Don't worry about a thing here."

"You do everything Heather tells you," Matt said.

"Oh, I think I can handle these two. I'm sure they'll show me around their world." One likely had her old room across the hall from the built-in linen cupboard. The room with a wide window seat that had doubled as a toy box. At least, until she was a teenager. Then it had become the catchall to hide random stuff when her exasperated mom demanded she clean up her room. Or else.

Along with the dog, she and the twins followed Matt and Stacey out the front door to the porch. Matt stopped and rubbed his chin, opened his mouth as if to speak and then changed his mind.

Going on a flash of intuition, Heather blurted, "It's a little odd being inside the house, but not difficult. No problem." She gave his upper arm a little push. "Go, go. I've got this."

"Of course you do," he said as he hurried down the stairs.

She stood with the kids and the dog and watched the taillights disappear down the long drive.

She hadn't lied to Matt. At one time, she'd have told Bethany and Jen it was unthinkable to be inside the house with memories of sounds and smells sharp with emotion. But it was a host of everyday images that flashed through her mind when she went back inside. She took a seat at the table while she and the kids she'd grown so fond of ate Stacey's homemade butter cookies.

Taking in her surroundings, she noted the old set of cabinets still lining the walls. Painted white and trimmed in dusty blue now, they stood out against the pale yellow walls. The appliances were new. No surprise there. Like so many things in the house, the old fridge and stove had been beyond one more repair.

Nick was busy licking the back of his cookie while Lucy was breaking off tiny pieces and letting them drop to the floor for Scrambler.

"I don't think I've ever seen kids take more time eating a cookie than you two."

"That's 'cuz when we finish we'll have to go to bed," Nick said, innocent as could be.

"No kidding!" Heather exclaimed. "But I know you'll settle right down. You don't want to get me into trouble with your gram or your uncle."

"You won't get into trouble," Lucy said. "They like you. Especially Uncle Matt."

Impossible to think a six-year-old could make her blush, but her warm face told a different story. When had she become a blusher?

"We *have* to brush our teeth before we read the story," Lucy said.

Amused by Lucy's note of authority, she readily agreed to follow the rule. "And when your teeth are so clean they squeak, we'll read. Now, for the most important question. What kind of stories do you like?"

"The ones with talking animals," Nick said without needing to consider his answer.

"Yep, and kids who have adventures." Lucy finally took a big bite of her cookie. "But the animals are the best."

"I understand," Heather said. "If you're

raised on a sheep ranch, you'll always have plenty of adventures."

Heather made a show of wiping her palms. "Finish those cookies, my friends. Let's get the story show underway." She looked forward to reading to them. On their sleepovers as kids, she and Bethany had taken turns reading to each other. Bethany liked mysteries and she liked historical novels, preferably involving mountains or prairies. Come to think of it, she and Bethany hadn't changed their reading preferences much at all.

The kids made quick work of the toothbrushing ritual, and both of them piled into Lucy's bed and moved around to make room for Heather. Scrambler took what Heather guessed was his customary place at the foot of the bed.

"Do you know you two are sharing the same room that used to be my bedroom?" she asked. "My mom and dad read to me in this room just like Gram and Uncle Matt read to you."

"Really?" Lucy handed her a book from the top of the pile on the nightstand between the beds. "That must have been a long, long time ago."

"It was." She pointed to the built-in bins under the window. "When I was about your age, I kept my favorite things in those bins, like I bet you do. I still remember a lot about growing up here on the ranch. You will, too. I know for a fact you'll *always* have good memories of being with the two people who love you most in the world." She tapped her temple. "You'll keep the memories up here in your brain."

"And we'll remember you reading to us," Nick said softly.

Without warning, her eyes filled with tears. She forced them back but at the cost of a hoarse voice forcing the words, "Well then, let's get to it." Heather cleared her throat and opened the book to a world of forest animals welcoming spring. In the next one, a couple of cows planned a birthday party for the lone mule on the farm.

Nick's head was heavy on Heather's arm and Lucy was yawning and settling in. "Nick likes to hold his bear up close to his chest," Lucy said, "but I like to have Molly next to me." Molly turned out to be an oversize cloth doll in a blue princess dress and a headful of yellow yarn hair.

"Did Uncle Matt call you because you're a nurse?" Lucy asked.

"Hmm…yes, but also because I'm a friend and a neighbor." Heather eased Nick into her arms, carried him the couple of feet to his bed, and settled him beneath the covers with the bear. She kissed his forehead.

She gave Lucy a quick kiss, too. "And he wanted someone you already know to come over and be with you."

"And Uncle Matt really, really likes you," Lucy said, her eyelids dropping.

"I like you, too," Nick said, his voice slow and sleepy.

"I didn't mean to wake you up," Heather whispered, turning to Nick and pulling the blanket up over his shoulders.

"Are you going to be our new mom?" he asked.

That beautiful thought came out of the blue. She tried to say no and let the moment pass, but something held her back. Much like she'd been holding herself back from accepting the job in Red Wing.

Nick's eyes closed again, and she was saved from answering his question. With

Scrambler jumping off the bed and following, Heather tiptoed out of the room.

She glanced at the closed door to the room that had once been Jeff's. Sooner or later, Nick would probably move into it and leave Lucy in the room with the bigger closet. Heather used to envy the windows in Jeff's room that offered a clear view of the corral. His closet made up for its smaller size by having more cubbyholes good for hiding things. Other doors opened to the two additional bedrooms, and behind a third, she'd find the stairway to the attic.

When she started downstairs, without the kids talking to her, she heard the familiar creak when her foot landed on the fifth stair from the bottom. According to her family lore, that same spot had "talked" ever since the new stairway was constructed around 1920.

Downstairs with Scrambler, the only noise came from the rustling of leaves on the trees in front of the house. A coyote's high-pitched cry broke through the night. The door to what had been the old TV room was open to reveal a bed and a desk with a laptop and a stack of books. The floral curtains led Heather to guess it was likely Stacey's room.

She walked under the scrolled arch into the dining room and stood in the space where her mother had painted at the tall bay windows, open now to let in the dry air. Mom's easels and paints had become the focal point of the room, with the elegant and elaborately carved built-in hutch at the opposite end. Her mom had favored painting in the dining room, so she could hear Heather and Jeff coming in after school or from the stables and chatting while they fixed snacks in the kitchen.

Everywhere Heather looked, the painstaking effort Matt and his mom had done to restore the woodwork was on display. That job had needed to be done years before her parents died. The hutch now gleamed like the polished gem it was meant to be. In the end, Heather and Jeff had possessed neither the time nor the money for anything other than DIY repairs.

Heather wandered into the living room to see that the three generations now sharing the house had turned it into a homey space. She could imagine Matt and Stacey sinking into the couch cushions while the twins played on the floor or sat in their child-sized chairs. Action figures kept company with library books and games on a coffee table. A good-size TV was mounted on the wall next to the fireplace, and a train set with bridges, crossings and a depot dominated the middle of the room. A dog bed was ready for Scrambler, who stayed by her side as she moved through the house.

Tingling in her arms and hands was undeniable evidence of her longings. She'd stepped into these lives for real, not just riding a horse over the ridge or eating steaks in the front yard. Or sharing carrots with the horses and kisses with Matt at the corral. She'd slipped into the images of their lives so easily. She rushed out of the room to stop her racing mind. No one had invited her to make herself at home.

She went back to the kitchen, passing the hutch on her way. The shelf caught her eye and she abruptly stopped in front of it. The manila envelope that sat on the edge had unfamiliar black lettering that said "Belongs to Heather."

She picked it up, at first puzzled. What could possibly be inside that was meant for her? The envelope was old and a little wrinkled and worn, but serviceable. It wasn't bulky, but pressing it between her fingers, it had more than one item inside. It wouldn't be snooping to open it. Or would it? She could ask about it when Matt and Stacey came back, but that might mean opening the envelope in front of them. It made her uneasy to think about other eyes on her as she discovered whatever this was.

Taking the envelope into the kitchen, she stood at the counter. Should she or shouldn't she? Finally, she opened the flap and peeked inside.

MATT FOLLOWED HIS mom through the side door into the kitchen. Heather raised her head, but her smile was more embarrassed than friendly. "I saw…this on the hutch. Where did these things come from?"

"The closet in one of the empty bedrooms," Stacey explained. "It was stuck between a bin and the wall. I went into the room to see what we'll need to do to move one of the twins into it, probably before school starts. We rarely go into the empty rooms, so I never noticed it before." She pointed to the counter. "I didn't know if these were important or not. Doesn't matter. They're yours."

"A couple of photos I thought were lost. Some memorabilia, I guess you'd call it." She held up the ticket stub. "Priceless objects like this memento from a first date, and dried flowers from my senior prom."

When her smile broadened, Matt took a relieved breath, but was still aware of the tension tightening the muscles all through his body. He reached down to pat the dog's head when Scrambler left Heather and came to sniff Matt's shoes for new smells.

She held up a white ribbon. "I once took third place in a herding contest. Not bad for a twelve-year-old." She shifted her gaze from Matt to his mom. "I'm glad to have these old photos of Mom and Dad and Jeff. But none of that is important now. What about you, Stacey?" She nodded to the stretchy wrap on Stacey's shoulder. "What's the verdict?"

"You were right. I'm battered and bruised, but not broken." She lightly patted her shoulder. "They gave me this contraption to keep me from moving my arm around, but they warned me I'll hurt for a few days."

"I imagine so." She frowned. "You'll have

to warn the twins. They can't throw themselves at you to get their hugs."

Stacey winced. "Oooh, that hurts just thinking it." She pointed to the envelope. "I meant to bring that to the shower the other night, but I forgot."

"As for the value, if the items mean something to you, then every item in it is worth a lot," Matt said, attempting to sound casual. He couldn't put aside the distressed look on Heather's face when they'd first come in. He wished she'd pass the photos across the counter so he could see them, but she kept them close to her in a little pile. His curiosity was selfish. None of it mattered now. In a few days, she'd likely be gone. He couldn't complain, not when he'd been inviting to her leave.

"I suppose that's true," she acknowledged in a thoughtful tone. "I haven't heard a peep out of the kids. Scrambler's been keeping me company." Heather waved her hand to encompass the kitchen. "You've done incredible things to the house. It looks beautiful. Because of you two, it has a new lease on life."

"Thanks—we love the house," Stacey said.

Heather held up her hands defensively, although neither he nor his mom challenged her. "I'm aware of how badly the house had deteriorated. When I drove down the driveway for the last time, I was embarrassed by how shabby it had become."

He hardly knew how to answer that. He had been able to afford the place with all the land only because the house and outbuildings were in bad shape and needed a lot of TLC to make them sound again. He doubted she wanted to hear that, and he didn't want to talk about it, either. Knowing he might have to put the ranch on the market down the road made some of his efforts seem pointless anyway. What good would restored woodwork do for a house someone else would demolish? Zoe hadn't been that explicit, but he could read between the lines.

"We understood the circumstances," Stacey said.

"On the subject of incredible things, your twins have found a spot in my heart." She made a little twisting motion with her hand over her chest.

Matt couldn't help but admire the skillful way she pivoted the conversation back to the twins, a safe topic of conversation.

"So those are family photos?" Stacey's curiosity wasn't subtle.

"Uh, yes. I'm not sure how they got separated from the others." She slid one across the counter. "This was always one of my favorites of Jeff."

Matt and Stacey studied the picture of the two teens. Clearly the older of the two, Jeff stood tall and broad-shouldered in his cap and gown and was grinning at his sister. Heather leaned into Jeff's chest. She was maybe fourteen and looking slightly self-conscious as teenagers usually do around that age. Her hair was shorter then, but the makings of the beautiful woman she'd become was present in her happy expression.

"Nice," he said softly, suddenly sad for himself over Susannah, but sad for Heather, too. Her brother was walking around alive and presumably well, but she hadn't seen him in over four years.

Heather stood straighter. "So, Stacey, you'll keep the ice up and take anti-inflammatories for a few days. And that's it?"

"Yes, then I'll be good as new." Mom made a pretense of looking at the clock on the stove. "I have a phone call to return," she said, "so I'll be in my room if you need me. Thanks, again, Heather."

"Absolutely," Heather said. "I'm glad I was able to come."

The sincerity in her voice was real. He was sure of it. When his mom disappeared around the corner, he said, "She's probably calling Grey back. They're friends. He's over in Cheyenne on business."

She flashed an amused smile. "Friends, huh?"

Now he regretted taking their conversation in that direction. He needed an off-ramp and found one in the white ribbon. "So you're a champion sheepherder. You didn't mention that, but I'm not surprised."

"It was at the county fair. Jeff talked me into entering. Our dog, Brody, was a real show-off, which is likely why I placed at all. Of course, Dad's horse, Blizzard, did his part. Velvet was still a filly."

"I would've enjoyed seeing that," Matt said, envisioning the awkward teen in the photo challenging herself and having fun in the process. A few years later, she was taking care of her mom in this rambling house all the while knowing her ranching days were over.

Heather held up a sheet of notebook paper. "I understand why I saved the ribbon, but why would I save a list of what I needed to do to complete my college application. I took charge of the applications for Bethany and me."

She got a faraway look in her eyes for a few seconds before she continued. "Bethany and I were the first in our families to be warned about finishing college with a career in mind. Turned out we both like nursing." She lowered her gaze and used her index finger to move around the items on the counter. "What I learned in nursing school came in handy later when I was the caregiver for my mom."

"I suppose these mementos bring all that back."

She pulled up to her full height, all five-feet-and-change of it. "I've spent too much time longing for the past, or some version of it. You've seen it for yourself." She pushed the items together and then, one by one, dropped them back into the envelope. "But I've surprised myself." She scanned the room. "The house sparkles…it's filled with energy and love. That's how it should be."

Wow. He had to take the next step before he chickened out. He didn't like lying, period. Misleading Heather took that to a whole new level. But all evening he'd been telling himself it was for the best.

"I should probably explain why I cancelled our ride and haven't been in touch the last few days." He took a deep breath, as prepared as he'd ever be to make up a story. "I… I realized that I've been neglecting things with the ranch. And with Finer Rides," he rushed to add. "One of our wranglers left suddenly. I may have to put Kenny in charge here and help out. And I have to consider the twins. You know, keeping them secure. Seems I've been not thinking ahead as much as I should." When he ran out of air, he stopped trying to string together a bunch of words that might be true but weren't his real reasons for avoiding her.

She stared at him with a frown deepening by the second. "I see." She picked up the envelope. "Well then, I guess I'll see you at the wedding. Lucky for us, there's not much to do."

"Charlie tells me you have a job offer. Is that true?" Matt blurted.

"Yes, it is." She clutched the envelope to her chest and stepped back from the counter.

"Are you leaving?" he asked as fast as he could. "Uh, can't you stay a minute and tell me about the offer?"

She looked at him as if she'd never seen him before. "No, no, I need to go."

"But…" But what? What did he expect now?

Like a streak of lightning, she came out from behind the counter and rushed past him to the door.

He'd mangled this horribly. None of it made sense. He managed to say, "I… I'll talk to you soon, then."

She had her hand on the doorknob, her upper body twisted to face him. She stared at him for a second or two. The next thing he knew, she was headed straight for him. She reached up and cradled his cheeks in her palms and drew his face down toward her. She kissed him once, and when she broke the kiss, his mouth found hers again. She splayed her palm over his chest and backed away. "I never meant for this to happen. But it did. I gave you a piece of my heart, too."

Then she was gone.

Matt went out to the porch. He called her name. He started for her, but what would he say?

Without looking back, she got into her SUV and drove away.

NOTHING WAS OPEN on Merchant Street, and only a couple of streetlights dimly illuminated the entry arch to the Adelaide Creek cemetery.

Heather left her car in the adjacent town hall lot and wandered along the curving stone path until she came to her parents' graves. They were next to her dad's folks and two of their children. Adelaide and William, along with their sons and their wives, were buried at the top of the hill. Like all the other Stanhopes, her parents' stones were simple, with only their names and dates of birth and death. Nothing ostentatious allowed in the Stanhope section.

She weaved through the rows, not so many graves given the generations of her family. For all Heather's identification with the family, it was clear more of her ancestors had left than stayed. Heather patted Adelaide's grave and smiled as if the woman could see her.

"I've learned a lot from all of you," Heather said out loud. She sat on the bench across from the Stanhope section and called Bethany.

"You're still up, I hope," Heather said. With the wedding days away, Bethany had started her time off.

"I am. Are you still at Matt's?" Bethany asked.

"No. I left." She gave Bethany a few details about Stacey and the envelope of odds and ends, and left it at that. "One of my favorite photos of Jeff and me was lost, but now it's found."

"Then where are you?"

"At the cemetery," Heather said. "It's dark and quiet. Very peaceful."

"Are you saying goodbye?" Bethany asked.

"No, more like saying hello." Heather filled her lungs. "When was the last time it rained? The air is so dry."

"You're being awfully mysterious," Bethany said. "Do you want company? I can be there in ten minutes. I'm not sleepy."

Heather considered the offer. "Yes, come on over to the cemetery, my friend. I've made some decisions."

Ten minutes later, Heather walked down the slope and met Bethany as she reached into her car and pulled out two bottles of water. She tossed one to Heather. "Speaking of dry."

"Let's wander a little," Heather said. "I'll fill you in."

Bethany fell into step with her as they started across the grass. "I hope that includes telling me how it felt being alone inside your old house."

Not fully understanding her own strange reaction, Heather struggled to find the right words. "It felt familiar, but not in a bad way. It's so *theirs*. Action figures and model train set and all. They've brought it back to what it should be. Lucy will grow up in my old room, and Nick will soon be in Jeff's." She took a couple of big gulps of water. "I liked seeing all that. The Burtons are exactly what that stale, run-down house needed."

Bethany chuckled. "I won't speak for Stacey, but at least three of the current occupants have come down with a bad case of affection for you."

Heather laughed. "It's no secret I adore the twins." She hesitated before stumbling over her words. "Nick asked me if I was going to be his new mom."

"Woo-hoo… I knew it," Bethany said.

Heather groaned. "He's six, Bethany. I never should have said anything. And what exactly do you think you know?"

"Before you got here, I was positive that Mathis Burton would take one look and want to know everything about you." Even in the dim starlight, Bethany radiated happiness. "He sees what the rest of us see. An intriguing, talented, really pretty and loving woman."

"Apparently not intriguing enough. He's gone cold and distant on me. What can I say?" She repeated his long list of concerns that justified backing away from her. "Business, the twins, a lot of blah, blah, blah."

"Pfft…no way. There has to be another explanation."

"I don't know," Heather said. "There was a lot of spark between the two of us. It was strong, too. New and sweet, but easy, like how we danced. From the start, it felt as if we'd been moving in each other's arms for a long time."

"Wow. That's what was obvious to everyone who saw the two of you together. Like I said, Mom and Dad are big Matt and Heather fans."

"Something happened that changed his mind. He asked about the job offer, but I didn't answer."

"So you're taking it, but you didn't tell him?" Bethany asked.

Heather let out a quick laugh. "No, I'm *not* taking it *and* I didn't tell him."

Bethany tugged on her arm. "What does that mean?"

"Matt ended whatever we had so fast, I could barely take the words in." Heather paused and gulped back almost half the bottle of water. "But I'd already figured some things out."

"You need to elaborate, because this sounds like a puzzle to me." Bethany poured a little water into her palm and splashed it on her face.

Heather stopped in front of her parents' graves again. "I have this feeling about home—and coexisting with the ranch as it is now, not as it was when my dad was a child. Even then its best days were over."

In a low voice, Bethany asked, "And what

about you and Matt and him ending things? Are you okay with it?"

She shook her head. "I was stunned in the worst way. For now though, I'm pushing away the sadness. I don't want to feel that hurt right now. But at some point I'm going to have to talk to him." She put her hand on Bethany's shoulder. "After the wedding. Nothing is going to interfere with your day."

"Thanks, sweetie, but I'm not buying this sudden turnaround. I'm with my dad on this. Matt's in love with you."

"We seemed to have exchanged pieces of our hearts, for all the good that's done," Heather said in as casual a tone as she could manage. "But nothing will drive me away from the place where I know I belong. I let a false belief that I failed my family drive me away for four years. Never again."

"Oh, Heather, good for you." Bethany wiped away brimming tears. "Here I am crying, and you're standing there stoic and strong."

"Maybe because it's really sinking in that I'm home for good."

"It's pretty gutsy to do that without a job in your pocket."

"As a matter of fact, I followed a hunch and called Tom Azar, the pediatrician I worked with at the wellness clinic. I told him I'd be interested if he ever had a job available for me. We're going to meet after the holiday to talk more about it. He can't take me on full-time, but he suggested one day a week in one of two satellite offices." Heather stretched her arms over her head as if releasing excess energy. "It's a start, and I'm in no rush."

She nudged Bethany. "Let's go home. You're getting married. You need your sleep." When she turned away from her parents' headstones, she said a silent goodbye. For now.

CHAPTER SIXTEEN

His MOM FOUND him in the stables, brushing Bo. "I've been looking for you, Matt. Have you heard from Charlie?"

"Bethany said they're still waiting for the final itinerary, but he was rebooked and is likely in the air now. No one knows for sure, but half the buffer day is already history. If he's lucky, he'll make the rehearsal dinner tomorrow night."

"Not the best news," Mom said. "Bethany must be frantic. Good thing she's got Heather with her. Nothing like a best buddy to keep you calm."

Matt kept his eyes on Bo but gave up trying to paste on a smile to cover up one of the two reasons he'd been brought down to this gloomy state. "Speaking of Heather, it turns out you were right."

"About what?"

Matt gave Bo another look and then patted his flank and the horse wandered into the corral to hang out with Pebbles. "You warned me about getting involved with her."

His mom's eyebrow arched. "And I've come to the opposite conclusion. I'm sure I was wrong and have been feeling bad about what I said to her at the clinic."

"Really?" Matt led the way outside to the picnic table, where they could keep an eye on the twins. "What brought on your change of heart?"

Stacey tucked wisps of hair behind her ears and looked over his shoulder at the twins riding their bikes around the yard. "There's so much more to her than I let myself see. All the things that drew you to her right away."

Matt grunted in frustration. "I don't mind saying it out loud. I've fallen in love with her. But like I said, you've been right all along. You about Heather, Zoe about the business. She never misses a chance to warn me about how risky this venture is. In the next breath, she's reassuring me that we're doing okay." He fixed his stance. "I've acted like I could make a go of the ranch because I said so. Zoe's been showing me red flags all along."

"Matt, c'mon, you're being too hard on yourself."

"Really? We've shaved it close—too close—for two years. Now we're facing an actual loss. Breaking even is hard enough." He'd had a couple of years like that in the adventure business, but it was harder with the ranch. "Finer Rides is having a better year than this place."

"I know you, so I'm positive you're not giving up...certainly not yet," Mom said. "You'll likely make it up—if not next year, the year after that."

"Maybe, maybe not." Heather was right about him leading with his facade of bravado. He could be so high and mighty sometimes, but he'd learned from this. "I acted like the Stanhopes failed from some personal flaw, like they were at fault. Lack of foresight, I called it. Turns out that was sort of true—two generations ago."

"Matt, that's the past. It's not the same world now."

"Maybe so, but no matter what, Mom, I will take care of the twins," Matt said. "If things don't turn around, then I'll take the hit and sell. I can work with Ruben or expand the horse business or find a job. The four of us will be okay."

"Then what's eating at you?"

He'd gone this far in spilling his troubles to his mom. He might as well fill in the blanks. "It's like you said in the first place. I played it out in my head, where I wanted things to go with Heather. But then, I had to stop that train. What if Heather and I got married…" He rubbed his forehead but couldn't get rid of his deep frown. "And she lost her home a *second* time. Not just any home." He pointed to the house. "This one."

Even though his mother's expression hadn't changed when he'd mentioned marriage, he added, "It's early to be talking marriage, I get it. But we were building something, the two of us. This wasn't a one-sided relationship." He shook his head to clear it. "So I ended it."

"*Ended* it?" Stacey scoffed. "Now? What did she say? You're the witnesses at the wedding in *two days*!"

"Zoe really spooked me. And Heather has a job offer in Minnesota. I asked her if she'd accepted it, and she didn't say one way or the other. I made assumptions and mistakes all over the place, but eventually, I poured cold water all over the possibility of the two of us being together. So she'll probably accept the offer and leave. It will be for the best."

Mom crossed her arms over her chest. "So your master plan is to avoid her, say hello at the wedding and hope she gets in her SUV and points it east?"

"That's stark."

"Yep. As intended." His mother reached over and said, "It was her gentle and fun manner with the twins that softened me. She embraced them from the start."

Matt nodded. The twins liked her, too. They talked about her and would miss her. Not as much as he would. "I know I sound like I'm made of ice or something, but I realized I couldn't allow my fear of causing another loss for Heather to hang over my head."

"I'm not going to change your mind—it's stubborn as always. But walking away from Heather is inflicting a loss and causing her pain anyway, assuming she feels the same way you do."

He tightened muscles in his neck and jaw. "Better now than later."

Stacey huffed as if helpless to say anything more. "Be sure you don't go making decisions based on anything other than the twins. Certainly not me," she insisted. "I'll be fine. In fact, in a year or two, I'll probably look for a teaching job."

First he'd heard mention of it, but it made sense. "It was a sacrifice to give up your job, so I understand you'd want to teach again."

"I have prospects, Matt, on other fronts, too. I'm not too old to change careers if no teaching job materializes. I also enjoy Grey's company…a lot."

Matt snickered. "Man, have I been blind or what? I mean I could see you liked him, but—"

"Don't add that to the list of failures you're compiling, Matt," his mom said, her tone serious. "This arrangement with us living together was always meant to be temporary. I never implied I was retiring. Not from teaching or from second chances. Four years ago, joining forces with you helped me cope with losing Susannah."

She got up, came behind him and wrapped her arms around him in a tight hug. "We're a good team, Matt, but this isn't all there is for you. And the same is true for me."

He could see that. But for the moment, the

twins and the business of making a living would have to define him.

Unless… He had one idea, a little far-fetched but worth a try. When his mom was out of sight, he picked up his phone and texted Zoe.

HEATHER HAD DONE all she could to prepare for this excruciating conversation, but it still left her sad and fighting back tears. To stay where she belonged, she had to hurt one of her favorite people.

Jillian brushed tears off her cheeks, but instead of lowering her head and hiding her eyes, she lifted her chin. Olivia, her arm around her daughter's shoulders, was speaking softly to her.

Sitting on the bunkhouse porch on the hottest day of the summer so far, Heather was facing Jillian, who'd been the wild card in all her decisions. Jillian was the one person unlikely to understand. She couldn't be expected to.

"But you said you'd be back. You broke your promise."

That wasn't literally true, but it was pointless to argue if a change in plans constituted a broken promise. To be fair to Jillian, from the start, Heather had described the trip to Adelaide Creek as limited to the wedding and a visit with old friends.

"I didn't expect this little place I was born in to feel like home again. But you've seen the Mississippi River your whole life and it's a part of you. What the river is for you, these mountains are for me." To reinforce the point, she added, "But I forgot that when I was off exploring those other places."

Jillian pursed her lips and crossed her arms. "Maybe so, but I might want to go away and see new things. There *are* rivers in other places, ya know."

Heather had expected some resentment and a little sarcasm. Good thing she and Olivia had already come up with a plan before this call. Olivia hadn't bought into Heather's reversal easily and struggled to understand the wisdom of turning down a job, a sure thing, when Heather didn't have solid prospects for full-time work. Ultimately, though, maybe Heather's willingness to go ahead anyway convinced Olivia of the depth of Heather's need to be in her true home.

"But what about being back in town?" Olivia had asked. "You said you were doubtful about how it would feel."

"It's not nearly as weird as I thought," Heather had explained. "I'd deluded myself. I built that up in my mind. There I was, riding into Adelaide Creek with a big F for Failure tattooed on my forehead. But I was so wrong. No one saw me that way. It was one hundred percent *my* problem."

Squeezing Jillian's shoulders, Olivia tried to put a positive spin on what had happened. "We've had a lot of practice with FaceTime. It's a wonderful thing."

Jillian sniffled. "I like FaceTime, but it's not the same."

"Right you are, Jillian." Heather cocked her head. "But it beats not being able to communicate at all." She sensed Jillian had turned a corner. She was more open and able to listen. "Your mom and I had an idea, and we want to see if you like it."

"What kind of an idea?"

Heather almost laughed out loud at the cute redhead's suspicious tone. "We were thinking that instead of camping up on Lake Superior later this summer, you and your mom could come here and stay in the bunkhouse with me. I've got plenty of room and lots of things to do."

"Really?" Jillian looked at Olivia. "Can we?"

"Like Heather said, it's up to you." She shrugged nonchalantly. "We could always camp another time."

"Could I see your old house and the twin kids, Lucy and Nick?" Jillian's face brightened. "And the horses and the Icelanders, too?"

No matter what happened with Matt, no way would he deny Jillian a chance to see the ranch. "Absolutely."

Jillian's smile boosted Heather's spirits. Matt or no Matt, she had a life and people dear to her. She leaned closer. "You'll love Bethany and her parents. Jen will let you help bring water to the Shetlands and Icelanders. Maybe you can help out at Farmer's Market, too."

"Okay, I like that idea. Let's go to Adelaide Creek."

"Are you sure?" Olivia said, cutting a quick glance at Heather.

"Positive." Jillian rolled two thumbs-up and laughed.

Seeing Jillian with her energy and sparkle back made Heather smile. "Meanwhile, I'll send you tons of pictures from the wedding."

"Don't forget the cake," Jillian warned.

"I won't. I'll want pictures of it to keep forever."

As they started saying their goodbyes, Jillian asked, "Even though I don't need a nurse anymore, we'll still be friends forever, won't we?"

"Forever," Heather said.

CHAPTER SEVENTEEN

CHARLIE WAS A NO-SHOW. It wasn't his fault, but this was the first and only glitch that had ruffled Bethany, at least so far. Jen had tasked Heather with helping keep Bethany calm, which wasn't grueling duty. Heather knew the difference between ruffled and frantic.

"We knew we were cutting it close," Bethany complained with a smirk. "That's the best reason I had for keeping this wedding small and simple. Turns out we needed more than one buffer day to make sure the groom got here."

"That was the one arrangement you couldn't control," Heather said. They stood alone at a spot outside the private dining room of the newish Tall Tale Lodge in between Adelaide Creek and Landrum. Its lobby was a classic great room with high ceilings, a huge fireplace and a tiered wrought-iron chandelier. "At least we have an elegant place to wait," Heather offered. "This lodge is really something."

"With live music every weekend and an indoor pool and spa out back." Bethany exaggerated a sigh of relief. "And an accommodating management staff. Charlie's parents warned the sales team this could happen before they booked it."

Ed and Cheri Goodman, Charlie's parents, had planned this small dinner. Since the wedding was taking place in the Hoovers' front garden, there wasn't much to rehearse, so tonight's gathering was really meant to be a family dinner with a couple of extra guests.

Charlie's original flight had been cancelled and he'd been rerouted. The first connecting flight had been delayed. Now they were waiting to see if Charlie would get a seat on a flight that would get him closer to home, but it would still mean he was a two-hour drive away.

Besides sticking close to Bethany, Heather's other immediate job was to avoid Matt. He'd approached her once since he'd arrived at the lodge and wanted to go off somewhere to talk. Insistent as he was, Heather cut him off with a curt, "It can wait. Tonight is about Bethany. She needs me."

In what Heather took to be a contrite tone, Matt said, "Of course. Sorry. You're right. It will keep."

Right now, Heather could see inside the room, where Dan, Grey, Matt and Ed sat at one end of the room with their eyes on their phones. That section of the room had been set up cocktail-lounge style, with couches and easy chairs. A table was set up for dinner at the other end. Lucy and Nick were at home enjoying the novelty of having a cool teenage babysitter. From what Heather could tell, Cheri, Jen and Stacey were sitting around the table killing time commenting on the lodge's menu of spa services.

"This is such bad luck," Bethany complained. "The longer it's taking, the more I want Charlie here."

"We need to stay strong. And to do that we should go ahead and have a fabulous dinner," Heather said. "Let's go talk to Cheri and the others and see what they think."

Everything happened quickly after Bethany approached Charlie's mom. She barely got the words out before Matt and Ed rushed toward them phones in hand.

"We just got word that Charlie is boarding the plane that will get him about two hours away," Matt said. "If we leave now, we can get there by the time he lands."

Bethany's eyebrows lifted as far as they could go.

"It's good news, Bethany," Ed said, clearly trying to reassure her. "The round trip will take us four hours tops."

The two were already out the door when Ed called out, "Don't wait dinner."

No one argued.

"Not how we planned it, but at least we know he's getting closer to home." Bethany smiled at Cheri and Jen. "Let's make the best of it."

Jen jabbed her thumb at Bethany. "That's my girl, Cheri. I have a feeling your son and my daughter will never have a dull moment, but they'll make the best of whatever comes their way."

Cheri laughed and linked her arm with Jen's. "Let's go talk to the food manager."

Heather watched the two women take off, knowing she wouldn't be able to avoid Stacey forever. For now, Grey was keeping her occupied. Once more, Heather could dodge small talk with a woman who was probably happy with Matt's decision. So be it. Heather had no intention of showing her disappointment over Matt.

With hours to kill before the guys could possibly show up with Charlie in tow, they took their time with their lake trout platters, one of the lodge's specialties. They sipped white wine and lingered over key lime pie and coffee. Jen and Dan toasted everyone at the table and Cheri thanked them all for coming.

Afterward, Heather staked out a place on the couch. The bride plopped down beside her. "Penny for your thoughts," Bethany teased.

"I was thinking that when Olivia and Jillian come for their visit, we should come here for lunch and a swim in the pool. And I'll be inviting my pals Bethany and Jen. We could even do a whole spa day."

Suddenly, Bethany cupped her ear. "The music has started in the bar." When Dan approached, she quickly got to her feet. "Okay, this party is on the move. We've got some dancing to do. While I've been working my little fingers to the bone on night shifts, the rest of you have been dancing." She grabbed her dad's hand and started for the door. There was no mistaking her arm gesture for a demand for everyone to follow.

The pairs headed to the floor and Heather stayed with Cheri and chatted about Charlie. Seeing Bethany and her dad crossing the floor triggered a wave of nostalgia for her own dad. She hadn't endured many shaky moments so far, but memories of her father forced her to look away or risk bursting into tears. Then seeing Dan and Jen dance reminded Heather of her mom and dad on warm summer nights just like this one.

When the music changed, she blended into the large and lively Friday-night crowd in the lounge. She could do the Cowboy Boogie and Cotton Eye Joe with the best of them and didn't have to force a smile through any of the line dances.

When the music shifted again, she took out her phone and swung into action fulfilling her job as Bethany's maid of honor and informal wedding photographer.

Since Matt had awkwardly pulled away,

she'd had moments of going wobbly about how the rest of the summer would go. Given her new part-time job, she'd likely run into Matt and Stacey and the twins. That wouldn't be the last time in this little place. But no negative inner voice would make a dent in her resolve to go after what she wanted. She'd never felt so sure about anything in her life.

She smiled seeing Dan approach with his arm extended. "C'mon, honey, put that phone away. You haven't danced with me yet. It's time to show off your Texas Two-Step."

Dan to the rescue once again. Heather, followed him to the floor and they soon moved in sync.

"I don't think the last word is in on you and Matt," Dan said, talking over the music as they rounded a corner and created distance from the band.

"You didn't waste one second before trying to make me feel better," Heather said in a mildly chiding tone.

"Trust me, honey, something else is going on with him. He's a good man, too." He cocked his head. "Your daddy would have liked him. He had a nose for good men."

That had crossed Heather's mind the first

time she'd seen Matt, the night of Spring Fling. But none of that mattered now. She kept her feet in motion but fixed her gaze on Dan. "You are an incredibly sweet man, but you don't need to think about me. I'll be fine."

"In the long run, I know that's true. But I'm thinking of you right now."

"Dan, really. Your glowing, brilliant daughter is marrying a man who will be as good to her as you are to Jen. *You* should pat yourself on the back for *her* choice."

"I'm just sayin', Heather, it's not over yet."

Heather had her doubts about that, but she'd never persuade Dan. Instead, she concentrated on the fiddles and keyboard while they circled the crowded floor with other couples and the band transitioned from one song to the next without stopping or changing the rhythm.

"Well, will you look at this?" Dan chortled and squeezed her hand. "Don't you ever doubt my hunches. Seems I'm a genius, kiddo. You'll never guess who's headed toward us. Like that time at Spring Fling, I'm going to get a tap on my shoulder."

Heather swallowed hard. "I don't know. I'm not sure I'm up for a big talk."

"Better make up your mind. Right about now."

Matt appeared next to Dan, but this time he didn't go through the motions of cutting in. He simply said, "Do you mind, Dan?"

It was obvious Dan was trying to keep a serious, even stern face. "Like I told you the first time, Mathis, it's up to the lady."

"It's fine, Dan. It's getting late," Heather said, giving Dan a quick hug. "Thanks for the dances. I'll talk to Matt, and then I should be heading home."

Dan took a step back and lightly poked his index finger in the middle of Matt's chest. "I hope you have your talking points sharpened up."

Heather scooted around some couples to get off the dance floor. Matt and Dan followed. "Whatever this is about," she told them, "I'm not having the conversation in the middle of a two-step." She leaned to the side to look behind her. "Bethany must be thrilled Charlie's here."

Dan aimed an encouraging look at Matt. "I'll see you later, Heather." He gave her shoulder a quick squeeze. "I'm going to say hello to Charlie. Unless Bethany won't share him." He hurried away.

"The bride and groom can take care of themselves for a moment," Matt said. "They aren't concerned with anyone except each other, as it should be." Matt patted the pocket of his sport coat. "Uh, would you come out to the balcony with me? I really need to show you something."

Heather yielded and wordlessly went with Matt outside. It was dark now, except for low lights marking the corners of the balcony. The music blared, the bar was full and they were alone. Just as well. Thinking about the eyes on them when they'd danced at Spring Fling and again at the steak fry, at least a few people in town were curious enough to note the comings and goings of Matt and Heather.

"I made a big mistake," Matt said when they got to the low brick wall at the far edge, "and I don't even know where to start."

"Oh, Matt. What difference does it make where you start?" For the first time, though, she considered what Dan had said. Something was up. "You were patting your pocket a minute ago. Why don't you start by show-ing me whatever it is you want me to see?"

In the dark, when Matt unfolded the papers and smoothed the creases, it was clear they were documents of some kind. Nothing else was clear. "What am I looking at?"

"It's an agreement," Matt said with a long exhale. "I need to tell you something. I wish I didn't have to admit this, but to make things right, I need to. I made up a story about why I had to focus on the kids and business and all that. That was mostly nonsense." He ex-plained his and Zoe's concerns about the ranch. "I got spooked when she told me the outlook for sheep ranchers isn't good this year and into next."

"I don't mean to be flippant, Matt, but that's hardly a headline, is it?" She made no effort to hide her impatience. "Haven't you learned that over these last four years?"

Matt stared out into the darkness. "Go ahead. I deserve your scorn. But in a way, that's my point." He shifted his gaze back to her. "It hit me like a boulder. My 'I can do anything' swagger worked to nudge me to take chances and start Finer Rides with Ruben. But when it comes to the ranch, that same cocky confidence doesn't fit. What can I actually *guarantee*? Nothing."

She mulled over how to respond. No matter what happened between them now, that had been a tough admission for Matt. "The realities of ranching are a world all their own. Maybe you'll make it, maybe you won't." She held up one hand to stop him from breaking in. She had more to say.

"But you can depend on yourself, and the way you're raising Susannah's twins. It's impressed me. I remember thinking, wow, what a good dad he is. They call you their uncle, but they're as much yours as any two kids can be." She crossed her hands over her chest. "When I watch you and feel your worry and see the fun you have with them, my whole heart fills up."

Closing his eyes, Matt put his fingertips over his mouth. "Coming from you…" He shook his head. "Let's just say it means everything to me."

Looking over the balcony, only vague outlines of trees and shrubs were visible behind the lodge. Even the mountaintop cutouts were hidden in the darkness. Music, laughter and conversation continued in the background.

Then the plaintive cry of a coyote in the distance divided the worlds in this wild place she loved so much.

"As it turns out, the real picture isn't quite as bleak as the one I painted. I panicked, and I can explain why. But I've got options." He smiled when he said, "Thanks to the stables the Stanhopes built, I can buy, sell, and lease horses. Demand is up."

Matt waved the documents. "But these papers aren't about that. They have to do with you and me."

She bristled at first and came close to making a sarcastic remark, but his earnest expression softened her attitude.

"It's complicated, but Zoe helped me negotiate a deal. I broke the one mortgage we had into two pieces. The house and the buildings are now separate from the bulk of the land." He ran his fingers down the page. "I can show you the numbers. I can explain how it will work."

Heather touched his arm. "Wait, don't do that. Your mortgages have nothing to do with me. I don't need to see paperwork for your bank loans." She took a step back and out of the corner of her eye, she saw Bethany come

to the entryway of the balcony, Charlie behind her.

The pair approached tentatively. "Can I
talk to you a sec?" Charlie said to Matt.

"Sure thing," Matt said. "I'll be right back.
Please, Heather, don't go anywhere."

When Matt went inside the lodge, Bethany,
sparkly and bubbly, gave Heather a big hug.
"Thanks so much for everything tonight."
She cocked her head toward Matt. "What's
going on out here? Looks pretty cozy."

"I don't know, but you don't want to waste
all your joy thinking about me." Heather's
rapidly beating heart was pretty sure what
was coming next, but she took nothing for
granted.

"Matt knows you're staying here in Adelaide Creek, right?"

"I don't know. I haven't told him," she said,
trying to smile. "He's been…let's just say he's
been explaining himself."

"I guess he's in for a surprise."

Heather shrugged. In this little town, the
news might already have spread.

"I WANTED TO see you before Bethany and I
leave," Charlie said, smiling broadly. "We're

going to take off and go hang out on the bunkhouse porch for a while before I come back here for the night. My parents booked a suite."

"Sounds good."

"Big, big thanks, Matt, for coming to get me. I think I'm finally relaxing a little."

Matt laughed. "No problem. We didn't want you driving home by yourself after such a long trip. You've got a big job to do tomorrow."

For the first time, Charlie's smile faded. "How's it going with Heather? Are you managing to convince her to give you another chance?" Charlie gave him a light punch on his upper arm.

"So far, so good. Thanks." During the last few miles to town, Ed had dozed in the back seat and Matt had sketched out the basics of the story of meeting Heather but foolishly letting her go. "I've explained the arrangements about the house and the property. Now, if I can only convince her to stay here and not go back to Minnesota."

"Huh?" Charlie frowned. "What are you talking about? I just got here, but Bethany can hardly stop talking about how stupendously wonderful it is that Heather is staying. She has a part-time gig with that new doctor in town. Joe or Tim—"

"Tom?" Matt braced his arm on the door-jamb.

"Yeah, Dr. Tom something. Pediatrician." Charlie frowned. "This is news?"

Matt threw his head back and barely re-sisted the urge to pump his fist in the air. This could turn out even better than Matt had hoped. "And here I was warming up for the part where I'd make my case to forget the Minnesota job and stay here…with me and the twins." Matt let out a long grunt. "I really have bungled it. I suppose everyone knows this but me."

"I can't say that," Charlie said, slapping Matt on the back. "I haven't been home for an hour yet. It might take me a while to get caught up."

When Bethany came toward them, Charlie took her hand. "We're outta here."

Bethany gave Matt a pointed look, and she and Charlie ducked through the back of the bar and disappeared.

Matt went to Heather. "It's true? You have a job with Dr. Tom?"

Heather's face lit up. "Yep, one day a week to start."

"Why didn't you say something?"

She drew back in obvious surprise. "We weren't talking to each other when I decided to call him."

"You called him about a job?"

"Right. I turned down the one in Minnesota. I'd already decided I'm here for good." She tilted her head to look him directly in the eye. "Whatever story you made up to pull away from me wasn't going to chase me back to Minnesota." She touched his hand, which still grasped the papers. "You were in the middle of explaining these to me—a new mortgage deal, you said."

Matt explained as fast as he could and put his hands lightly on her shoulders. "It all came down to this. With things being the way they are now financially or in the future, what if we were together and I was forced to sell the ranch and we had to move out of the house."

Heather closed her eyes and shook her head.

"You lost your home once, and I could never, ever, live with myself if I caused you to lose it twice." He leaned in. "The image of us packing up and driving away from the house and the barn and the corrals was too painful. I couldn't risk doing that to you."

"That's why you came up with those reasons?"

Matt nodded. "It was wrong. I hope you'll forgive me. It seemed like I had to risk hurting you one way in order to protect you from a different kind of devastation down the road." Matt frowned. "When I put it like that, it sounds so messed up. I'm really sorry."

Heather leaned forward and rested her forehead on his chest. "You better be. I *was* hurt. It was even worse because I never got to tell you that the ranch isn't holding me in its vise grips anymore."

She lifted her head. "I learned something so important. I rode Pebbles on your land, read stories to the twins in your house. The earth didn't cave in. It wasn't my house anymore, Matt. I never got a chance to tell you that I've put my family's past to rest."

"I am so sorry, Heather. I started falling in love with you the night I asked you to dance—well, cut in. You challenged me with your 'Okay then, mister, show me what you've got.'"

"It turned out you had some moves to show off." She narrowed her eyes. "You didn't need a mortgage scheme to convince me to stay." Her face suddenly became serious. "It's not a bad idea, mind you. You can give the twins some extra security."

"It was part of my argument to win you back," he said, his heart beating fast. "Even with my fears blinding me, I never lost the vision of us together raising the twins. I know it's a lot to ask, but those two already think you're special." He smoothed his fingers down her soft cheek. "But putting my little cubs aside, I *love* you, Heather."

Her serious expression stayed put. "We'll need to take it a little slow with them—and us—but I can picture it all, too. And I love your little cubs. They like it when you call them that."

"Right." He shook his finger at her. "You heard them yourself. No more tykes."

"I'll remember that." She took a couple of steps back. "But here's what you need to know. With or without you, I'm staying. Because this is my part of the world. This basin, the mountains and hills with their craggy ridges and raw beauty." She stepped forward, cupped his face and gave him a light kiss. "And as luck would have it, I love you back. You are the coconut frosting on my chocolate cake."

He gathered her in his arms and kissed her soft lips, holding her in a tight embrace until the sound of the music grabbed his attention. They didn't need more words for her to entwine her fingers with his or for him to place his hand on the small of her back and waltz across the balcony.

CHAPTER EIGHTEEN

Matt clapped Charlie on the shoulder again. "Are you going to keep that ear-to-ear grin on your face all day?"

"That's the plan." Charlie took another sip from his glass, but then put it on the table. "I think that's enough champagne for me. I'm so jet-lagged I barely know what day of the week it is. But the flags in the flower beds remind me it really is the Fourth of July."

"Jet lag didn't make your mind go blank when you said your vows. Nicely done."

Charlie patted his chest. "The words came from right here." He twisted around to scan the area. "Speaking of hearts, a lot happened since the maid of honor arrived in Adelaide Creek. If you don't mind my saying so, you're wearing a sappy smile yourself."

Matt tried to hide the smile but found it hard to do so. "I learned a lot from all this, but right now, Heather and I are planning the summer. More rides on Bo and Pebbles, more time for Heather to get to know the twins. Her starting a new job. A visit from friends in Minnesota." He gestured to Heather and Bethany, who sat on a bench eating slices of wedding cake, high-heeled shoes in the grass by their feet.

"Maybe we'll be eating the same kind of cake at your wedding," Charlie said. "You do know they decided on chocolate with coconut icing when they were about twelve. It's like a pact between them."

"Whew. Thanks for saving me from yet another blunder," Matt said, pretending to swipe his forehead. At the moment, Lucy and Nick sat on chairs on either side of the two women, licking frosting off their forks. Heather's soft expression as she watched his twins made Matt's chest fill with the kind of joy he could easily become accustomed to. "Heather and my two are off to a good start."

Charlie nodded and smiled as he pointed to the flags in front of the house. "I won't have an excuse to forget our anniversary, will I?"

"No, man, you aced that one." Matt patted Charlie on the back again. "Your delay was the only glitch."

"It was a close call," Charlie agreed, glancing around. "I suppose Bethany and I should help clean up the yard and then be on our way."

"Don't even *think* about it." The booming voice came from Dan Hoover, who approached with Ed. "I don't care how simple you wanted this wedding to be, you're not on the cleanup crew." Dan smirked at Matt. "That's what the best man is for. And Mathis here got off easy. He hasn't had to do a thing except hand you the ring at the right time."

"I got my orders, son," Ed said. "You have to indulge your mom and get the group together for a few more pictures." He raised the video camera. "It's a little overkill if you ask me, but she told me to record us taking pictures."

"Mom can have whatever she wants," Charlie said.

Matt and Charlie ambled over to the bed of black-eyed Susans, where Jen and Cheri waited.

Matt hung back for a minute. He couldn't keep his eyes off Heather, who was laughing with Bethany as they held up their shoes and shook their heads before slipping them on.

The two stood and smoothed their dresses. Then Heather put out one hand to Lucy and another to Nick, and they walked toward Jen. When Heather saw him coming her way, her face lit up like sunshine. He'd never forget that look.

HEATHER STOOD NEXT to Matt and the twins and waved goodbye to Bethany and Charlie. Jen and Dan had their arms around each other, and Charlie's dad kept recording until the SUV disappeared down the road.

As if they were disassembling a movie set, the caterer arrived and took away everything, including the plates and champagne glasses. It took only a few minutes to put the yard to rights. As dusk fell, the guests drifted away, including Stacey and Grey.

"Do you want to see the special path to the bunkhouse?" Heather asked the twins. They stood close to Matt as they waited for her to tie her sneakers. "It's more fun than driving, and it's not too far. And then you can sit on my porch and we can all talk about the wedding and maybe look at the pictures on our phones. You can help me choose which ones to send to Olivia and Jillian."

"Those are the friends we'll meet when they visit in a few weeks," Matt added. "It's going to be a busy summer."

"Uncle Matt says you are our new special, special, special friend," Lucy said.

"Wow, *three* specials. That makes me so happy." She crooked her finger at them. "Follow me."

Heather and Bethany had kept the path mowed and easy to navigate. Nick hadn't been on liquid iron for long, but already he had color in his face and was keeping up with Lucy as she skipped on the path and jumped over patchy spots.

Excited to see Jen's sheep, they had sharp eyes and noted that the Shetlands and Icelanders weren't the same as theirs.

"It's a little house," Lucy said when they'd reached the bunkhouse.

"It was the perfect size for Bethany, and now it's perfect for me." She picked up Lucy and sat in the rocker.

"Until you and Uncle Matt get married," Lucy said, putting her head against Heather's chest. "Then you'll come and live in our house."

"Whoa, let's not rush things too much,"

Heather said, meeting Matt's gaze. His eyes, more greenish than blue in the dimming light, were full of fun.

"That's what Gram told us," Nick said. "And she said Heather is going to work with Dr. Tom." He pointed to himself. "*My* doctor."

"Mine, too," Lucy added.

"Yep, that's all true." Matt picked up Nick and took the other chair. "First, we're going to spend more time together this summer."

Matt extended his hand across the space between the two gently rocking chairs. "We have a lot to talk about, don't we?"

Heather took his hand and smiled at him. "This feels so right."

"Almost," Matt said. "You're a little too far away to kiss."

Heather looked down at Lucy, her eyes closing. Nick was drifting off as well. "Not for long," she whispered, her eyes filling with happy tears. "They can sleep on my bed for a while. It's been a big day."

"Big for us, too, huh? And many more beautiful days to come."

Still holding his hand, she said, "I love your twins, Matt, and I love you." She looked toward the mountains, violet and lavender washing over them like watercolors.

"Think of it, Heather, we can watch the sun go down behind those mountains every day."

She smiled. "Yes. For the rest of our lives."

* * * * *

*For more great romances from
Virginia McCullough and
Harlequin Heartwarming,
visit www.Harlequin.com today!*

Get 4 FREE REWARDS!

We'll send you 2 FREE Books plus 2 FREE Mystery Gifts.

FREE Value Over **$20**

Both the **Love Inspired®** and **Love Inspired® Suspense** series feature compelling novels filled with inspirational romance, faith, forgiveness, and hope.

YES! Please send me 2 FREE novels from the Love Inspired or Love Inspired Suspense series and my 2 FREE gifts (gifts are worth about $10 retail). After receiving them, if I don't wish to receive any more books, I can return the shipping statement marked "cancel." If I don't cancel, I will receive 6 brand-new Love Inspired Larger-Print books or Love Inspired Suspense Larger-Print books every month and be billed just $5.99 each in the U.S. or $6.24 each in Canada. That is a savings of at least 17% off the cover price. It's quite a bargain! Shipping and handling is just 50¢ per book in the U.S. and $1.25 per book in Canada.* I understand that accepting the 2 free books and gifts places me under no obligation to buy anything. I can always return a shipment and cancel at any time. The free books and gifts are mine to keep no matter what I decide.

Choose one: ☐ **Love Inspired Larger-Print** (122/322 IDN GNWC) ☐ **Love Inspired Suspense Larger-Print** (107/307 IDN GNWN)

Name (please print)

Address   Apt. #

City   State/Province   Zip/Postal Code

Email: Please check this box ☐ if you would like to receive newsletters and promotional emails from Harlequin Enterprises ULC and its affiliates. You can unsubscribe anytime.

Mail to the Harlequin Reader Service:
IN U.S.A.: P.O. Box 1341, Buffalo, NY 14240-8531
IN CANADA: P.O. Box 603, Fort Erie, Ontario L2A 5X3

Want to try 2 free books from another series! Call 1-800-873-8635 or visit www.ReaderService.com.

Get 4 FREE REWARDS!

We'll send you 2 FREE Books plus 2 FREE Mystery Gifts.

The Charming Checklist — HEATHERLY BELL

A Rancher's Touch — ALLISON LEIGH

FREE Value Over **$20**

The Wrong Cowboy — Melinda Sheppers

A Cowgirl's Secret — Melinda Curtis

Both the **Harlequin® Special Edition** and **Harlequin® Heartwarming™** series feature compelling novels filled with stories of love and strength where the bonds of friendship, family and community unite.

YES! Please send me 2 FREE novels from the Harlequin Special Edition or Harlequin Heartwarming series and my 2 FREE gifts (gifts are worth about $10 retail). After receiving them, if I don't wish to receive any more books, I can return the shipping statement marked "cancel." If I don't cancel, I will receive 6 brand-new Harlequin Special Edition books every month and be billed just $4.99 each in the U.S or $5.74 each in Canada, a savings of at least 17% off the cover price or 4 brand-new Harlequin Heartwarming Larger-Print books every month and be billed just $5.74 each in the U.S. or $6.24 each in Canada, a savings of at least 21% off the cover price. It's quite a bargain! Shipping and handling is just 50¢ per book in the U.S. and $1.25 per book in Canada.* I understand that accepting the 2 free books and gifts places me under no obligation to buy anything. I can always return a shipment and cancel at any time. The free books and gifts are mine to keep no matter what I decide.

Choose one: ☐ **Harlequin Special Edition** ☐ **Harlequin Heartwarming**
(235/335 HDN GNMP) **Larger-Print**
(161/361 HDN GNPZ)

Name (please print)

Address   Apt. #

City   State/Province   Zip/Postal Code

Email: Please check this box ☐ if you would like to receive newsletters and promotional emails from Harlequin Enterprises ULC and its affiliates. You can unsubscribe anytime.

Mail to the Harlequin Reader Service:
IN U.S.A.: P.O. Box 1341, Buffalo, NY 14240-8531
IN CANADA: P.O. Box 603, Fort Erie, Ontario L2A 5X3

Want to try 2 free books from another series! Call 1-800-873-8635 or visit www.ReaderService.com.

*Terms and prices subject to change without notice. Prices do not include sales taxes, which will be charged (if applicable) based on your state or country of residence. Canadian residents will be charged applicable taxes. Offer not valid in Quebec. This offer is limited to one order per household. Books received may not be as shown. Not valid for current subscribers to the Harlequin Special Edition or Harlequin Heartwarming series. All orders subject to approval. Credit or debit balances in a customer's account(s) may be offset by any other outstanding balance owed by or to the customer. Please allow 4 to 6 weeks for delivery. Offer available while quantities last.

Your Privacy—Your information is being collected by Harlequin Enterprises ULC, operating as Harlequin Reader Service. For a complete summary of the information we collect, how we use this information and to whom it is disclosed, please visit our privacy notice located at corporate.harlequin.com/privacy-notice. From time to time we may also exchange your personal information with reputable third parties. If you wish to opt out of this sharing of your personal information, please visit readerservice.com/consumerschoice or call 1-800-873-8635. **Notice to California Residents**—Under California law, you have specific rights to control and access your data. For more information on these rights and how to exercise them, visit corporate.harlequin.com/california-privacy.

HSEHW22

COUNTRY LEGACY COLLECTION

19 FREE BOOKS IN ALL!

Cowboys, adventure and romance await you in this new collection! Enjoy superb reading all year long with books by bestselling authors like Diana Palmer, Sasha Summers and Marie Ferrarella!

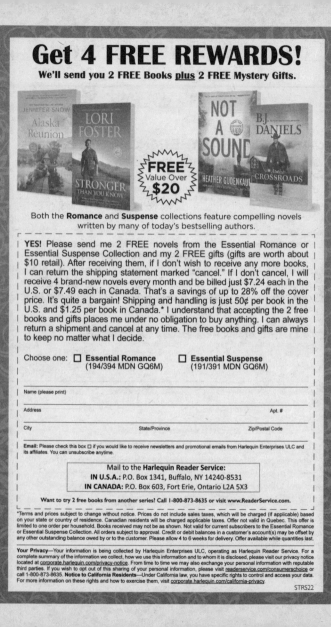

Visit
ReaderService.com
Today!

As a valued member of the Harlequin Reader Service, you'll find these benefits and more at ReaderService.com:

- Try 2 free books from any series
- Access risk-free special offers
- View your account history & manage payments
- Browse the latest Bonus Bucks catalog

Don't miss out!

If you want to stay up-to-date on the latest at the Harlequin Reader Service and enjoy more content, make sure you've signed up for our monthly News & Notes email newsletter. Sign up online at ReaderService.com or by calling Customer Service at 1-800-873-8635.